Praise for Errant Blood,
the first book in the Duncul series.

'...beautiful writing about landscape, about cruelty, about loyalty'

- Catriona Macpherson

'Themes of family, mortality, morality, love, and betrayal are examined in a fresh and invigorating manner'

– Scots Whay Hae!

'It's a crime for a debut to be this good'

– Criminal Minds

'Reminiscent of Ian Banks and I do not say that lightly'

– Alistair Braidwood

'The author's voice is very distinctive. he has that rare ability to create a world which is recognisable and real but not quite like anywhere else.'

–Kate Vane

Longlisted for the People's Book Prize 2019

THE PURIFIED

By

C. F PETERSON

Scotland Street Press
EDINBURGH

First Published in the UK in 2021 by
Scotland Street Press
100 Willowbrae Avenue
Edinburgh EH8 7HU

A CIP record for this book is available from the British Library.

ISBN 978-1-910895-56-6

This is a work of fiction. Names, characters, business, events
and incidents are the products of the author's imagination. Any
resemblance to actual persons, living or dead, or actual events is
purely coincidental.

Typeset by Antonia Weir in Edinburgh
Printed and bound by CPI Group (UK) Ltd, Croydon, CR0 4YY

For my father, Peter J. Findlay.

Prologue

On the hill above the village the thin figure moved in the dark, capturing light. From the shadows of the pines he could see into thirty windows. He felt safe up here, armed with a long lens. They were all in their boxes, beneath him. Some drew him in more than others. Mhairi Macintosh in her bedroom, for one. But there was not only that. There was Freda Macrae, an old woman, sitting in an armchair in front of a television, with her eyes closed, slowly dying. Tom Blackett, in high-waisted trousers tight around his belly, watching soup boil. The Camerons; the mother with dark hair and a sphinx smile, playing board games and drawing with her children; the father in his shed, spinning bowls and candlesticks from his lathe. There was a Macdonald child on his stomach in a bare room in Tarr Bow, eyes inches from an iPad. All there, all safe, all his. Apart from the ones at the manse. They did not make sense. They were flies in the ointment. They were men that were not men. They had no routine, and would not stay in their box. They were strangers, and they crept about, by day and night, stealing things. He had to get closer, into the trees behind the manse, to see through their window. Tonight he was going down there to watch, knowing he would see things that should not be. He was going to catch their light, and put it in a box.

Malky had been hearing stories about 'The Chosen One' for months and was prepared to be disappointed. When she took the bag of his head he saw that she was just a girl, as he had heard. She had a flat face and a turned-up nose and her blonde hair was matted into dreadlocks. The lips were slightly parted and the face thoughtful. She was wearing jeans and scruffy trainers and a baggy jumper with over-long arms that hid the shape of breasts and thighs. She wasn't making any attempt at beauty, but something was shining from somewhere inside, brighter than the single bare bulb hanging from the ceiling. The four young men with scarves over their faces who had tied him to the chair loomed behind her. She gestured to the tallest and he handed her a bolt-cutter. This was what she was known for; getting to the point. Her accent was a strange mixture of East London and German.

'If you really believe in something, you are prepared to die for it. These will help you decide if you are for us or them.'

'False dichotomy,' said Malky in the accent of a lowland Scot. 'I'm not for them or you. Maybe what I choose is just to keep things hidden.'

'I do not believe you. We have your map.'

'Maybe what I choose is silence.'

'That is not likely,' she said. He smiled, but she did not.

She moved behind him and he felt the cold of the cutter on his hands. He clenched his fists, but two men held his arms while a third stretched out one of the fingers. He felt the jaws tighten on the bone. He swallowed as she squeezed the handles with her girl-strength, which was enough. The wave of pain had the familiar effect of clearing his head. He breathed fast through the nose and bit blood from his lip, trying to stop the explosion from his lungs, but could not stop himself howling at the bare bulb. No, there was nothing disappointing about Brigitta Neilsen, he thought, as the darkness returned.

Chapter 1

It was the end of a hot June day in the Highlands and after a long and timid approach a soft, half-night had settled upon the hills and forests that surround the village of Duncul. Among the handful of streets and lanes the not-quite darkness skirmished with street-lights, warmth-filled windows and the cold flames of televisions, but recovered itself about the lawns of Duncul Castle at the edge of the village and beneath the avenue of beech and elm that lined the drive, raising strength for an assault upon the one light high up in the ancient sentinel, and upon the dim lamp that glowed outside a small cabin in the Ash Woods to the south. Beyond the door beneath the lamp Eamon Ansgar was looking at the broad back of his gardener, Mike Mack, who sat hunched before a pot-bellied stove. Eamon's phone buzzed.

'The police are up at the manse,' said Rona. 'I thought you might want to know.'

'Thanks. I'll be back soon,' said Eamon. 'Something up at the manse,' he said to Mike. 'Probably something to do with those boys. You were up there yourself lately. What's the story?'

'A hollowed out sycamore at the back. Could fall on the house,' Mike said to the stove. He was more taciturn than usual, if that was possible. At one point during the evening he had seemed on the verge of weeping.

'You don't have to live here,' said Eamon, looking around the one-room wooden hut that Mike had built. He took in the smell of woodsmoke, the neat bed, the sagging armchair, the store of firewood, the gardening tools in the corner. It was a real man-cave. Perhaps that is why I like it, he thought. Like his brother Stevie's caravan in the quarry on the other side of the village, it had become a refuge from the castle, which had become the domain of women and a child; Kirsty the housekeeper, his wife, her mother, and his infant son. He was being ousted by a six month old; the heir already taking over. 'There's a house in the village, a proper house, that you can have.'

'This suits me,' said Mike.

'How is Finlay?' said Eamon, getting round to the subject he had been avoiding for an hour. Finlay Mack,

Mike's brother, had been taken to the mental hospital in Aberdeen for the second time in a year.

'Not good,' said Mike. Eamon waited but knew he would not say anything more. Mike Mack had never spoken much for the forty years he had known him. He needed companionship right now, but it would not come from conversation; it would come from silent, hard work. The way forward was not into the subject, but around and alongside it. He reminded himself to concentrate on the practical, the details of doing things.

'I've got to go. But tomorrow we can start chopping that beech. Is the chainsaw sharp?'

'Aye.'

'Have you put a new handle on the axe?'

Mike nodded.

Eamon walked back to the castle through last year's crisp-dry beech leaves, entering the gardens by the door in the south wall and crossing the yellow lawn to the tower door. Perhaps Mike was still annoyed about not being allowed to water the lawn. They had plenty of water from the castle's private supply, but after thirty days without rain the village had been warned of imminent mains rationing, and it didn't seem fair to water a full acre. 'Let it burn,' Eamon had said.

Rona was in the study on the fourth floor, half-watching the television while Harry gurgled next to her on the couch. A man with short blonde hair and a long fringe was being interviewed in a studio, his name 'Acturus McBean' was displayed beneath the smirk like a scar in the long, pockmarked jaw. A sinister face; a jovial, fruity voice.

'I was born in a council house in Fife,' said Acturus, 'I know everything there is to know about deprivation…'

Rona switched him off and she and Eamon moved to the bay window. The cold police light was flickering through the trees around the manse on the other side of the village.

'How's Mike?' she asked.

'Taking it bad.'

'Looks like someone finally complained.'

'Bit heavy handed though. Why the lights?' said Eamon.

'Do you think they'll be arrested?'

Eamon shrugged in reply and thought about making a call, but it was after ten and they had a rule. He switched off his phone, placed it with hers on the desk and closed the shutters.

But at the manse a small crowd had gathered, and the consensus was that now was not the time to sleep. Now was very much the time, in part because the night was warm, for standing around in knots of twos and threes and talking in low tones. It was the time for good old-fashioned smoking, and for clouds of strawberry, mint and banana vapour; for flapping arms in defence against the midges and for bathing in the flickering blue, for catching the rays on camera-phones and re-distributing them, so that the whole wide world could be touched by that marvellous colour that speaks of urgency, violence, and the fact that makes us all important; death. Sergeant Peters, who had a neat black beard and a chest and stomach that were one big barrel encased in a yellow stab vest, set to his designated task as colleagues opened the front door of the manse with a sledgehammer. With gentle fluctuations of his fat hands he drew the gathered citizens together.

'Can you stop that?' he said to a young woman. She lowered the phone and paused the video. 'It's very important, for legal reasons, that you tell me now if anyone took any photos or video through the windows before we arrived. Anyone?

Siobhan Macdonald raised a hand halfway to her shoulder then drew hard on the remains of a Lambert and Butler, thinning her thin face, and tossed the butt to the ground.

'OK. Anyone else? You need to know you can be charged.' He stared at blank stares and a few nods.

Peters took Siobhan out of the midges and smoke into the car and began asking questions and clumsily writing down the answers. She had posted a photograph of what she had seen through the back window of the manse to her one hundred Twitter followers, and had to be persuaded to delete it, and Sergeant Peters noted that

there had been four re-tweets and someone, probably
him, was going to have to get in touch with Twitter,
and he cursed. He received a second-hand monosyllabic
approximation of what Siobhan's eight-year-old son,
Angus, had seen. But he had a good enough imagination,
and despite her evasions began to piece together what had
happened to the boy, and why. He could see the light in
Angus' eyes as he pulled with his fingertips on the high
sandstone sill of the window at the back of the manse
until he could see into the living room. It had been ten
p.m. and Peters understood what the boy had hoped for,
even craved; those forbidden possibilities of the body. He
had seen for himself what the boy had got instead. He had
got the moment of un-recognition, when the body is no
longer a body but merely an accumulation of oddness;
of limbs at wrong angles, of flattened light in the eyes, of
tangled and blood-stiffened hair. He had got chairs and a
table overturned, blood-spatters on the walls and broken
glass on the floor of the high-ceilinged room, his own
unrecognisable whine and a vision that would stay with
him for life. Sergeant Peters had a son of his own and he
felt pity as he imagined Angus howling, and dropping
down, and running.

To those who slept through the howl of the boy and
the curses of his mother and neighbours and the curt calls
and the anxious wait for the police, the news only broke
with the sun rising over the mountain to the north-east

and glancing from the surface of Loch Cul. It came as an avalanche of bright texts breaking into the greyscale of sleep.

It was morning before Kirsty brought the news. Eamon was in the kitchen, making porridge, while his wife slept off the effects of Harry's unearthly routine.

'Did you hear?' Kirsty said as she shuffled into the room with a pale, blank face. She was dressed in blue overalls, but he could see she would not be doing any work that day.

'Were they arrested?'

'Arrested? No. Eamon, they're dead.'

'Dead?' said Eamon, with his mind going blank like her face. 'Both of them?'

'Aye,' she said, holding his gaze. He put a hand on her arm and brought her to a chair at the table.

'Who found them?' he asked, and he was later to wonder why, then, he thought only of suicide. Kirsty avoided his eyes. He repeated the question, but she shook her head. He was moving to the door when she spoke.

'Eamon, they were killed.'

'Killed?'

'All smashed up.'

'Who told you that?' he said, sounding irritated, as if dismissing village gossip.

The old woman recovered herself and spoke to him as she had done since his infancy, with kindness, but impatiently. 'They were killed, Eamon.' She took a phone from the pocket of her overall, touched the screen and held the picture up to Eamon's face. The image was divided by the soft focussed grid of astragals on a big window, taken from a high angle, a brightly lit room in chaos; broken furniture, a body face down on the floor with long blonde hair stained dark with blood.

'What is that?' asked Eamon, reaching for the phone. Kirsty put the phone in her pocket. 'Show me. No, don't. Is that, at the manse? Is that…? You shouldn't show people that. How…?' He didn't know which question to ask. He went out into the hall and was about to run up the main staircase to his own phone when the doorbell rang and he opened to the thin figure of Detective Superintendent John Maclean and a short round policeman with a neat beard, the latest incumbent of the Aberfashie beat.

'David Smart and Kosma Milosz,' said Maclean when he and Sergeant Peters had settled into wingback chairs in the study on the fourth floor.

Eamon stood in the window then moved behind his desk, then back to the window. He suspected he was developing some sort of allergy to police interviews. His grey eyes flicked at random objects around the room: the painting of his father above the desk; the ormolu clock on the mantlepiece; the patterns of the Persian carpet beneath the policemen's feet. And he found his hand repeatedly dragging through the thin blonde hair high on his forehead. He wanted to smoke. He looked out along the avenue of beeches that were green and growing warm and bright with life.

'It seems that you knew them,' said Maclean, who had aged more than the year since Eamon had last seen him. The dark eyes had sunk further into the skull, and the skin was thinner, offering less resistance to the light. The hair was still dyed black; an odd vanity in a man who was otherwise so austere.

Eamon shook his head, half in incredulity, half in denial. 'They were here. They were here the night before last, for dinner. What happened?'

'What do you know?' said Maclean, raising eyebrows.

Eamon let out a sigh and tried to conceal irritation. 'I know what everyone in the village knows. They're dead. I've seen a picture.' There was a long pause.

'Where?' asked Sergeant Peters.

'On my housekeeper's phone.'

'I'll need to speak to her about that. The deceased were friends of yours?' said Maclean.

'I wouldn't say that. I'd only spoken to them a couple of times. People think that I own the manse, so they complained to me. But it belongs to the church. I went

to speak to them.' He leant on the window frame,
wondering if there were any cigarettes in the desk.

'Why did people complain?'

'You can ask anyone about that. There had been break-
ins. Not really break-ins. People don't keep their doors
locked around here.'

'They were homosexuals,' interrupted Maclean, almost
forming a question.

Eamon inwardly winced at something that was not
quite right with that description, but he let it pass.
Maclean was an old man. He shrugged and sat on a
couch.

'They came to Duncul about three months ago. The
manse has been empty for years. The church had been
looking for tenants, but the building is too big and there's
no furniture. I thought perhaps it was leased to them out
of charity. They were just kids, and with no jobs as far as
anyone could make out. Odd kids. One of them liked to
wear makeup. They didn't seem to be very sociable. But
you would see them walking all the time, in the woods,
up the hill and in the village. They were stealing stuff.
Mrs Macdonald found one of them in her kitchen one
day. They came in here. The front door is never locked,
normally, and they took that thing.' He pointed to a small
bronze and silver statue that stood on a table next to the
fireplace; a naked Atlas, twelve inches high, straining
beneath the weight of a cosmic sphere.

'How do you know this?'

'Because when I went to visit them I saw it all. For some reason they were sleeping downstairs in the living room, on the floor, in sleeping bags. And all around their beds was the stuff that they'd nicked. That statue, and all kinds of things that had gone missing from houses in the village. They'd stolen bottles of shampoo from Mrs Macdonald's bathroom. They'd taken a china dog from one of the gardens in Tarr Bow, a peg-bag from Peggy Smith. Garden ornaments. They had a thing for people's garden ornaments. All around their beds, gnomes and things. They weren't trying to hide anything. I saw all this through the front window.'

'Is it valuable?' Maclean pointed at the statue.

'I really don't know.'

'Is it an heirloom?'

'I suppose.' He moved to the statue. It says here, "Presented by DM on behalf of the tenants of Duncul Estate to Adoman Ansgar Laird of Duncul, in gratitude, 1888". I suppose that makes it an heirloom. It belongs to the estate, to the castle, like everything you see around you.'

'And you confronted them?'

'I rang the door-bell and the one with long blonde hair, David, came to the door. He was very polite and friendly. I told him there had been complaints, and he said he was sorry about it. "It's a problem," he said, and he said he would put the things back.'

'Did you not think of reporting this to the police?'

'He said they would give the things back. I did say someone would phone the police, probably, eventually, if they didn't.'

'And did they? Put things back?'

'Some of them, certainly. I'm not sure about everything.' Maclean took notes. 'They were odd. Gay, as you say. Perhaps.' Eamon shrugged again. 'For here, they were odd. David wore women's clothes.'

'And you invited them to dinner.'

'It was Rona's idea.'

'And?'

'I went there last week and David answered the door again. He seemed keen to come, and asked what time, but then Kosma came out, and he was polite but I really got the feeling that he didn't want to come at all.'

'But they did come.'

'They came. Late. We thought they weren't coming. We had dinner.'

'And?'

'You know. Dinner. Maybe we made it a bit too formal. But they did have a good time. Kosma got so pissed he fell off his chair. He didn't talk much. I don't know if his English was very good. David was a bit more talkative. He told us he was an art student. From Peterborough. Said how much he liked it here, all the nature and everything. Said it was his first time in Scotland. He asked about Rona's cattle. He was interested in the paintings.'

'You didn't confront them again about the thefts?'

'I didn't want to. It didn't seem polite. I had already told them once. And the funniest thing was, the next morning, yesterday morning, it was Rona who noticed; they'd put the statue back, exactly where it had been, here. I don't know how they smuggled it in, but they must have done it while they were here. It was like a magic trick.' He paused. 'How did they die?'

Maclean exchanged a look with Sergeant Peters, who shifted his weight. 'The pathologist will let us know,' said Maclean. 'Did they speak of anyone threatening them?'

'Not to us. But I'm not the one to ask. I don't hear everything. With Harry the last few months have been terribly busy.'

'Of course. Congratulations. How is Rona? And the boy?'

'Thank you. They are well.'

'Good. Give her my regards.'

'Kirsty says they were all smashed up. What happened?'

'There was a degree of violence.'

'John, I want to help.'

Maclean looked at him steadily. 'How would you do that?'

'I can talk to people. I can find out.'

'And end up doing more harm than good.' Maclean got up. 'Eamon, this might seem hard to believe, especially for you, but usually these things are quite straightforward.' Sergeant Peters got up.

'John. Johnny Murachar...' began Eamon, but Maclean held up a finger to stop him.

'You leave Johnny Murachar to me.'

Eamon was at the door putting on his walking boots when Rona came down into the hall.

'Leave it,' she said. 'Let the police do their job.'

'I'm going for a walk,' said Eamon, taking a stick from the rack.

Chapter 2

The sky was cloudless and the day already warm. At first
Eamon walked through the village towards the manse,
but there was yellow tape across the drive and an officer
in the shade of the beech and sycamores. Maclean's little
blue car was parked at the front door. Eamon walked
back towards the castle, then took the single-track road
that led west, towards the head of Loch Nish. He knew
the five miles would take an hour at his pace. He could
have driven, but the anger building inside him needed
the release of feet and walking stick pounding on the
warming tar.

'All smashed up,' Kirsty had said. All smashed up. He
thought of David Smart's delicate face. It was not difficult
to smash up a boy like that. He thought of his thin arms

and legs. He thought of Kosma; an elegant young man
with long dark curls and deep-set, dark eyes. A young man
wearing a cardigan and skinny jeans, with filed nails. All
smashed up. Eamon cursed.

The road followed the river's curves as it searched
through the levelling glen for the head of the Loch.
Eamon took off his jacket and left it behind a gorse bush
to pick up on the way back.

The metalled road came to an end at a slipway and
a weed covered shore. A steel bridge crossed the river
and the road continued untarred along the southern
shore. Dust rose from his feet into the still air. 'Quite
straightforward,' Maclean had said. There would be
nothing straightforward about it to the boy's families,
to their friends, and to others like them. To the south
of the road a twelve-foot-high chain-link fence formed
a straight band of grey marching up over the hill to the
south, cutting off the forested Ardven peninsula from
the rest of the world. In the other direction, ahead of
him, the fence ran along the hill side, hemming the track
against the shore. White plastic signs were attached every
fifty meters, declaring in inch-thick red lettering: 'Ardven
Re-Wilding Project. Beware Wild Animals. Trespassers
will be Prosecuted.' Eamon followed the track for a mile
with the loch to his right and the fence to his left, until it
turned up and south into the forest. Here the fence ran
close along both sides, forming a steel-lined channel into

the trees. The track rose and fell for a kilometre inland until it arrived at the high steel gate to Johnny Murachar's croft.

The wooden platform behind the gate was manned by a young man holding a small calibre rifle. His blue eyes looked too wide-open for comfort.

'Shem. Really?' said Eamon, looking at the gun.

'Hello Mr Ansgar,' said Shem. The gate and the platform were on a rise and Eamon looked down upon the croft which lay in a clearing in the forest. It was several acres of small fields, vegetable patches, polytunnels, sheds and caravans, criss-crossed with paths and spread out over rising ground to the croft house on a small hill in the centre. Smoke was rising straight up from the chimney. Behind the house rough ground recently cleared of trees rose to the encircling steel fence. The old oak forest beyond formed a green bowl in the purple hill. There were wooden platforms like the one at the gate around the perimeter of the croft, and below the house a taller watchtower which was topped with a wooden cross twice the height of a man. Among the vegetable patches and fields there were several women wearing long dresses, white bonnets or headscarves. There were children playing between the vegetable patches and greenhouses, and there was a group of young men in dungarees fixing a barn roof. The high sun was making the whole picture of peace and pastoral contentment shine.

Shem spoke into a walky-talky, then climbed down from the platform to escort Eamon through the gate. Eamon had visited the croft several times and had always been impressed by the beauty of the place and the atmosphere of peace and simplicity. But the anger that had propelled him along the road from Duncul was still coursing through him as they walked towards the hill and house in the centre and for the first time he could feel the superficiality. It was as if the vegetable patches, women in their smocks, children happily skipping, sun-dappled paths and groves were all plastic thin, like a film-set. The women were smiling at him to order, the children laughing on cue and the hammers knocking on the roof of the shed were a part of an orchestra of fraud. Even the birds in the trees and the wind rustling the branches were playing their part, and the conductor was walking towards him accompanied by two young men armed with heavy sticks. Eamon let his anger rise unchecked.

Johnny Murachar was a vigorous looking man in late middle age with thick white hair and a red face. He carried a stick in one hand and as he approached he held his arms open in greeting. He smiled as he began to speak, but his eyes were narrowed. Eamon's pace quickened within the last few steps and he swung his stick, aiming for Johnny's head. Johnny ducked like a man twenty years younger and Eamon felt a blow on his own shoulder that collapsed his legs. Four more young men appeared around

Johnny. Eamon looked up at sharp implements and faces silhouetted against blue sky. Johnny rubbed his chin and smiled without any warmth. 'Take him to the kitchen,' he said.

Eamon was surrounded by a cloud of breath and sweat and felt strong hands beneath his arms, a hand in his pocket taking his phone, and his feet walking fast up the little hill to the croft house. They ducked his head under the lintel into a cool, dark passage, then a kitchen smelling of mutton and leeks.

A woman was chopping vegetables at the table before the stove but seeing Eamon and some signal from one of the men she put down the knife and left. The men put Eamon on a chair beside the stove and left him under the guard of Shem and a boy carrying a spade. The pain in his shoulder settled into an intense flame. He was glad to be sitting and had no desire to speak. He listened to the clock above the mantlepiece and felt the warmth of the stove. A woman came into the room and whispered something to the boy before taking him out. Another woman opened the door and stared. Shem closed the door. After about an hour Johnny came in and sat on a chair in front of Eamon.

'He who lives by the sword will die by the sword,' he said, leaning back with a faint sneer. 'When we met I was taking a look about the croft. We are trying to grow enough food to last the winter, but it is not easy now that I have lost my grazing. I was supposed to be thinking about green-beans and tatties, but I had to be thinking about Eamon Ansgar. Eamon Ansgar who has never said a word against me when everyone else has condemned me. Eamon Ansgar who has always treated his own crofters with dignity and justice. Eamon Ansgar who has a reputation as a good laird; the laird who stood up for the poor and against the rich and powerful. The kind of laird who would never clear his land of people to make way for a pack of wolves. "Blessed are those who hunger and thirst for justice, for they shall see God," saith The Lord. Of course, it came to me as I was inspecting the cabbages, he blames me for the death of those two queers in the manse. Do you really believe I have something to do with that?'

'I've read your blog.'

'Good. I hope it made you think a little.'

'I think you are wrong.'

'About what exactly?'

'About everything.'

'You don't believe in God?'

'That is not the question you address.'

'You don't believe that there is such a thing as sin? As wickedness? As decadence? You don't believe that our society is rotten?'

'What you say is poison, nothing but poison.' Eamon sensed strength draining from him. He did not want to discuss this subject with Johnny Murachar. He looked

at the flagstones. Rona had been right; he should let the
police deal with him.

'Tell me Eamon, are you speaking as a Christian?'

Eamon shrugged, and winced at the pain in his
shoulder. 'I was brought up a Catholic.'

'Catholic! When was the last time you went to church?'

'How often I go to church is not the point. You ask if
I am a Christian. Well, I am, like most people, whether I
like it or not.'

'What you are, whether you like it or not, Eamon
Ansgar, is a Liberal. You believe in nothing but your own
comfort. You believe, above all else, in Not Rocking The
Boat. You are safe in Duncul, in your fairy-tale castle,
owning all the land for miles around, safe for centuries,
safe, and kind to strangers. You are not out here,
threatened with eviction and surrounded by wolves.'

'No-one is making you leave. Nyst can never force you
to sell. The council, the planners, the government, are
never going to clear you off your croft. And he is probably
never going to get permission to release his wolves. All
that stuff you write is crap and you know it.'

'He *has* surrounded me and he *is* strangling me, and
I am not only fighting Nyst. I am fighting the forces of
darkness.'

'Aren't we all?' Eamon looked up and gave a weak smile.

'You have a son now. Would you not care if he grows
up to be homosexual, or trans-sexual?'

'If he did I would want to protect him from people like you.'

Johnny Murachar shook his head and stared hard at Eamon. '"If you are not for me you are against me." You would let your own son fall into the pit.'

'I have to go home,' said Eamon.

'You will. But first I want you to spend the night here. Consider it your punishment for trying to knock my head off. Someone will call your wife to tell her you will be home in the morning. One of the boys will drive you back then.'

'Why?'

'You'll see.'

When Johnny had gone strong hands and tense faces returned to guide Eamon to a bedroom and lock the plank door behind him. He sat on the neat bed. The floor was bare wood and the rough plastered walls were painted a dull grey. The furniture was a shaker chair and a crude chest of drawers. Apart from the cross on the wall and the bible on the pillow it reminded him of the Airbnb he and Rona had hired in Sutherland six months ago, just before Harry's birth. Johnny Murachar, religious fanatic, cult leader and culture-war champion, was on trend with his interior decoration. As Eamon lay down his eye caught a movement at the small window and he saw the top half of a child's face, then a swift adult hand scuffing the head and lifting a tuft of hair. The face disappeared. Eamon closed his eyes and felt tiredness begin its war with the pain in his shoulder and the pain emerge from the dark as a writhing blade.

The bare bulb had been switched off and Malky Macleod was alone. He opened one eye, smiled into the darkness, and thought about the politicisation of the body and the role of the neo-liberal state in the manufacture of the spiritual narrative. These were important subjects but not easy ones and his hand hurt where the finger had been cut off. He moved his tongue around his teeth and was surprised to find they were all intact. He spat. The film of dried blood on his face cracked as he opened the other eye. The only light came from the faint outline of a trapdoor in the ceiling. He could see the stairs leading up and as his eyes adjusted, the rough walls and floor.

There was the smell of earth, and the sickening tang of dogshit. He could hear nothing. He listened and breathed and closed his eyes but re-lived the shouts and felt a slap across his face. He opened his eyes and tried again to think: Why his finger? What did the cutting off of a finger mean? A finger was an indicator, a button-pusher, a signaller. She had cut off the finger that could push the button. Did that mean he could no longer push the button and she could? What had she done with his finger? Did she keep it? Did she have others? A collection? That wasn't the point, he told himself. Maybe it was a phallic symbol?

Why didn't she just cut off his dick? Too much blood. He
would have died. Then there would have been the political
significance of the corpse. This was all conditioning of
course, he told himself. They wanted you to think like
this. And they wanted you to think of Jesus. But this was
no time for spiritual contemplation. The real revelation,
the revolution that Malky Macleod was undergoing,
concerned The State. For the first time in his life he could
see the point of it. Yes, now that he had had his finger
cut off he was going to go to the police. He groaned at
the pain. The question was, did knowledge come from
the outside or the inside? From within or without? From
within, of course. It was lucky Brigitta didn't know
that. But Malky Macleod was a man of action, not just
a thinker. He was a situationist, and this was a situation.
Over there to the right there was a machine of some kind,
a lawnmower or something that had sharp edges that
could cut cable ties. He was going over there. He rocked
the chair and fell hard on his side to the floor.

Chapter 3

In The Old Schoolhouse Guesthouse in Inverish, Mohammed Landa leant back and put his feet up on one of the three unmade beds that over-filled the bedroom. The view from the window was to the north over the waters of Loch Houn and the forests of the Ardven peninsula, but the view was half-obscured by a sixty-five-inch screen where a half-machine half-man was spraying aliens with laser beams.

'She's pregnant? What makes you think she's pregnant?' he said.

'I can tell,' said Solomon Matobela, spraying a monster with three jaws and tossing a grenade into a cave.

'That's what I'm asking you. How?'

Solly grinned and made a gesture that expressed the heaviness of an imaginary breast.

'You have experience of these things?'

'I read books,' said Solly. 'You should try it sometime.'

Mo laughed. The third man in the room, Qualin H Bremner, was rolling pairs of socks gathered from the pile on his bed and throwing the balls into an open drawer.

'Why do you make your socks into pairs Qualin, when they are all the same colour?'

'That's his pastime,' said Qualin, 'Making babies. Am I right Solly?'

Solly grinned and blew up a house. Lazy stereotypes one-oh-one, he thought. The black man goes around getting girls pregnant, scattering his seed like chicken food. Let them think what they wanted. He was not going to break the illusion and let them know that this was his first.

'Tell me this Solly,' said Mo, 'If she has a child, what will that child be? A Scottish or a Zulu or a Coloured?'

'A Zulu.'

'But it's a Coloured eh? Half-white, half-black.'

'How can it be Coloured?' said Qualin. 'To be a Coloured your mother must be a Coloured and your father a Coloured, like me.'

'So I am not a Coloured?' said Mo.

'You an Indian. Your father's an Indian.'

'My mother's a Coloured.'

'You a Muslim. A Muslim Indian. Forget it, you can never be a Coloured.' Qualin emphasised his point by throwing a sock-ball into the drawer.

'I can be what I want,' said Mo. 'This is the UK. Multiculturalism. Both of you are trapped in the apartheid mindset. You need to de-colonise your minds.'

'In the UK you are all Black,' said Solly. 'Coloured, Indian, Muslim, Zulu, Xhosa, Nigerian, Eskimo, all Black!'

'S'true,' said Qualin. 'In Scotland, Muslims is *kaffirs*.' Solly tutted, hissed at the word and shot an alien.

'You see,' said Mo, 'that's what I'm talking about! How can a Muslim be a *kaffir*? You know what *kaffir* means?'

'*Ja, Ja, ek se*!' said Qualin, 'I know all that. What I'm saying is, in this country, everyone that is not white is B.A.M.E! That is what you are, same as him, same as me! BAME!

'And this baby?' said Mo. 'What is this baby now? BAME? His mother is white, but he is BAME? Now you see how they're dividing us? *That* is racism.'

'My baby, any baby that is mine, will be a Zulu, no question.' Solly tossed the controller onto the couch as the half-man was devoured by an octopus.

Mo picked up his buzzing phone from the bed and held up a hand for silence. 'Brigitta?' he stood up as he listened. 'I'll tell you what we're doing today. We're doing what we do every day. We're going to get everything in the RIB and go out to the barge. We're going to go out to the barge and sit around for four hours smoking *zol*. Then we are going to come back here and go to the pub. Then when we finished in the pub we are going *jolling*. Brigitta, I work for Pik. If Pik wants me to do something different you tell him to call me himself.' He tossed the phone onto the bed.

'What she want?' said Qualin.

Mo held up his hand and counted the seconds with a nodding finger. Fill your boots. He had never heard this expression until he had arrived in the UK, but now it occurred to him every day. The boots, the bank accounts, the pockets, his Dad's bank account, they were all being filled. At the count of ten the phone buzzed and he took his time about picking it up.

'Uhuh. It's five hundred each.' He listened and nodded, smiling at the others. When he ended the call he announced: 'Boys, you must be grateful you have a Muslim brother who knows how to make money.'

'Anyone can make money when you are surrounded by white people who have too much,' said Solly.

'S'true my *bru*,' said Mo, 'but the *wit o* stole it from us, we *mus* take it back. It's *The Case for Reparations!*'

Solly snorted. *The Case for Reparations* only perpetuates the self-denigration of internalised victimhood, he thought, but didn't say.

'You know she is pregnant,' said Qualin, 'but why doesn't she *tell* you she is pregnant? If a woman wants your baby, she's gonna tell you she is pregnant, *neh*?'

Solly shrugged and stared out of the window. Of course, Qualin was right, he thought. Of course she wants to be sure that she is loved, first. I would, if I was pregnant.

At Johnny Murachar's croft-house the sound of the lock in the bedroom door woke Eamon. There was a long moment when he did not know where he was, but when he remembered he was surprised at how well he had slept, and how little he felt the pain in his shoulder.

A woman entered, put a bowl of soup and a glass of water on the chest of drawers and left without meeting his eye. He ate and drank as the last of the sun withdrew from the window, abandoning the floating flecks of dust. Then Shem came in, carrying a heavy stick instead of a rifle. He was somehow managing to keep his eyes wide open and frown at the same time.

'Come on,' he said, 'It'll start soon.' He led Eamon outside.

The hush of dusk had descended on the clearing and in the forest undergrowth it was already night. There were men in the watchtowers and men walking the path along the inside of the fence. They were carrying homemade clubs, shinty sticks and baseball bats. They were looking out, beyond the fence, into the dark beneath the trees, and batting midges from around their heads. Shem led Eamon up the rising ground towards the back of the croft.

'Dad said to show you these,' he said. He pointed with his stick to the corpse of a small deer lying in the undergrowth next to the fence. A little further on he pointed out a tangle of animal intestines. 'They have come in before and pulled up our crops. But we caught one and gave him a good hiding, and they are more cautious now.'

'Who is they?' said Eamon but Shem did not answer. The silence was complete, and unnatural. There was no birdsong and the men spread out around the perimeter were moving without a sound. They were small figures in a fading painting. Eamon stared into forest and thought he saw movement. Shem called him to look at something else lying on the path and as Eamon turned a curl of animal innards slapped against the fence next to him and blood wet his face. He heard a girl's giggle from the trees.

'Stay back from the fence,' said Shem. 'They can only throw so far.'

As the last flickers of light disappeared from the treetops a long, drawn-out wolf-howl sounded from the forest, and in the silence that followed Eamon felt the hairs on the back of his neck stick up. There was an element of self-consciousness in the howl. It was almost too good an imitation of a wolf. It was a method actor's

wolf-howl, and this made it at the same time ridiculous
and more sinister than the real thing. The howl echoed,
and there was a moment when the sound carried over the
croft and vanished somewhere in the centre as if diving
down a well, when it seemed that time surrounding
the cry dilated, and the thick, warm, still air and all it
contained: columns of hovering insects, leaves poised
movement-less at the end of branches, darkness creeping
inwards from the forest towards the points of light in
barns, croft-house and caravan windows, the smell of
wood-smoke and the dry ground, the soft motion of the
men at the perimeter and the gathering of women, the
old and the young in the centre beneath the black lines
of the platform and the cross, a moment when every
detail presaged some unknown awful thing, as if the
world knew, like animals running before an earthquake,
that something ugly was about to rise. Then the howl
was answered by a score of others from all sides of the
compound, and a chorus of barks, screams and yelps.
Powerful lights lit up the tower and two men in suits and
ties appeared on the platform. They were Johnny, carrying
a bible, and a small, old man carrying a microphone.
Johnny raised his hands, the little man sang into the
microphone and the voice emerged from the row of
speakers above them, loud above the howls. It was a
high, thin voice, and Eamon recognised the Gaelic. The

man sang the first line of a psalm, and the congregation beneath answered.

'*S e an t-uachdaran an ciobair agam*,' sang the man.

'*S e an t-uachdaran an ciobair agam*,' sang the people. Something kindled in Eamon's memory and the meaning emerged, like flickers of light beneath the trees.

'The lord is my shepherd, I shall not want;

He makes me to lie down in green pastures…'

And in response the cacophony from the shadows increased; catcalls, curses, wolf-howls and dog-barks. The precentor responded:

'Thou preparest a table before me in the presence of my enemies

Thou anointest my head with oil

My cup overflows'

Eamon could feel the missiles parting the air above his head. Shem handed him a torch, but the beam was caught and reflected in the mesh of the fence and lit little beyond.

'They throw shit,' said Shem, and in the same moment Eamon felt the impact of something soft on his arm and the smell hit him. He took cover behind the trunk of a slender ash. Again he heard the laughter of a girl. Then a new cry came from the forest;

'Crucify him! Crucify him!' in an accent that was either foreign or deliberately strange.

'Surely goodness and mercy shall follow me,' sang the congregation.

'All the days of my life…'

'Crucify him! Crucify him!'

Eamon thought he saw movement in the shadows and he tried to follow a dark shape with his torch. The singing ceased and the distorted voice of Johnny Murachar boomed over the croft.

'"For we wrestle not against flesh and blood, but against principalities! Against powers! Against the rulers of the darkness in this world!" Brothers and Sisters, Our Lord warned us about demons and evil spirits! He warned us about possession! He cast out the demons and put them into the swine, but they still roam this world, and when we speak the truth, the demons emerge from the darkness! We have gone from a god-fearing nation to a nation that worships animals! And here in Ardven they have gone from worshipping Our Saviour to worshipping The Wolf! A predator and devourer of children that was driven from these shores three hundred years ago!'

As Johnny went on in this vein Eamon thought at first it was having a calming effect on the voices from the trees. But then they began to hiss, and this was followed by the screaming of a real animal, an unmistakeable sound; somewhere in the trees higher up they were slaughtering a pig.

'I thought he said they worshipped animals,' whispered Eamon to Shem, not wanting to be the target of any more missiles. 'Does this happen every night?'

'A lot of nights,' said Shem. 'But the pig-sticking is new.'

The pig screamed until it was done, and then the psalms started up again. But after a few verses there was a collective indrawing of breath and a cry and the psalmists were silent. The spotlights trained on the tower were shining from the ground behind the crowd. A woman was holding her head.

'Probably an egg,' said Shem. A bloodied pig's trotter slammed against the trunk next to Eamon's head. He swung his torch, saw the human form in black, and ran for the fence. The rattling of the steel links drowned out Shem's voice calling him back as he climbed, rolled over the top, caught the other side, remembered that he had once been taught how to do this, and tore open a finger as he swung down. He saw a leg disappearing from his torchlight into the undergrowth and chased, tripping and flailing arms at bracken as high as his head. 'Bloody kids,' he thought as he heard mocking laughter ahead of him and ran through a thicket of hazel on the edge of the forest to shine his torch wildly around a clearing. Then he was into the woods, chasing the sound of running feet. Behind him the psalm singing started up again and it already seemed far away when the first blow caught him on the back. He swung the torch beam but saw only trees. There was laughter to his right, then movement to his left, many feet and breaking undergrowth crashing towards him. He shone the torch into yellow eyes; it was a stag; a full twelve-pointer, coming straight at him, then stopping, mist bursting from its nostrils in the cooling air. There was movement behind and another blow on his shoulder, as if the assailant knew about the one he had received earlier in the day, and he sunk to his knees as the stag stumbled into the trees. Eamon turned to see the figure standing over him, baseball bat raised; a tall man dressed in black, his mouth covered with a scarf printed with a skull. Eamon raised an arm, and as if at his command an explosion came from behind him. The flash lit up the canopy of trees, the man with the bat, and where the stag had been, the thin figure of a girl with long blonde, matted hair. In slow motion the bat descended, and, finally, the darkness that had been in abeyance since sunset, an age before.

Eamon became conscious to the sound of an engine. He was five years old and lying on the back seat of his father's car, trying to make sense of the pressures on his body and the lights moving on the ceiling. He closed his eyes. He was a teenager, drunk out of his mind, as his car swung and his gut heaved. He was sitting up, head out in the hot desert wind as a lightless Humvee churned dust into the star-thick Helmand skies. The contents of his stomach leeched a trail down the door. He could smell the vomit and someone else's shit, then the comfort of a thick wool jumper permeated with a man's sweat and a decade of cigarette smoke. The man's strength gentled as he unbuttoned Eamon's shirt and he felt the cold on his chest. He recognised the curses encouraging him to take a step, then another, until he was covered in a blanket and sitting in an armchair. He was in the living-room of Stevie Van's caravan, his big brother's home, in the quarry just north of Duncul village. He watched Stevie roll a cigarette.

When he next opened his eyes he was staring into a bright studio. Two men were sitting at a coffee table formed from a slab of red and white light. Stevie's beard and sticking-up hair were silhouetted against the television and the curl of smoke from his lips was parting into tendrils, forming a fog that filled the room and Eamon's lungs. Stevie saw him move and tossed over the packet of tobacco.

'What happened?' said Eamon.

'Rona called me. Your phone was off. She was worried.'

'Did you fire a shotgun at them?'

'How could I? You know I don't own a shotgun.'

Eamon felt the lump the size of a tennis ball on the back of his head. Stevie nodded at a six pack of lager. Eamon slaked the ache in his throat.

They both stared into the TV, leaving behind the cramped caravan and the smell of cigarettes and last night's pasta. The presenter was a Scot and he was interviewing Acturus McBean.

'I was born in a council house in Fife,' said Acturus. "My father was unemployed for most of my childhood. I come from a world you can barely imagine.'

'I'm not going to get into comparing childhoods. Can you explain to us what the so-called *Alt-Scot* movement actually is and why you are having your first conference in an obscure village in the North-West Highlands of Scotland?'

'I'm only too happy to do so Andrew,' said Acturus.

He's a Scot too, thought Eamon, but he didn't sound as if he had grown up on a council estate. He had the barely recognisable remnants of a Scottish accent, the ever-so-slightly rolled 'r' and that continual drone somewhere at the back of the nose. It was the voice of a posh Scot, a privately-educated Scot, an officer Scot, Anglo-Scot, Scot of the Castle, Hunt Ball and Shoot. A never-quite Scot, like me and my ilk.

Acturus made his signature move, sweeping the straight flop of blonde fringe away from his eyes. 'We are an alternative for Scotland. An alternative to the neo-liberal, elitist, internationalist, left-leaning chattering-class consensus. We are the future! The Alt-Scot Convention or *Cruinneachadh*, is a gathering of a diverse group of voices. But not fake diverse! We don't all agree with each other, unlike you lot!'

'I didn't know you were into politics,' said Eamon.

Stevie shrugged. 'Don't seem to have any choice these days.'

'We have speakers from the *Scottish Identitarian Movement*,' continued Acturus McBean, 'and *The Climate Acceptance Group*. We have myself and others from the *Scottish Independent Conservatives, Siol Nan Gael*, guest speakers from down south, *The Irish Freedom Party*, and many of our European cousins will be there.'

'Many would say these are neo-fascist groups from across Europe. White-supremacists and climate-change deniers,' said Andrew.

'There you go again, those weasel words, "climate-change deniers"! As if they are denying the Holocaust! What about diversity Andrew? What about free speech? What about listening to an opinion that you might not agree with? What about listening to the science? And you say, "white supremacists"! Try saying that to the *Kampala Christian Brotherhood*, one of our most welcome African groups!'

'Well what *would* you say unites all of these groups?'

'It's very clear. There are three themes, Religion, Family and Property, which amount to a resistance to the intrusion of the dead hand of the state and the liberal hegemony. I could say that what also unites us is that we are intensely "problematic".'

'And why Duncul? Of all places, in the middle of nowhere?'

'Because the convention is going to be held in that
nexus of the culture wars, on Johnny Murachar's Croft,
where one man has been standing alone against the
onslaught of the eco-fascist, anti-family, anti-Christian,
anti-property-rights arch-liberal internationalist Denis
Nyst. Johnny Murachar's croft is a symbol of all that we
stand for; the lone crofter, standing his ground against
International Capital. The lone crofter surrounded by the
howling wolves, resisting! And before you ask, no, I don't
agree with everything he says, but I stand by his right to
say it. He is a devout Christian, and he has a right to his
beliefs.'

'He has been accused of hate-speech, against Muslims,
against homosexuals, against Jews, you name it.'

'I defy you to find one example of hate in any speech
Johnny Murachar has made.'

'I could give you a score, and you know it. As for
international capital, would you like to talk about who
funds you and the SIC?'

'Now you're changing the subject, because of course,
you don't want to talk about the issues.'

'I don't think I can take any more of this crap,' said
Eamon.

'You're going to be hearing a lot more,' said Stevie. 'Just
wait 'til Acturus gets here. He's one of your lot isn't he?
Won't you be entertaining him at the castle, old chap?'

'One of our lot makes him one of your lot, *bruv*. Please, switch it off.'

Stevie grinned. Acturus McBean swept away his fringe and faded to black. They sat still in the sudden silence.

'Why didn't you take me home?' said Eamon.

'Because you're covered in blood and shit, and you were hardly conscious. You want your wife to see you like that?'

'Do the police know about what's going on at the croft? Apparently it happens regularly.'

'You think Johnny wants it to stop? It suits him fine. He livestreams it. He's got everyone there stirred up to a frenzy. They think they're in the backwoods of Michigan, about to make a stand against The Feds. Check this out.' He swung his chair around to the wall of bookshelves that lined one side of the room and switched on a computer screen.

'You've entered the twenty-first century.'

'Have you heard of *Call of Duty*?'

'No.'

'Didn't think so.' Stevie played a video of Johnny Murachar standing on the platform in the floodlights.

'…surrounded by the demons of hell, the screaming demons, crying the name of Satan, because here on Johnny Murachar's croft, here in the woods and hills of Ardven, in the peace of the Highlands where men and women of good-will have come together to form a brotherhood steeped in the blood of the lamb, even here, in the far north of the country the stinking stench of the corruption that envelopes the nation has crept like a foul mist!

'Yeah. I've read his blog, and now I've seen him live.' said Eamon. 'I'm going home. Give me a shirt.'

Stevie went through to the bedroom.

'Who are those people on the other side of the fence?'

'Employees of Mr Nyst,' said Stevie, throwing a t-shirt at Eamon. 'German anarchists apparently. They call themselves "*Autonomass*". Anti-state, anti-police, anti-whatever you've got. In Germany they used to call them *Autonomen*. Or Black bloc. In America they call them *Antifa* now. In my experience, trustafarians, the lot of them.'

'Trustafarian?'

'White kid with dreadlocks and a trust fund. Middle class, smashing the system, as long as Daddy keeps sending the cheques.'

'That's you isn't it?' They both grinned.

'You got me, 'cept, definitely not middle class. My mum was a cleaner.'

'Your dad was the Laird of Duncul. You're half-toff, half-cleaner, puts you bang in the middle.' Eamon rubbed the bump on the back of his head. He leant back in the chair and thought of David Smart with his thin limbs and bright smile.

'What does Detective Maclean think happened at the manse?' said Stevie.

'He won't tell me anything.'

'If it was one of Murachar's lot, Maclean will catch them pretty quick. From what I heard it must have been a hell of a fight. The whole place was smashed up. It looks like they were beaten to death. Their will be DNA everywhere. But Murachar's not the only one around here who hates gays.'

'How do you know what happened?'

'It was the Macdonald kids who saw the bodies through the window. They were sneaking around the back, peeking in the windows, and then their mum, Sonya, went up. By the time the cops arrived half of Tarr Bow had had a look. And someone took pictures. Here,' he took out his phone and tapped. 'That's weird. It's gone. It was on Siobhan's twitter.'

'Not weird. Sergeant Peters has had the pictures deleted.' Eamon closed his eyes and thought about going home, to his beautiful wife, to the wisps of hair on his son's head.

'There was graffiti all over the walls, "Fuck Fags! Kill the Gays!"'

'I didn't see that.' said Eamon. 'Who else hates gays?'

'Let's see. Half the Catholics. Pretty much all the Free Churchers. Probably all the Muslims. And no, before you get any ideas, you can't evict them all.'

'There's no Muslims in Duncul.'

'There's three in Inverish.'

'Since when?'

'Since months. Divers apparently, here to salvage the *Eloise*. But they haven't made much progress. They smoke a lot of weed.'

'Customers of yours?'

'Customer of a customer. Malky buys for them.'

'But you can't know that all these people hate gays, not like that.'

'Maybe not obviously, but the prejudice is there, deep down. David and Kosma were kind of obvious, and they pissed off a lot of people, going around choring stuff.'

'Did they take anything from you?'

'No. But I was coming down from the hill one day, a couple of months back, looking down on the quarry, and I saw the dark one, Kosma, leaving the caravan and going back along the track to the village.'

'Didn't you say something?'

'Nah. I'm not like you, I don't like confrontation. And he kinda' seemed, you know, harmless. Besides, the caravan is never locked. He didn't actually break in, and he didn't take anything.'

Eamon took a torch and went out into a night lit by three-quarters of a moon moving in and out of the clouds. At the end of the track to the quarry he turned

away from the road that led through the village to the
castle and walked up the hill towards the manse.

The wind was unsettling last year's leaves beneath the
trees and bouncing the police tape that was taught across
the gate. He ducked under the tape and switched on the
torch as he left the reach of the streetlights. There was
a police car parked at the front door. He stayed off the
drive and crept through the trees around to the back of
the building. The manse backed onto the hillside and
was separated from the slope by a narrow alley. Eamon
shone the torch through the living-room window onto
a broken table and chairs and upended sofa, smashed
coffee-table and tossed up sleeping-bags and mattresses.
The epithets that he hadn't noticed in the photograph
were on the wall, in marker pen. It was as if a tornado had
torn through the room. The light made the broken glass
that covered the floor sparkle between the odd collection
of things that David and Kosma had pilfered; remains of
garden gnomes, a bird-table, a dog-basket, potted plants,
a child's fishing rod. He switched off the torch, rested his
forehead on the sill and felt tears swell beneath his eyelids.
Words emerged from some long forgotten childish
version of himself: 'God Bless David and Kosma.' He
stood up and was leaving the alley when he was startled
by a small, white face hovering ahead of him. He fumbled
for the torch but by the time he switched it on the face
had gone.

He stumbled to the corner of the house and swung the beam, trying to catch something other than tree trunks and bushes and caught the gloss of a raincoat and the scything of quick limbs on the beech-covered bank beyond the drive. He followed, but saw only trees until he reached the high wall to the manse garden and was about to turn back when he noticed the door in the wall.

The road beyond was empty and carried on uphill, to where what the village knew as 'The Avenue' ran along the contour of the hill behind the manse. Here larger houses and 'villas' were set among gardens and old trees. When Duncul had had a doctor he had lived here, as had the butcher, the vet and the headmaster, but they had long since gone and the avenue had been extended by retirees and refugees from the property prices of the South. 'Economic Migrants' he had heard them called, or by those with less subtlety, 'White Settlers,' and 'Colonists'. The figure in the raincoat walked briskly through the gateway to a white bungalow set among unkempt rhododendrons and lupins. Then it turned the little face to shine on him again, like a little moon fallen into the shrubbery, and he raised a hand, but she did not return the wave. He recognised Mrs Murray; Edwina or Edina or something like that.

You know the tall, thin man, running through the trees. It's the Laird. The lens is good even in this light. You recognise his long head and jaw jutting into the darkness. What does he want at the back of the manse? What does he want with the watchers? Catch him, put his light into darkness. Keep him. Never let him escape. No, that was a mistake you would never let happen again, letting one escape.

Chapter 4

At Endpoint House, at the westernmost tip of the Ardven Peninsula, the fresh east wind was tossing the tops of the pines at a cloud-scraped moon. In the over-heated study the air smelled of sweat, dust and something chemical. One table lamp and a small TV screen barely lit the oak panels and mahogany desk. Denis Nyst, a heavy-faced man in his seventies with long curling grey hair, wearing a floor-length grey smock, sat before the screen pressing hard on the buttons of a remote control and jabbing it at the nodding, grinning image of Acturus McBean. He stood and cursed as he hit the side of the screen to switch it off. Breathing hard, he tossed the remote to the tall man with short blonde hair standing in the doorway.

'Get me batteries for this thing,' he said with a Dutch accent.

'Sure Boss,' said Pik, with a South African accent.

Nyst rubbed his face with his hands. 'Why is she not here? Must I wait for her now?' He scowled as he went into the darkness by the far wall to lie down on a creaking camp bed. Pik waited. Nyst closed his eyes and could see only Brigitta, little Brigitta, girl Brigitta, woman Brigitta. Was she really a woman? Was there anything womanly about her? After a life full of so many achievements, riches and pleasures, all he could think about was this miserable child! On a table in the centre of the room a large plastic box attached to a computer made a whizzing sound. Nyst grinned at the distraction and moved to the table. The box whizzed, paused and whizzed.

'Is it working OK now?' said Pik.

'Yes, thank you, working fine. It all depends on the filament. I think I have found the optimum. Look!' He held up a figure made of shiny grey plastic.

'That's great Boss.'

'Don't you recognise him? Look closely at the face.'

Pik looked and smiled, but shook his head.

'It's Acturus McBean!' said Nyst. 'But of course you are not political. I have a very clever programme that can make a 3D representation of any photograph. Here's the leader of the Highland Council. Here's the Director of Scottish Natural Heritage. Here's Johnny Murachar himself.' He lined up the figures on the table.

'What are those?' Pik pointed to some grey plastic cubes and cylinders.

'Oh, nothing. Just experiments. I'm still learning the ropes. Look at these. Aren't they wonderful?' He held up a pair of model wolves. 'Come. Let's go to the sheds.'

Nyst looked up at the moon and muttered curses as they walked across an overgrown lawn towards a steading of grey stone and slate roofs. As they approached the cobbled yard between the buildings, they passed a group of young men and women gathered around a bonfire, sitting on garden chairs and a decrepit sofa. Music was playing. As Nyst and Pik crossed the yard there were shouts and the sound of a bottle smashing. Pik looked back with a frown, but Nyst did not turn his head. He kept his eyes fixed on a door into one of the barns and shut it firmly behind them.

They had entered a corridor that ran the length of the building and was lit only by the moon beyond the windows. Nyst took a deep breath and tried to release the tension in his shoulders. It was not a remarkable smell. It was merely like a dog, but stronger, but he was sure that it was mingled with the smell of a forest; sunlight scattered over moss beneath evergreens.

'You must not worry. They are fine,' said Pik.

'They are not fine. The keeper says I should send them back.'

Pik shrugged his shoulders. 'Get another keeper.'

'This is not Africa Pik. You can't just get rid of people.' There was a long silence before Pik spoke.

'You know, that's funny, coming from you.'

Nyst smiled weakly. 'You think I'm a murderer?'

'No Boss, I think you are a great man. I think the world has been waiting for you for a long time.'

'You are wrong. Everybody hates me. But I don't care. You know,' he jerked his thumb in the direction of the youths around the bonfire, 'They think the world has been waiting for *her*.' He waited for a reply, but Pik only shrugged. 'Go and speak to them. Get their *"Chosen One"* to come to my office. I have feelings, feelings, feelings.' He rubbed his face. 'I always trust my feelings.'

'Yes Boss.'

When Pik had gone Nyst put his fingers in his ears to block the sound from outside and let the cool of the barn and the smell of the wolves fill him up. He stretched out a hand to place it against the steel door in the wall before him. There was something wrong with him, he was sure. He had not found a doctor that could say what it was, but he knew there was something decaying inside. He went to the end of the corridor, opened a wooden door and climbed the narrow stair beyond. At the top there was a small room which looked down through a thick glass

pane into the straw-carpeted wolf-room. There was little
light, but he could see two of the wolves that had come
in by the hatch that led to the compound in the forest.
They were lying down but awake, with their heads up,
watching the darkness. Nyst felt the familiar, never-failing
quiver of excitement. His lips parted. He did not move,
but as he watched they began to unsettle and at first he
thought he was the cause. He knew they could smell him
even through the glass. They began to pace; two huge
shadows circling each other. Then one began to paw at
the steel door. Nyst heard a low bumping, like a door
knocking, coming from below. He descended the stairs,
trying not to make them creak. The bumping was coming
from the end of the corridor, from a wooden trapdoor
in the floor. He watched it move slightly against the bolt.
He watched it move several times and considered the
possibility there was a wolf under the floor. But all the
doors and gates to the compound were made of steel,
because wolves had one overwhelming instinct; to be free,
and a wooden door posed little hindrance to them. They
would gnaw and scratch through it. In the dark and silent
barn the knowledge began to emerge in Nyst's mind that
there was something in the basement, and that something
was trying to get out, and that something could only be a
person. The door moved again, a matter of millimetres,
and was held by the thick bolt. He added the facts
together again. Someone was in the basement, and that

someone was trying to get out, against the will of a draw-bolt, and that draw-bolt had been drawn by someone else. There is an unerring equation; for every prisoner there is at least one jailor. No-one had told him about this. No-one had told Denis Nyst that there was a man locked in *his* basement. There was someone locked in *his* basement and it was disturbing *his* wolves. He bent his tired frame and slid back the bolt.

It was only when he had done so that he considered the alternatives and found them more sensible. He could have gone to find Pik. He could have demanded an explanation from Brigitta, because of course this could only be Brigitta's business. He stepped back into the shadows in retreat from his decision and watched the door rise and the man climb the steps. The moonlight was all that lit him, but Nyst saw enough to make him draw in breath and hold it. The man was small, with close-cropped hair, swollen eyes, a bulging lower lip and blood thick on the face and hair. There was blood that was still red and blood turned black and stiff in patterns that merged with the tattoos that crept up his neck and covered his bare arms. The man held up both hands in a placating gesture and twisted the lips in what Nyst thought might be an attempt at a smile. One of the hands was bandaged with a sock and one of the feet was bare. The man stood still, watching him, and Nyst watched back as he approached with his arms raised and edged along the corridor wall.

Nyst was about to speak when the man turned and ran out into the yard.

'Hey!' shouted Nyst. 'Hey!' The man darted beneath the arches of the implement shed on the other side. 'Pik!' shouted Nyst, and standing in the centre of the yard yelled against the east wind and the music and laughter that came from the bonfire, 'Brigitta!' Men from the fire began walking towards him. Nyst was raising his arm to point and begin an explanation when the sound of a motorbike erupted from the implement shed, and the machine lit them with its headlight, scattered curses in its wake and tore into the night. Nyst spun to follow it and spun again as the men ran to the shed and two bikes roared out of the yard in pursuit.

Chapter 5

Malky Macleod had grown up working on two-stroke engines and the sound drilled into his memory as it pierced the darkness of the loch to his left and the forest to his right, like a machine-gun spitting out gobbets of childhood. The bike was an old one and he was braking with a foot in a sock, changing gear with a bare foot, and pulling the clutch with two of the remaining three fingers on his left hand, but the beam from the headlight seemed to be pulling him into the night over the track and the wind was easing the pain in his face. He grinned. He could hear the bikes behind but he doubted they would catch up. His only disadvantage was that although he knew where he was, he only knew how to get there by boat. They had taken him in a van, with a sack over his

head, and then on a RIB. He had felt the soft gunwale
as they dragged him on board and he had heard the
outboard, a four-stroke Yamaha with electric start, at least
fifty horse. They had taken him west from his caravan on
the shore of Loch Houn, ten miles up the loch to the end
of the Ardven Peninsula, to Endpoint House. They had
taken him by boat because there was no road to Endpoint,
but there had to be paths of some kind.

He slid to a stop as the track ended at a turning circle
and a gate in the wolf-fence. The bikes behind were
screaming closer but there was no lock on the gate and
he followed the path on the other side that ran uphill,
away from the shore, along a firebreak in the forest. The
bike bucked and crunched beneath him. The firebreak
led south, across the peninsula, and he knew he needed
to turn east, into the wall of trees to his left. It was hard
to keep his eyes far enough ahead on the twisting path,
and he almost crashed into the pile of stones; a newly
built cairn right in the middle of the path, made from
clean stones that shone in the headlight. It was topped
with a large flat stone and a kind of large stone cup stood
in the centre. Even in his panic Malky was struck by the
oddness of it. He cursed and made the engine scream
as he manoeuvred around. The sound of the two bikes
behind were louder. He thumped the baseplate on rocks
as the path rose steeply. A hundred yards further brought
him to another cairn, right on the path, flat topped, newly

built, with another cup on the top, and he had to skirt around again. But then the forest opened to his left with a firebreak leading up the hill to the east, and the path became smooth and wide. He took off, flipping up the gears. The engine crackled back at him from the tunnel of pines and he felt the wind on his face again.

Malky the anarchist was going to the police. This was something to do with Jesus and something to do with Kosma. But the moment of decision had come when she had cut off his finger. So it was above all to do with her, he had to admit. He had finally met her. He had never believed all the bullshit about Brigitta being weird and special, but they had been right. Somehow she clarified things. She made you think. She made you feel small. She was not like him. She was not even like them.

Ten of them had walked into the pub in Inverish, about a year ago, dressed like himself in skinny black jeans, scruffy t-shirts, baggy jumpers and leather jackets. They had come in and ordered beers in German accents and a couple had started smoking. Eilidh the barmaid had ordered them out and they had sworn at her in German, and if they had stayed even a second longer there would have been a fight, because Big Dougie had an unrequited thing for Eilidh and although it was only late morning he was red-faced pissed and brooding in his corner at the end of the bar. But one of the Germans had answered a phone and in the last second before war broke out they had

walked, leaving burning cigarettes on the floor. They had
never returned.

Until that day Malky had been the only anarchist in
the glen and he had been not a little disappointed when
they left. He knew a German anarchist when he saw one,
because he had spent a lot of time studying them on
YouTube. The German anarchist was a pretty high class
of anarchist, not quite as hard-core as your Spanish or
Greek, but definitely a cut above your French, who was
merely decadent and whose idea of political action was
to make love in the catacombs. A German anarchist was
infinitely superior to the English, whose idea of political
action was to get drunk and swear at a policeman. And
they were a species of demi-god to the Scottish anarchist,
of whom there were ten in Glasgow, ten in Leith, and five
in the Highlands.

When they had left the pub Malky had assumed they
had gone back to Germany. He had assumed they had
been tourist anarchists, with an interest in romantic
landscapes and pastiche medieval castles. After a few days
he had become used to the disappointment that he had
not been able to get to know them, and had even begun
to think that this was for the best, because he suspected
they might have not quite lived up to his expectations, and
vice versa. He had begun to be a little bit disappointed
in himself, as an anarchist. When he wasn't making a lot
of money diving for scallops all he did was get stoned,

play long hours of *Call of Duty* on Stevie Van's computer, and eat frozen pizza. He had noticed a total absence of political action. The only things anarchist about him were his tattoos and clothes, and then the Jesus thing had started, and that was the beginning of the end. Once that idea got into your head, that *thought-worm*, working its way through everything, it wasn't going to stop. He wouldn't have wanted the German anarchists to find out about *that*. So it was just as well they had disappeared. But then they had re-appeared, not in the flesh, but by report. Because who else would be throwing eggs and rabbit guts over the fence at Johnny Murachar's croft? That was German anarchist behaviour, for sure. He had watched them online, throwing rocks at the police, every second weekend in Berlin. This was protest as performance stuff, 'propaganda of the deed'. And it made sense that Denis Nyst had hired them, because everyone knew anarchists like nothing better than getting paid for their anarchism. He had hired them to get rid of Johnny Murachar. Whether they would succeed was another matter, because perhaps even German anarchists were out of their depth when it came to Scottish Calvinists on a midge-infested croft. And yes, he had to admit, this present situation, with the kidnapping and the finger cutting, was only his own fault. He had approached them. He had wanted to impress, despite how much he had changed, and had gone to them bearing gifts, and offering a weed supply.

Pathetic. Anyhow, that was all irrelevant now. Now all that mattered was that he was going to the police. As soon as she had cut off his finger. That was the definitive end of anarchism, once you went to the police. He twisted the throttle to its limit and the bike screamed at the forest.

He was chasing the edge of the reach of the headlight, like a missile fired down the tunnel of trees, glancing over his shoulder at the jerks and flashes of the two lights behind. He found the fifth gear with a bruised toe and took control of the bike to a higher level, guiding it by instinct and faith, with minute twitches towards the line of the path. But the gate in the deer fence at the edge of the forest appeared above him and he had to stand the bike, get off, open the gate, and by the time he was back on and through, the lights of the pursuers were touching him. Beyond the forest he tore up a steep and twisting route through the heather and then out into a straight run beneath the moon. He did not know where the path led, he did not know how much fuel was in the tank; it was all faith, moonlight, cold wind and the bikes behind like hunting wolves.

At the top where the heather was only ankle deep he looked out beyond the beam of the headlight and could see where the hill descended into forest again. Below to his right lay Loch Houn, below to his left, Loch Nish, and further on, beyond the forest, the lights of Duncul. He fired the bike downhill, losing the path,

bucking and thumping and finding it again. The lights
behind shifted like blades against the black sky and fell
around his wheels, making the heather gleam. Malky
reached the ancient forest of oak and Caledonian pines
that surrounded Johnny Murachar's, and he cursed as he
remembered the fence around the croft, and the fence
beyond running all the way across the peninsula. Before
he could think of a plan the wire mesh loomed up before
him and he had turned down the hill towards Loch Nish.
Even as he found a path and the forest opened, doubt gave
birth to fear, and the fear grew in him like a tide rising
through the weeds at the edge of the loch. The lights of
the bikes behind were snatching at his back. The fence
that surrounded Murachar's croft ran unbroken into Loch
Nish. He cursed his own stupidity as he caught glimpses
of the water through the trees and smelt familiar salt and
rotting weed, the smell of his living. The tide was low, but
the fence extended far out, marching down into the little
waves that tossed the moon back at itself. Whoever had
built the fence for Denis Nyst had spared him no expense.
The glimmer of hope that had sustained the run over the
hill vanished. But Malky did not slow. He clattered on over
the weed and rocks, through the low-tide pools, onto the
sand, and twisted the throttle so that the bike sliced into
the sea, casting up a plume that glittered in the following
beams. He rode until the bike was underwater and
suffocated. Then he put his chin out and launched into the

arms of that old, most treacherous of friends and swam towards the invisible far shore; out, out beyond the fence, straight out above the deep like a bird above the hill. The pursuing beams stopped and shone across the wave-tops. Malky turned, grinned, and turned again to face the dark. He felt the little waves fall against his face, and let the myriad tendrils that embrace the world caress his limbs, hold him up, pull him down, and let the trillion spirits of the sea gently explore every aspect of himself, and swam a hard, fast swim, pitting determination and faith against the cold, forming a resolution for Duncul; lights, a house, the police station at Aberfashie and the unburdening of all he knew and how it all made sense. And his numbed three-fingered hand rose from the surface and reached and dove, reached and dove, thrusting the darkness behind him, while the trillion spirits curled about each limb and considered as they have considered since long before the first man swam, the fate of all living things.

'Who wins in the battle between the neo-liberal hegemony and the sea? The trouble with me is the same as with all good Christians,' spluttered Malky the lonely anarchist against the waves, 'It's that I have something within me that shouldn't be there. What I need,' splutter, cough, 'is for the police,' splutter, cough, 'to perform an exorcism.'

Chapter 6

As Eamon walked up the drive to Duncul Castle he
looked towards the Ash woods and the faint glow from
Mike's shed. He knew that Mike slept little and wondered
if he was awake, keeping watch. Mike was like a golem
at the gates, guarding Duncul. A faithful servant, like his
father and grandfather and his father before that. Mike
Mack, Archie Mack, Alasdair Mack, and his father, also a
Mack, in the time when the castle had had five gardeners.
Eamon tried the front door of the castle and found it
locked. At the back he tried the tower door and found it
open. He locked it behind him.

In the bedroom he lit a candle and cast the light over
her face and the face of his child. He went downstairs to
shower and when he came back to the room Harry was

crying and she was sitting up to feed him. She saw the purple bruising on his shoulder and neck.

'What happened?'

'It's a long story.'

'I've got all night.'

Half an hour later in the study Rona was staring at the frozen image of Johnny Murachar on the laptop screen. 'He should be in jail,' she said.

'It's not illegal,' said Eamon, standing by the fire and sipping his second whisky.

'Why not? It's poison!'

'There is freedom of speech. You don't have to listen to it.'

'But thousands of people do! I thought there were laws about this sort of thing; hate-speech on the internet?'

'It's his own website. He's not doing it on Facebook or Twitter.'

Rona closed the laptop. 'All that in the name of God? No wonder no-one likes God anymore.'

Eamon sat on the couch next to her and she put her feet on his lap.

'But still, it doesn't mean the Murachars killed them,' she said. 'I mean, which one? Shem? Melchizidek? Daniel? Abraham? Abraham is fourteen years old! Johnny Murachar himself? Really? He's going to march over there in the middle of the night and beat two boys to death?'

'There are other men there, at least ten others, older
men. We don't know anything about them, apart from
them being religious fanatics.'

'Maybe it's nothing to do with Johnny Murachar?' said
Rona. 'We don't know anything about David and Kosma.
I mean, what were they doing before they came here?
Why did they come here? For a start, who leased them the
manse?'

'You told me to let Maclean do his job.'

'I googled David Smart. There's very little. A few
Facebook pictures of him at parties. There's nothing at all
on Kosma. No pictures. Nothing.'

Eamon rubbed his neck. 'What about these
Autonomass?'

Rona opened the laptop and tapped the keyboard.
'Kids in face masks and black hoodies. Throwing rocks at
police.' She turned the screen to him. 'All these pictures
are from Berlin.'

'That's them.'

'Antifascists. Beating up neo-Nazis. They hate the
police too. And the army. They don't like people like you.'
Eamon closed his eyes and she read on in silence. Eamon
saw Mrs Murray's little white face, turning towards him
out of the dark beech trees, turning away, like the moon
going in and out of clouds.

In the study at Endpoint House Nyst rubbed his eyes
and studied Brigitta from between his fingers, crushing
her limbs with shadows, allowing the light from the table
lamp to set fire to her hair. Somewhere behind the façade
of her face he could see the smile of a twelve-year-old in
an incongruous bikini, feet dangling in the pool. Straight,
ghost-white hair; a face that never stilled, leaping from
smile to laugh to frown. His memories of Brigitta the
child were confused with memories of sore teeth and the
squealing of the Berlin U-Bahn. Her father had been the
best dentist in Europe.

Brigitta had been born to wealthy parents; she had
been a clever, well-educated, only child, in a wealthy
country, brought up with success and achievement in
mind, but something had gone wrong with this project.
Perhaps there was an event; perhaps it involved the father.
Perhaps no event; only an idea. She had been febrile,
vivacious, cute; then not, between a cracked molar and
a replacement cap. Sometime not long after the dangling
of the feet in the pool this child had stopped smiling and
had begun to move deliberately, without spontaneity. He
remembered her presenting herself in another study; her
father's, in the top box of that pile of glass and steel boxes
in Wannsee. Brigitta with her homework, with sleeves of
a sweatshirt pulled down over her hands, covering bitten
down fingernails; nervous, fearful even, of two big men
drinking whisky from big tumblers. And somehow her

disaffection had mirrored his own. He could not track the genesis of the *angst* in himself; how could he discern it in her? What had turned him from a big man with a big whisky in a big tumbler, devouring life, devouring men, women, children, families, mines, factories, towns, into this determined, obsessive, depressed shell? Some thought, some bug, some bacteria or virus? Some cancer that had entered him, and begun to gnaw. Something that no doctor could see. His eyes had been opened in the time it took for her to grow from twelve into a woman. Sometimes, thinking about it deeply, lying on his camp bed with his head in his hands, he considered that it was only the sight of her in the study and her father calling her forward into the light reflecting in the whisky glass and the image of the strong hand, adept at pulling molars, rubbing her spine; the tentative smile pushed out of her that had pushed something out of, or into, himself. Somehow, at some point, Brigitta had looked at him and done what no other woman had ever done; she had pricked his conscience. But, he realised, this could all be his imagination.

He had had many occasions to visit her father as his teeth crumbled over the years from her pubescence to adulthood. She had become interested in politics; the environment, capitalism, sexism, racism. She had gone on marches. She had been arrested. She had moved out, into a squat; she had dropped out of her university. She had thrown a bomb at a line of policemen, and was on the run. She had been caught, and jailed, and released on a technicality. All this he had learned from her father. Then she had disappeared from his life for a year, then another. Then Denis Nyst had had her found, because no-one can disappear from Denis Nyst. Pik had tracked her down to a housing estate in east London and Pik had delivered the information with a list of warnings. Topmost, she had killed a boyfriend, somewhere in the Ardennes, and burned his body in the house. Secondly, she and her friends had kidnapped a woman and child, and received the ransom, all without the police finding out.

'Perfect.' Denis Nyst had said. 'She is perfect. She has always been perfect.' But she still made him uneasy, because in spite of his principals and his projects, he was still the enemy. One of those who had sat in the dim light of her father's study, tumbler in hand, conscious of their power and her perfect fragility.

She had removed a pair of filthy trainers and curled her feet beneath her on the sofa.

'You are here to help me get rid of Johnny Murachar, to maintain the fence, to prepare the forest for the wolves, and for that I am paying you a lot of money.'

'But we don't do it for the money.'

'No, of course not.'

'We are volunteers. We are autonomous.'

'Who was the man in the cellar?'

'His name is Malky. He is a scallop diver.'

'Why was he in the cellar?'

'He has information about a source,' said Brigitta.

Nyst frowned. 'Really? A scallop diver? A source?'

'Yes.'

'That is intriguing,' said Nyst, 'Tell me more.'

Brigitta watched him. 'I don't think I should. Also, it may not be good information.'

'And if it is good information? What then?'

'We will make use of it.'

'Using my method?'

'Yes.'

A grin spread across Nyst's face. 'Perhaps we are on the same page, you and I.'

'Maybe. It is an accident.'

'A happy accident,' he grinned, but frowned again. 'The two men in Duncul…'

'They were not men.'

'Boys then…'

'They were pigs.'

'You mean police?'

'I mean pigs.'

'It was you?' he asked.

She stared at him. 'What does it matter?'

'If you kill people it matters. The police will investigate.' Nyst paced the room, sat down on his bed and rubbed his face. 'How soon will you have the source?'

'I don't know. We will need more money.'

'That is not a problem. Speak to Pik.' Nyst stood up and began arranging the plastic figures on the table. 'They will see. All of them. Speaking of pigs, what about the other one?'

'We have followed him.'

'To where?'

'To a house in the hills. It belongs to your neighbour, the Arab.'

'What is his business? Why is he watching us?'

'It doesn't matter. We will deal with him. I am going now, to find Malky.' She left the room. Nyst called Pik.

'Have you found a source yet?'

'Boss, there are difficulties.'

'For you! Not for her!' There was a long pause.

'What kind?'

'A source. That is all she will say.'

'Boss, I am happy for you. That is a good thing.'

'Yes, yes, a good thing. A wonderful thing!'

By morning the wind had fallen, Loch Houn had reclaimed a perfect reflection of the hills and forests of Ardven and a blue sky had been adorned with the faintest of clouds. The *Kelpie*, a square, rusting barge anchored above the remains of the wreck of the *Eloise*, towards the end of the loch and half a mile from both the mainland and the peninsula of Ardven, moved against its moorings.

Ripples spread out, buckling the image of sky and hills.
A ten-metre RIB dive-boat squeaked against the tyres
that ringed the barge, '*Sea Wolf*' emblazoned on her
grey inflatable gunwales, and on the deck, busy with a
compressor and a collection of yellow air bottles, three
men, causing the ripples.

'Put on your *kufi*,' said Mo. 'They going to be here *now
now*.' Solly emitted a disaffected syllable as he put on the
white prayer cap, matching the other two. The bottles
were charged and stowed; weights, suits, jackets, fins,
masks, all checked. The three rested against the wall of
the wheelhouse, looking to the west. Qualin lit a joint and
passed it to Solly.

'Here she comes,' said Qualin, watching the developing
tear in the surface of the loch as another grey RIB with a
powerful outboard emerged from between the hills. 'She
could have come to Inverish. Why didn't she come to
Inverish?'

'Obvious my *bru*,' said Mo. 'She don't want anyone to
know.'

'This woman is some woman,' said Solly. 'This woman
is very…white. You know?'

'What do you mean?'

'I dunno. Just…not BAME.'

'Remember not to stand too close Solly,' said Qualin.

'Why?'

'She don't like toothpaste.'

'Toothpaste?'

'Apparently she thinks it's a conspiracy.'

'A toothpaste conspiracy?'

'Just don't stand downwind.'

'And don't mention *halal*, how you *slag* those sheep. She is strict vegan.'

'I don't *halal* nothing. I'm a Zulu.'

'That's even worse my *bru*. Don't mention it!'

'Quiet man! Be professional,' said Mo as the boat approached on a silky bow wave that bent the sky back beneath the hull. Brigitta stood at the bow, a figurehead with waving hair. The boat slowed precisely, guided by the three crew, and as it kissed the side of the barge she stepped on board without waiting for the mooring rope. She landed on the deck in front of them as if she had floated from the air, with her face glowing. Solly tossed the joint into the water. Mo smiled but she did not, as she looked at them with grey eyes.

'Which one is Mohammed?' Mo raised a hand, like a schoolboy. 'Horst,' she said and the tallest and thinnest of the crew stepped onto the boat in front of Mo and showed his crooked teeth. He presented a grey box with a shiny screen and wires protruding from the back. 'You know what this is?' said Brigitta.

'Chart-plotter,' said Mo, taking it. 'I have one.'

'You will use this one. It has all the dive sites.'

'How many?'

'Thirty four.'

'Thirty four? That's going to take a while,' he grinned, doing the arithmetic.

'How long?'

'Depends. We do two a day, that's three weeks. Depends on weather. Depends how deep.'

'You can do three a day.'

'Maybe. Three a day at five hundred a dive is fifteen hundred a day.' He watched Brigitta's blank face. 'What are we looking for?'

'AUV. You know was *ist* AUV?'

'Autonomous Underwater Vehicle. What kind? What does it look like?' Horst waited for a nod from Brigitta before handing Mo a sheet of paper. It showed a sleek yellow tube about three metres long, with guidance fins and a transparent nose containing a camera. The AUV was suspended on a line above a tropical sea. There were palm trees in the background. Mo read the Google Images address at the top of the page. 'OK,' he said.

'Only this one is grey, not yellow.'

Horst held out his hand for the picture.

'OK,' said Mo as he handed it back.

'And you don't know what you are looking for. *Ja*?' said Brigitta.

'*Ja Ja. Verstanden.* We don't know nothing.'

The next day the dives began from the deck of *Sea Wolf*, and they found nothing but scallops, but the boots were being filled, as easily as if they were being pushed under the surface of the loch. If Mo Landa had been asked, he would have grinned and said he was happy, and would have at least have half-meant it. But Brigitta did not ask, and despite Mo's grins and salutations she expressed only distrust and dissatisfaction.

She was not happy that she could not watch each dive in real time because the video camera could not be wired to the boat and she could only watch a recording when the dive was over. She was not happy that only two divers went down together and one remained on board, fully kitted out, in case of an emergency. She was not happy that they had to wait for hours to decompress between dives and would not dive more than three times in a day. She was not happy that the decompression tables said so, and she studied them to make sure the divers were not mistaken. She was not happy that the weather was fine; she was not happy when there was a three-hour journey to the dive site, and not happy when it took five minutes. Brigitta did not smile, nor speak except to give an order. She spent the whole day on the boat without eating, drinking or smoking. Sometimes she would rest on a coil of rope in the bow, tucking her legs under her and leaning her arms on the gunwale beneath her chin as she gazed out to sea, and Mo could see then, for a moment,

how like any other girl she was, but most of the time
she was in the wheelhouse, studying the touch-screen of
the chart-plotter, zooming in and out by pinching thumb
and forefinger together, studying the yellow dots that
marked the dive sites and the red lines that marked the
movements between them as if searching for some cryptic
significance. And when she was not doing that she was
on deck, watching everything they did with her blank,
flat face. She watched every belt being buckled, every zip
being pulled, every tank being filled and clamped; how
the fins and masks were put on, how the compressor was
started, and once, when they were resting, Mo caught her
pushing buttons on his dive computer, and he snatched
it away from her because his life depended on it. But his
smile soon returned, because in general he was pretty
damn happy, because apart from the extra money on
top of the money that Pik was already paying, they were
actually doing something.

They had been in Scotland for three months and at first
Mo had been happy with being paid for doing nothing.
There were however several problems with this set-up,
not least of which was that it gave him too much time
to think. Mo Landa was sure that his forty years had
bestowed at least a little wisdom, and among the hard-
won precepts he considered thoroughly resolved was that
thinking was an activity that should be undertaken in
moderation. He had relatives that thought too much. In

some it inspired them to go to mosque a little too often. In his father's case it meant that he had never made any money. In his daughter's (he had to admit that he admired the trait in his daughter) it meant she was going to have to spend her life overthrowing the patriarchy. But when your working day consisted of sitting on a barge in the middle of a loch surrounded by mountains slowly interweaving patterns of purple and auburn with patterns of grey and green beneath an ever-churning sky, while you smoked the most fantastic weed and money poured into your bank account, you couldn't help thinking. You couldn't help going back to the beginning, to even before the beginning, to when Mo had first met Pik.

He had first met Pik beside a dirt road in Zambia, and Pik had been pointing an automatic rifle at his head. That was a younger Pik and a younger Mo. That was a Mo ambitious to buy copper ingots at a discount from truck drivers out of Kitwe, and a Pik who had the job of preventing such transactions. It had turned out to be a profitable relationship, albeit with inherent structural faults, firstly because copper ingots are heavy and not easily missed, and secondly because Mo knew Pik regarded him as a farmer regards a dog: useful, but with no prohibition on execution. It was as if the automatic rifle had never really been lowered. Perhaps that was why, after the ingot business had run its course, they had not seen each other for ten years, until the day last year when

Pik had appeared among the racks of Chinese t-shirts and shelves of Chinese shoes in Mo's father's shop in Nelspruit; a white guy with a blonde crew-cut, in clothes that were not quite military and never completely not.

'*Salaam Aleikum howzit*?' Pik had grinned.

Mo had taken him to his cousin's café further down the street. Pik had been friendly.

'How's business?' he had asked.

Mo had replied with a shrug. Pik had been the first person to enter the shop that morning, and he wasn't going to buy anything.

'Not in the scrap business now. I'm retired.' Mo had said. This was not entirely true, but a big part of the scrap business was not talking about the scrap business. 'Too much competition,' he had said, which was true, and 'Everybody has a gun,' which was also true.

Pik had told him what he was doing now, which was working security for some guy with billions who had been in gold mines but had sold them and become a conservationist and was now spending his billions on game parks in Ghana and Scotland, and how he was glad to be out of South Africa where the *darkies* think they are all that, how the *darkies* in Ghana are almost as bad, but at least there are no *darkies* in Scotland. Pik had always been racist. He was a white South African 'security operative', and he was as Dutch as a tulip; just stepped out of a covered wagon and descended from Piet

Retief Dutch. Pik's racism had never been surprising nor
even disturbing. Everyone in South Africa is some kind
of racist, but it seemed Pik had newly discovered a racist
creed; he had become a born-again racist, an evangelising
racist. Mo did not interrupt or encourage him as he went
on for a while about the *darkies*. This was more from Mo's
store of accumulated wisdom; when it came to this kind
of racist most of the time you just say nothing, there is no
point arguing. and they will tire of it themselves. Pik had
finally got around to how he needed someone like Mo to
do a salvage job on a boat in a loch in Scotland; a diving
job, a clean-up job, cleaning up the environment, and the
money was not in the metal but in a wage and everything
would be paid for and plane tickets, work permits, boat
and all equipment provided, and Mo had started to have
that feeling that he hadn't had in a long time, the feeling
that you got when the steel price was sky-high and you
stumbled on a T34 in the bush in Mozambique; that
electric feeling, like a long, slow bolt of lightning was
reaching down to you, when you had cut into a vein of
easy money. He hadn't shown this feeling. There had been
twenty questions buzzing through his head as he stirred
his coffee and closed his eyes. He knew better than to ask
most of them.

'What kind of boat?' he had asked, 'How deep?'

'A small cargo vessel, at thirty metres, went down only
a few months ago, in a loch. You know what is a loch?'

Mo knew what was a loch. 'Twenty metres down. Calm water.' Pik had repeated that there was no risk for Mo, because he was going to be paid a wage. Mo had stared at the coffee swirling around the spoon and had asked how much and had doubled it and made it for each of his crew which would be minimum two by the time the coffee stopped swirling. Yes, there had been definitely something not quite right about it. Mo Landa had been a dealer in scrap metal all over Southern Africa, and there was always something not quite right about what he did, but this job wasn't even properly crooked. The questions he didn't ask were about who owned the boat, why they didn't use local divers, and what was, or had been, the cargo. The answers he got about the money side of things were enough for him to forget those questions, at least for the time being. They were to be provided with a dive-boat, a barge, and all the dive equipment they needed, all bought new so nothing would have to come with them. They were to have work permits, all above board, as employees of 'Ardven Estates'. There was no competition; the wreck was already claimed and the salvage barge in place. Pik had told him that in Scotland nobody has a gun, which turned out to be not strictly true, but it was certainly not like South Africa, where every second o had a pistol in his waistband. Pik had asked for his bank account details so that he could send the first wage to get things started, and he had used his phone to set up the transfer right there in the café. Of course it was all too good to be true, but that did not mean it was not. Plenty of things that were too good to be true had happened to Mo Landa, along with plenty of things that were worse than could be imagined. There was only one small catch. Pik had added it as they got up to leave and shook hands.

'Your team. No *fockin' darkies* eh? You bring your own people.'

Mo had nodded his assent, thinking of his team, which would always and only be Solomon Matobela and Qualin H Bremner, who would without a doubt fall into this category. It was a catch, but not the end of the world. Pik was a racist; a hard-core AWB endorsing, Hitler admiring, old-school racist, but he was a South African racist, and as far as Pik was concerned Mohammed Landa with his skin the colour of a strong cup of coffee, at least as dark as Qualin's, was not a *darkie*, because he was a Muslim; a *salaamse*. Solomon Matobela was half-Pentecostal-half-communist, he thought, and Qualin was a Catholic that actually went to church, but none of this would be a problem when they heard about the wage. He had got over the catch by the time he had walked back to his father's shop, which among many kinds of hats stocked *kufis*. His dad would give him a special price. But the colour bar had not been the only catch.

They had flown into Glasgow and had been driven out of the city in a taxi by a man who spoke a strange language that for part of every twentieth sentence sounded like English. Their reaction to the landscape, after they had left the suburbs of the city, was to stare in silence, with faint smiles. Somehow it evoked memories, but of a dream they had never had, built of colours they had not known existed; soft greens, browns, purples, intertwining, swirling in three dimensions, up, until they blended with mists both chaotic and sublime. As they travelled over Rannoch Moor and through Glencoe the sense had grown, a palpable lightness in the chest, that they were nearing both an earthly heaven and some kind of earthly hell; as if the peaks and dark glens between them pierced the thin mist between this world and others beyond. By the time they had passed Fort William they had been stunned into a state of transcendental contemplation, a state that would have been impossible to maintain, it seemed, without some part of the mind breaking, so that they were glad of nightfall and the relief that the slow drawing down of darkness brought.

They had awoken in the Old Schoolhouse Guesthouse, to the view across the loch to Ardven. Pik was waiting for them downstairs at the breakfast table. They wore their *kufis*, and Pik let his eyes rest on Solly's dark face for less than one telling second before grinning and shaking hands. He enquired about the journey, and hoped the accommodation was satisfactory. He reassured Mo that

the equipment was all the best quality and that they
would be very happy with the brand-new *Sea Wolf*.

'You can start in a couple of days. There is no hurry.
But first you must come stalking.'

'Stalking?'

'Hunting a buck, a red deer, here on the estate. Have
you ever shot a red deer?' He was assured that they had
not. 'The boss will not be there but it is his way of saying
thank-you for coming all this way. Don't worry, I will
provide you with the gear and rifles.'

So later that same morning they found themselves high
amid those green, brown and purple swirls ascending
into the sky that had entranced them on the journey. And
intoxicated by the hunt, the sensation of high-powered
rifles in their hands, the pure air, the camaraderie induced
by the kill, and the surprising friendliness of Pik, the
photographs that he insisted on as the twilight encroached
captured the three grinning unrestrainedly, holding rifles
across their chests with the waters of Loch Houn in
the background forming a silver twisting snake below a
gleaming Ben Briagh.

'Come now, stop grinning, this is a serious business
this hunting; a manly business. Look like men who have
conquered the world!' said Pik. They made an effort, but
went down the hill to the lodge and across by boat to
Inverish with smiles that refused to diminish.

They made the first dives a few days later, and the job was to take pictures of the *Eloise* and Pik was to order the specialist airbags which would be used to raise her. That first reconnaissance was all the work they had done, in three months.

'There's a delay with the airbag company. Don't worry, you get paid as normal. That is not a problem. Just keep turning up at the barge every day. I don't want the boss thinking he is paying you to sit around doing nothing.' And that was the unforeseen catch; that was exactly what they were doing. The scrap metal business was sometimes about making money out of nothing, sometimes, when it was too easy, and that left you with a hollow feeling, even when it was not illegal; as if you had stolen, when in fact you hadn't, strictly speaking. It left you with a feeling of being filled with hot air. Too much money too quick.

'It's called a guilty conscience,' Qualin said. There was a solution of course, and it was to give alms. You filled up with that hot-air feeling, like a tyre overfilled, and then you let out enough of the air until you felt comfortable again by giving some cash to the ladies at the mosque who took pots of food to the township. It didn't take much until you felt comfortable, but you had to do something. It was like indigestion; indigestion of the bank account. So he was used to that, and knew how to deal with it. But this job was like nothing else.

For the first week they spent the whole of every day on the barge, and in the evenings went home to bed, as instructed. And on the seventh night of passing the only pub in Inverish, *The Clachan*, on their way from jetty to accommodation, Solly took the lead and ducked his head under the low lintel. Mo and Qualin followed. They were not supposed to fraternise with the locals.

'They're a bit Islamophobic around here,' Pik had told them.

By the end of the second week Solly was sleeping in the barmaid's apartment above the pub and hadn't spent a night in the Old Schoolhouse Guesthouse since. It had taken a week for Mo to recant the vow he had made while working for his father and start drinking whisky again, and a few days later the three of them had come across Malky Macleod smoking a joint in *The Clachan* beer garden, which consisted of one picnic table between the single track road in front of the pub and the shore, and so weed supplies were taken care of, and the weed was good. Malky told them it was genetically modified and grown in high-tech conditions in an underground factory in Glasgow. So they had weed, drink, and what the locals called *ceilidhs*, a new form of entertainment to them, that involved sitting around in someone's living room and listening to fiddle, guitar and *boran*. Scottish music, which was like Boere music whiskied up so that the fast tunes were like being caught in a tornado, and the slow ones made death and sorrow into a delicacy to be savoured like a fine malt. *Ceilidh* music, at a push, when you've had a few drams, could even be described as having soul. And there were women. But Qualin was engaged to a Catholic girl back in Durban, and Mo, who had a teenage daughter and attendant complications, was really, definitely this time, not interested. All that was waiting for him, if he wished, in a heartbeat. All he had to do was go back to work in his father's shop. But Solomon Matobela whose mother was from Ulundi, who had not worn shoes nor spoken English nor slept in anything other than a genuine mud-hut until he was an adult, was in love with Eilidh Murachar, daughter of a Free Church minister. So there was plenty to do outside of work, where there was nothing to do.

Every day they would go out to the barge, sit around smoking weed, and fill the boots. So Mo was glad when Pik had okayed the diving for Brigitta. They were at least doing something, even though they didn't know what this something was. Only Mo had seen the picture of the 'AUV'. He described it to Qualin and Solly when they were back at the Old Schoolhouse, sharing a joint.

'It's a tube, a pipe. As long as this room.'

'What colour?' said Qualin.

'Grey.'

'It's not an AUV. An AUV is yellow or orange, so that when you lose it you can find it. Also, what does this girl

want with an AUV? She doesn't even know how to dive.
What is this girl here for? To chase the holy guy, Eilidh's
dad, who's stopping Pik's boss from releasing his wolves.
How or why would she lose an AUV? These things are
expensive, sometimes even one million. And if you lose
an AUV you know pretty much where you lost it. You
know the ballpark. You've seen the points on the satnav.
They are all over the place; all the way out towards Eigg,
some on the other side of Skye. Come on! No way are we
looking for an AUV.'

'What then?'

'I know what it is.'

'What?'

'It's drugs. This is a way of smuggling drugs; coke or
heroin or something. I have seen a thing on Netflix. They
put the drugs not in the boat, but under the boat in a tube
like this, and the boat makes its move, from Columbia
or whatnot, and if the coastguard catches up to you and
wants to come on board and have a look it's all cool. The
coastguard can look around inside and even on the hull
of the boat with a camera or whatever but you are safe
because you dropped it, pulled a lever or something and
the tube drops down, sinks to the bottom. All you have
to do is put a marker on the satnav and come back for it
later. This is the moves of whatshisname.'

'Who?'

'Escobar. Pablo Escobar. His moves.'

'What if you drop it and the sea is three miles deep?'

'Then you screwed. Pablo Escobar kills you and your whole *familia*.' Qualin took a long drag and passed the joint. Mo took a long drag and passed it to Solly. Solly took a long drag.

'So who's Pablo Escobar, here, now?' said Mo.

'I don't know. Nyst? Pik? Brigitta?' said Qualin.

'Nyst is a billionaire. He doesn't need to smuggle drugs. Pik hates drugs, thinks they are for *kaffirs*.'

'So, Brigitta then.'

'Still doesn't make sense. You drop it. You mark it. How many times do you mark it? She has thirty-four markers. Spaced out over hundreds of square kilometres.' They sat in silence for a long time. Solly suggested the pub.

'Whatever it is, it's worth a hell of a lot of money.'

The Clachan Bar consisted of one low-ceilinged room, with dark furniture and dark wood-panelled walls, a pool table and a dartboard at one end. The customers were all locals in winter, but in the summer the room suffered bouts of hillwalkers in bright anoraks, coming on like a rash, filling the dark space and the till. The locals had been bearing these invasions for decades, and had evolved a nonchalance, so that conversations, games of darts and pool, and the routines of round-buying carried on without interruption, so that on a busy evening when these men and women in work clothes from fishing boats

and crofts were outnumbered they became a species
of ghost in their own pub, a haunting from another
time, holding pints aloft like torches as they threaded
immutable paths through the crowd. That afternoon the
tourists had yet to descend from the hills.

Eilidh Murachar was moving with graceful vigour,
carrying plates of fish and chips from the kitchen and
drinks from the bar. Mo and his crew sat at a table on
the other side of the room and Solly settled back in his
chair to watch her work. It had become an almost formal
pleasure to him, to watch her; as elevating as making
love. She was a consummate artist of a barmaid. She was
beautiful without any hint of fragility; never severe, yet
carrying a glint of steel in her eye to deter the abusive
word or hand, and when it did come, as it must, she did
not flinch. Solly had seen her slap men a head taller than
herself and push them out of the front door, before he
or anyone else had had a chance to intervene. This was
a gift; to be able to throw out a drunk without her smile
failing. Solly had watched and thought for hours about
the wonder that was this woman who ran a bar at the
end of the road into the middle of nowhere, lived on her
own in a one room flat above, late into her thirties, with
no husband nor children and no contact with her parents
or siblings. This woman who lived a solitary life, who
was great at her job because she felt a genuine warmth
towards everyone that ducked their head under the low

door and took the step down into The Clachan. There was something complete about her; she did not need anyone else to complete her; she was full of herself in the only way that is good, without thinking much of herself. He didn't think he had anything to do with this. She had been like that the day he had first met her, the day that she had filled his heart up. He had fallen in love with the way she moved, the way she spoke, with her warmth and ease, and with her untidy dark blonde hair, her large breasts and her large, high bum. She was ten years older than him, and he had fallen in love with that; she had had her heart broken by an arsehole who had worked on oilrigs, and he had fallen in love with that. Solly was thin and not tall, and Eilidh was not thin, and he had surprised himself with his strength when he first picked her up and lay her on the bed in the upstairs room.

Eilidh had liked Solly from the moment she had seen him. At first she had thought that this was just because he was different, and it was true, she had never in her life seen a black man up close; she had never spoken to one. She had been working in The Clachan for three years and had never had a black customer. It seemed that black people did not hill-walk. Of course she had seen black people on the street in Glasgow, and of course on television all the time, but she had never touched one until the first time Solly had held her hand. So she could not deny that fascination. But it was not only that which had drawn her to him. He had a gentleness that she had never seen in a man. The men she had known were always restless and full of energy. The boyfriends and fiance that she had known before she came back to Inverish were typical; thrusting and dynamic, full of get up and go, trying to make money and wrestle life to the ground. Solly knew how to take his time, but without diminishing that thing that you would call masculinity one bit. Was that a black thing?

'I am not black. I am a Zulu,' he told her. Was that a Zulu thing? She had no way of telling. He was a beautiful man. His face had an elfin finesse, with the heavy eyelids of a sleepy cat. He had a wide broad smile, and his lips; she just wanted to bite them, all the time. It was not that he was not interested in money, or lazy. She knew how much money he was making, for doing nothing. So there was love, lust, joy, pleasure, curiosity, and now there had to be more, because she was pregnant. She reckoned about eight weeks pregnant. And the fact, or perhaps the hormones, (she could not remember if this was how she had felt the last time) had frozen everything and made everything seem like it was moving at two times normal speed. It was as if her whole life were condensed to that fact, and at the same time, everything else mattered twice as much.

The child was inside, only inside, only about her, but it was outside too, because her life had expanded outwards, back into the lives of those she had tried to leave behind. It was not only her child. It was her mother's and father's and everyone that she had escaped; the child was bringing it all back in. The child was a Murachar. She was certain it would be a good pregnancy and a good birth and a healthy child. But the birth would draw in shadows.

Solomon Matobela was the father, and his strangeness was part of why she loved him, but he was much younger, and free, and flown in from some far quarter of the world, and could fly out. He was not a definite thing, he was a faerie thing. What was definite was her own family; four brothers and two sisters and mother and father across the loch and aunties and uncles on Skye and in Edinburgh and Glasgow, and they would all be closing in. She would have to know them and live with them again and they would not think much of Solomon Matobela. Inside was joy and love, outside, encircling pain, and the child was bringing it all in. So she lived for the time being on the cusp of not knowing and not deciding. This could be the third child that she would not give birth to. All it would take was a visit to the doctor in Mallaig and a bus journey to Inverness. Twice was enough to make you familiar with the routine. The pain would pass, and the faeries would go back to their lands, both the one inside her and the one smiling at the corner table waiting for his beer.

Chapter 7

It was late morning before Eamon descended from his bedroom. At breakfast Kirsty reminded him that she needed help lowering the chandelier in the hall so that the bulbs could be replaced. He remembered that he had arranged a meeting later with the builders who were renovating the cottage on the other side of the Ash Bridge. There was a question about the stonework that he had to decide on, and the council had sent a complaint about the colour of the drainpipes. When a white van pulled up on the drive and Shem Murachar stepped out Eamon was relieved by the distraction. Shem had brought his phone.

'Dad wanted to know if you were alright,' he said. Eamon invited him into the hall. 'Dad said not to go in if you invite me in, and not to talk to you.' He got back into the van and gravel spurted from beneath the wheels as it headed for the gate.

When Eamon was back in the hall Rona called down to remind him about the new tenants who were coming to look at Burnum Farm. Eamon called DS Maclean but got voicemail. Then the factor called, wanting to talk about annual accounts. While he was still talking to the factor Mike Mack filled the gothic arch of the front door. He was carrying an axe and Eamon remembered the arrangement of the day before that he had missed. Mike did not speak. Eamon told him to start with the saw without him and watched him walk across the south lawn. He would have liked nothing better than to go into the woods and spend the day chopping and stacking logs with the calming silence of Mike Mack.

Eamon called Reverend Farrawell, in Aberfashie. The man was, as always, delighted to hear from him. He mentioned the upcoming garden-party and Eamon assured him he would be there.

'I wanted to talk to you about the boys that were killed in the manse,' said Eamon.

There was a long silence before Reverend Farrawell replied in a benevolent tone. 'Yes, of course.'

'What were they doing there?' Again, there was a long silence.

'The police are investigating this, aren't they?' said the minister.

'Yes, but perhaps you could help me. David and Kosma left something at my house. I was hoping to be able to get in touch with their parents or whoever is next of kin.'

'Oh, yes, of course. You'll have to speak to the estates committee.'

'How would I get in touch with them?'

'The local presbytery would be your first port of call.'

'And who would be the contact?'

'That would be Edwina Murray. You perhaps know her?' Edwina Murray, the little white face in the moonlight.

The meeting with the builders could not be put off, so it was late in the afternoon by the time he knocked on the door at the end of a path crowded with rhododendrons and lupins. Mrs Murray, wearing a baggy tracksuit, did not greet him with a smile.

'Eamon Ansgar,' said Eamon, offering his hand.

'Dr Farrawell said you would visit.'

'Do you think I could come in?' She hesitated before stepping back. He followed her along a dark corridor. There was an echo of the garden inside the house; floral scents condensed into powder and spray. The furniture was nineteen-seventies artificial wood, fading beneath doilies and cacti. There were watercolours of birds on the walls. In the sitting room she gestured to a sofa covered in a crocheted rug and sat in an orthopaedic armchair. She smiled thinly as he sat.

'He didn't leave any address for next of kin,' she said.

'None at all? Neither of them?'

'No.'

'No previous address?'

'No.'

'But they signed a lease?' Mrs Murray did not reply. 'Normally, a lease would require an address, I would have thought...' he tailed off as her gaze shifted from his face. He turned to see a shadow in the doorway. The shadow stepped into the light and became a short, well-built man with a white beard and hair.

'Hi,' said the man. He wore a thin smile like Mrs Murray's. 'Justin,' said the man, and extended a hand. Eamon stood to shake it, and waited for someone to speak.

'You wanted to return some property?' said Justin.

'Are you on the estates committee too?'

'Maybe. The property, may I ask what it is?'

'It's a statue.'

'Of a man with the world on his shoulders?' said Justin.

Eamon nodded. 'Atlas. Holding up the Cosmos. How did you know?'

'But that belongs to you, does it not?' said Justin. 'David stole it from you, and then returned it.'

Eamon wondered if he should persist in his lie. 'It was a gift. We gave it to them.' he said. Justin indicated that they should both sit.

'Eamon. I am aware that you have some form helping the police. You helped them last year with the thing about the poor Africans. Are you helping them again?'

'I'm just trying to return the statue.'

'The statue that was never his. I am sure you are well intentioned but are the police aware that you are helping them? Does Detective Maclean know?'

Eamon took a deep breath. 'Look, all I want to do is find out what they were doing here. Why did they come here?' There was another long silence.

'Perhaps we can talk hypothetically,' said Justin. Eamon waited. 'Imagine a young man who is troubled. He has problems. Psychological, and spiritual, problems. His friends, his family, his teachers, those who care about him, they see him in trouble and see him getting into more trouble. They arrange for him to get away, to extricate himself from the mess he has got himself into, the bad influences. They arrange for him to go somewhere peaceful, where he can have time to reflect and ponder his future.'

'That makes sense. Up to a point.'

'And his parents are not proud of the way their son has been behaving. They want discretion. You can understand a need for discretion can't you?'

Eamon nodded. 'You mean you are not going to tell me his parent's address.'

'We are not obliged to tell you anything. We will co-operate with the police.'

Eamon got up and moved towards the dark corridor. 'How do you know? About the statue? That it belonged to me?'

'You were not the only one telling David to put things back.'

Eamon called for Rona as he climbed the stairs but knew she was in her mother's bedroom when she did not answer. He was pacing the study when she came down.

'Who is Justin? Short, beard, old. Friend of Mrs Murray?' he said.

'That will be Justin Simmonds.'

'What is he? What is he doing here?'

'Well, he lives here. He doesn't need a reason. As far as I know he's just someone that's retired. Like lots of people in the village. He's on various committees.'

'Like what?'

'He's on the Decorating the Village with Hanging Baskets Committee, whatever that's called. He's the guy you go to if you want to hire the hall. He holds the keys for the tennis court. That sort of thing.'

'I've never seen him before.'

'Well, that's not his fault.'

'David was the one who was nicking stuff wasn't he?'

'I don't know. Perhaps it was both of them.'

'Yes, but it was David that was seen. By Mrs MacDonald, in her kitchen? Wasn't it? And she told Kirsty and Kirsty told us. Am I right?'

'I think so.'

'Because they were always talking about "he". Singular. Not "them". And I was trying to work out which one they meant. They meant David. It was as if Kosma didn't exist.'

'But Stevie saw Kosma going into his caravan.'

'Yes. But they only talked about David.'

'Who?'

'Mrs goddam Murray and her friend, Justin. Not her husband?'

'Not as far as I know.'

'No husband? Who is her husband? Who was her husband?'

'No idea. When she came here she was alone.'

'When did she come here?'

'About two years ago.'

'Two years ago?'

'Yes. She bought the house when Donald McKillop died. The butcher.'

'Two years ago?'

'Yes,' said Rona, frowning at him.

Eamon paced to the window and thumped the frame. 'Her house. It looks like she's been there for a very long time. Everything in it is old, and dusty. Two years ago? Why don't I know these things?'

'Because you're a bit of a misanthrope, perhaps.'

He smiled, and sat, and told her about his visit.

'What they said kind of makes sense to me,' she said.

'OK. I suppose it makes sense if you consider they are talking about David. David is getting into trouble, so somebody knows somebody who knows Mrs Murray or Justin and they arrange for him to have a holiday in the manse. In a big old, cold house with no furniture, but fine, let's go with that. But who the hell is Kosma?'

'His boyfriend. He comes plus-one. That's all.' Of course she was right. 'It's called Occam's Razor. The straightforward explanation is generally right.' The faint sound of her name came from the stairwell. Mother. 'When I come down we need to go to Borlum, to meet the Piggots,' she said. She kissed him and went upstairs.

At Burnum he let Rona do the talking, with Harry strapped to her chest. The Piggots were grinning at the prospect of the tenancy. Eamon stopped wondering if the rent was too low and wandered across the field to the river. He saw two marked cars and Maclean's little blue one on the single-track road on the other side, going in the direction of Loch Nish and Murachar's croft. Let him see how straightforward things were down there.

It was the beginning of evening and Kirsty had removed her blue overall and was walking down the drive when her phone rang.

'Granny, it's me.'

'Aye.'

'You need to delete the photo.'

'What photo?'

'You know. The photo.'

'I don't know how to do that.'

'I'll be at yours when you get home and do it for you.'

Eamon had dined with his mother-in-law when his phone lit up with Maclean's number.

'Yes?' said Eamon.

'Shem Murachar took off from the croft this afternoon when he saw the police cars. Up the hill, on to your ground. Towards Glen Feshie we think.'

'You were going to arrest him?'

'No. We wanted forensic samples.'

'You want me to look for him?'

'I didn't say that. I've put in a request for a helicopter. I want to know where you think he will go.'

'There's hundreds of square-miles of hill out there. I have no idea. He's lived here all his life. He'll know the ground as well as anyone.'

'He will need to find shelter.'

'Not necessarily. Not in this weather.'

As soon as Maclean ended the call Eamon went down to the hall. He put on a heavy jacket and walking boots and took a stick and binoculars. He was about to leave from the tower door when he turned back, climbed the stairs and found Rona in the bathroom cupping water over the wriggling boy. He expected her to try to stop him from going but she smiled when he told her.

'He'll have to stick to the path until the top of Ardven,' she said, 'but then if he goes down the other side to Loch Houn, there's no path, the forest is thick, and he'll just reach the shore. He knows that, so he'll come along the top of the hill.'

Eamon drove over the Ash Bridge and past the abandoned Misty Glen Pub. The light was fading as he took the road that led along the hillside towards Ardven, sidling up to the summit. He stopped the car in the passing-place at the top and looked along the road that doubled back east and down towards the pier at the head of Loch Houn, where it turned into a dirt track that led on to the remains of the dam, and the graveyard. Behind him the sun was setting beyond the hills to the north of Loch Nish, the light just touching the tops and casting beams and deep shadows over Glen Cul. The village was already signalling to the cosmos with orange streetlights. But Loch Nish, and below him Loch Houn, were dense black in the shade, cold fingers extending from the Atlantic. He looked through the binoculars along the

Ardven peninsula and could see the grey line of chain-link
fence cutting it off, about three miles to the west. Shem
would have come up inside the fence, Eamon thought,
but would have climbed over it, this way, because he
wouldn't want to be inside the fence at night, alone, with
the protesters and their baseball bats and road-kill bombs.
That was enemy territory to Shem Murachar. So he
would have come over the fence, and then he could have
gone towards Duncul, but that would have meant straight
into the arms of the police. So, over towards Loch Houn.
What was down there? Thick plantations until the loch, as
Rona had said, and not even a beach. Only a shore of bare
rock until you came east and found the old boathouse.
Close to the boathouse there was a converted ambulance,
painted black, with a stove pipe protruding from the
roof, *chez* Malky Scallops. But was Shem, a born-again
Christian-fundamentalist, going to seek shelter with the
anarchist weed-head, Malky? There was no-one else down
there, not a soul. Nothing. Further up the glen, what was
there?

There had been an archaeological dig at the Pictish
tomb, but it had stopped because of lack of funding.
Beyond the graveyard where the dam had been there was
Tarvin Lodge, but all boarded up now because no-one
could work out who it belonged to. A long way further
up the glen in the forest there was Duncan Fraser's
abandoned bothy, but Eamon doubted Shem knew about

that. Then beyond that was hill, moor, hill, forest; nothing
for thirty miles inland, except for a couple of derelict
shepherd huts. Perhaps Shem knew about them? The only
way out was in the other direction; a ten-mile trek along
Loch Houn, to Inverish, and then by road from there to
Mallaig, or past Inverish, out to sea, if he had a boat, but
what boat? Eamon could still make out the barge moored
over the wreck. The barge that had been there for a year
but hadn't raised anything. The barge couldn't move.
He turned his gaze to the pier and could see the bright
orange of Malky's RIB. If Shem was trying to get away
he would take it. Eamon thought about driving down and
doing something to the boat to make sure it couldn't be
used, but reasoned Shem might see him. He tried to work
out where Shem would be by now. Maclean had not said
what time he had left the croft. He thought about calling
Maclean. It was almost eleven and the sun had just gone.
It would be light by three. If Shem saw him at the boat
he would hide. Eamon closed his eyes. If Shem was going
to Inverish he would take the RIB. If he was going to
Inverish. He would have to go to Inverish, to get out. He
would have to get out.

Chapter 8

The three o'clock light came from somewhere just to the
right of north. Eamon had slept with his head against
the window. The sun had been reluctant to leave and was
just as reluctant to return, and it was still as dark as the
dusk he had drifted from, but his binoculars picked out
the RIB, still at the pier. Perhaps it was padlocked and
chained? Malky the anarchist was known to be an astute
businessman, and that was a twenty-thousand-pound
boat. Eamon thought about driving down to find out, but
he waited for the sun.

It was an hour later, and the glen was filling up with
a glow that tinged gold the thin mist that lay over the
head of the loch, when Eamon saw Shem through
the binoculars. He had moved fast, perhaps walking

throughout the night, and was on the other side of Loch Houn, heading up the hill. He was wearing a yellow t-shirt and blue jeans. Eamon imagined him seeing the police-car at the croft and running, without thinking, without picking up a jacket. He was not quite running now, but walking fast, his arms and legs moving with stiff jerks as he climbed a sheep path. Eamon called Maclean.

'Where's the helicopter?'

'It's coming from Glasgow,' said Maclean. 'It'll take about three hours. I'll send a car, but it's going to come from Inverness. You'll have to follow him. Don't approach him, just keep him in sight and you can direct us.'

Eamon set off down the hill towards the pier. He tried to keep one eye on the tiny figure but had to keep stopping to look through the binoculars. He tried to make out the trajectory of the path Shem was on but as it rose into the heather it disappeared. He put the binoculars away and sped up. When he stopped again to look he saw the jerking figure disappear into a gully. Shem was on the low first rise before the slope of Ben Briagh, and at its top it broke up into a tumult of boulders and hillocks. There was nothing for Eamon to do but get out and walk fast. He crossed a ford in the river, getting his feet wet, half-ran over sheep-cropped grass on the flat, and took a guess about the path. He guessed right; there were fresh prints of trainers in the mud.

The path was steep and he surrendered to the effort of
a stiff pace as the sun rose and the day stood still beneath
a windless sky. Eamon didn't see how he could gain on
the boy so he kept his head down and looked for prints
but as he moved higher the ground was dry and there
was nothing to see. It took him an hour to get to the
top of the first rise and see the path lose itself among
others, between boulders which had looked like stones
from the other side of the glen but were here as big as
houses. He climbed one and took another look through
the binoculars. The face of Ben Briagh was one unbroken
wave of heather, poised for a million years, bearing down
on him. If Shem had wanted to go to Inverish he would
have turned to the west by now, and would be walking
along through the boulder field above the shore of Loch
Houn, but he was not going to Inverish. He was going
straight up the hill, without slackening pace. Eamon had
gained a little and could see him more clearly. White
trainers, blue jeans, yellow t-shirt, and he was carrying
something, in his right hand. It was a blue something
that swung back and forth as he walked. Eamon could
not work out what it was, and he watched through the
binoculars for a long time before Shem made a brief stop
and he saw that it was a coil of rope; a couple of metres
of rope. Shem was at least a mile off and he doubted that
he could hear him, but the day was as still as if it had been

frozen, and Eamon called with all the force that fear could raise.

'Shem!' the word echoed back from the hill and before it could come back from the other side of the loch Eamon had raised the binoculars to check if he was heard. The boy did not stop or slow. Eamon made a futile wave, then dropped his jacket and stick and started to run up the hill.

But it was useless. Shem was moving just as fast and Eamon could see that when he rounded the shoulder of the hill he would be out of sight. He listened for the sound of the helicopter but it was not there. He searched back towards the head of the loch for the promised police-car but the pier was out of sight now behind the boulder field, and what could they do, being a mile behind him? There was nothing to do but walk, and speed up to a trot when the path levelled off, and curse his unfitness as the path grew steeper and his breath got away from him and the sweat poured. He kept at it for another hour, until he was up at the shoulder of the hill, and could see over the boulder field and low rise behind him that there was a police-car at the pier. He called Maclean again and told him about the rope. Maclean cursed. Eamon sent his location to guide the two officers who were getting out of the car at the pier, then carried on around the shoulder of the hill into the steep-sided glen that led south, bringing a tumbling burn down from the corries between slopes of ancient oak and pine.

Eamon searched with the binoculars but Shem was not in sight. He was in there somewhere, in the light-filled spaces between the trees, among the grass and moss and heather singing to the skies, a frightened boy, wanted for murder, with just enough rope. Eamon sprinted into the forest calling the name. At first he followed the path that ran along the contour of the hill, then he took a fork down, not following any reason or plan, just calling and running, searching with maddened eyes, wiping sweat from his forehead and trying to catch his breath. He might not have gone into the trees at all, Eamon considered, might have carried on higher up, along the face into the corries, up into the peaks, but why? Why this way where there was nothing and no hope of escape? He called and listened, but after the echo there only came the sound of the burn below. There was only forest, still grass, the sound of his own blood in his ears and his heaving chest. He sat and tried to phone Maclean, but there was no signal in the shadow of the hill. The nearest mast was beyond Inverish. He cursed, lay back and closed his eyes. When he opened them again he saw the colour of Shem's t-shirt below him through branches and leaves, and he called out and ran, jumped, and slid down the slope.

Shem was hanging from a thick oak limb that twisted like a snake over a shady hollow. His back was towards Eamon, and the neck was stretched to an unnatural length. Eamon found himself shouting the name angrily,

suddenly possessed by the voice of a sergeant on a parade
ground. But Shem was still, his arms stiff by his side, at
attention, staring at a burning sun without narrowing his
blue eyes. The tongue was out, thick and purple. There
was a smell of shit. He must have climbed the tree, and
out along the branch, because his feet were at the level
of Eamon's head. There were already flies around his
mouth and at the stain on his jeans. Eamon put down the
binoculars and climbed the oak. He shimmied out along
the branch to untie the rope but the knot was tight. He
felt in his pockets for a knife and found only a pen. The
branch was thick enough for him to turn on his back and
look up at Shem's last vision of blue sky and sunbeams
coming through the leaves. He thought about the boy
with the wide blue eyes the day before, awkwardly
holding the gun at the gate. The boy that he had known
all his life, not well, but whom he had met now and then;
a child on the croft, playing with his brothers, a boy who
had been home-schooled, who had not come into the
village often. A boy who had been brought up on his
father's peculiar brand of salvation and hate for breakfast,
lunch and dinner every day, for every one of his eighteen
years. Was that enough to make him into a killer? A good-
looking boy; a blonde, tall, rippling-with-strength, blue-
eyed boy.

Eamon must have been on the branch for a half hour
before he heard the chopper coming from the direction

of Loch Houn. He remembered the two cops who were
coming up the hill and he climbed down and began
walking up through the trees, meaning to get out into the
open and then back to where the police could see him.

He could not believe that the police had already
climbed the hill when he glimpsed a figure in black above
him, disappearing behind the trees where the forest
thinned out and the heather began, but he called out and
waved. There was no way they could have made it up
the hill so quickly. He climbed to the edge of the trees
and up into the heather, and saw the chopper circling to
the north, above the loch. He thought perhaps he had
imagined the figure, or had mistaken the dark brown of a
deer for black. He walked a little towards Loch Houn and
up onto the shoulder of the hill until he could see the two
tiny policemen, who were not in black but in luminous
yellow vests, slowly climbing. He went further up to try
and catch the phone signal and looked out over the top in
the direction of Inverish, down onto the flat of the top of
the next hill. The figure had walked fast and was at least a
mile off, moving through peat bogs. Eamon took out the
binoculars.

He was a small, nimble man, in black hillwalking
gear and a blue beanie, carrying a backpack. He was
on a path that Eamon could not make out, weaving in
and out of peat hags, without hesitating, like someone
who knows where they are going. He was not going

to Inverish, thought Eamon. For Inverish he should be heading north, down the face of the hill to the shore. He was going in the direction of Mallaig, a good thirty miles away. There was nothing but open country between here and Mallaig. Eamon's phone buzzed. He answered, told Maclean about Shem and sent him the location. Maclean put him on hold. Eamon took another look through the binoculars. At first he could not find the man among the stains of peat bogs and clusters of boulders. When he saw him again the man had stopped and was taking off the backpack. Eamon noticed that he had light, dark skin. Maclean's voice emerged from the phone.

'This helicopter can't take a body. It'll have to be the mountain rescue.'

'Can the helicopter take me?' Maclean put him on hold again. Eamon took up the binoculars. The man was among a collection of boulders, kneeling, and Eamon could just see his head and shoulders, coming down, into view, and then as he sat up, disappearing behind a boulder. Instead of the blue hat he was wearing a white prayer cap, a *kufi*. The man was praying, on a prayer mat. Muslim praying, on his knees, bowing to the East. Maclean spoke.

'You'll have to wait for the Mountain Rescue. The police chopper isn't authorised to pick you up. We'd appreciate it if you could guide in the officers on the hill.' Eamon ended the call. He looked down and guessed that it would be at least an hour before the police arrived

at the forest. He recognised Sergeant Peters, who had
taken off his yellow vest and police hat. He hoped that
along with the pepper-spray and cuffs and radios at least
one of them carried a knife. He turned the binoculars
to the man in black again and watched him until he had
finished praying. Then he found a convenient spot in the
heather where he could rest the glasses upon a rock and
watched the man for a long time, packing up the prayer
mat, putting the backpack on and changing his hat, then
walking off, not to Inverish, but to the south-west, into
nowhere. He watched until he could hardly pick him out,
and he vanished behind a ripple in the sea of heather and
rocks.

It was late evening before Eamon got back to the castle.
He set about showering and drinking away the day, but
the memories would not begin to fade; the smell of the
body in the hot wood and the smell of the two clumsy
policemen struggling to cut it down, and then the long
wait with them as the midges descended and only the
birds spoke, until the mountain-rescue helicopter thudded
above them and brought the trees to life. Then the
loading of the body into the stretcher and having to drag
it up out of the trees before it could be sent up on the
winch, and then, once they had found a place where the
chopper could land, the journey with the grim men in the
flying barrel of noise to the pier and at last the solitude

of the drive home, when he had to stop twice to let his breathing and heart subside. He had already spent a long time giving Maclean a statement but was glad when the detective called and asked him to come down to the front door, because Eamon knew he would not be able to bring himself to wake Rona, and he was going to have to talk to someone. Maclean stayed in his seat and opened the passenger door.

'It looks like I need your help again,' he said, with a sad smile. Eamon got in and shut the door. 'We went up to the croft to tell Johnny Murachar. He came up to the gate and refused to let me in, so I told him there and then. "Your son is dead," I said, and before he could think otherwise, "By his own hand." It is not the first time I have had to say that to a father and it is the same each time. You see a man break, in an instant. It is like you've killed the man in him or cut everything that is manly away, and all that is left is weaker than a child. He cast his eyes down when I told him, and for a moment it was as if he did not see us, and I was afraid he was going to turn around and walk back into the dark. I was afraid that I was going to have to call him back, to bring him to his senses, and I did not want to have to do that. But then he raised his eyes and asked how it happened, and again I asked if I could come in and sit with him somewhere, but he made me tell him everything there, standing at the gate in the torchlight with the blue light on the car going, and the

officers and young men from the croft standing around,
all in earshot. He made me tell him about how he died
and who had found him and how he was taken out of the
wood. I explained to him that we needed to come in and
make a search of Shem's room, but he shook his head
and turned away, and went back into the dark. Now here
is the problem. I can call Inverness and get the negotiator
to come down and talk to him. Then if that doesn't work
I can get a warrant and he will have to let us in, or else
we knock down the gates. But you and I know that there
are firearms in there, and you and I know that he is not
going to shoot anyone, probably, but in order to get a
negotiator or a warrant I have to fill out a risk-assessment
and that means that there will have to be armed officers
and Lord knows what else; the helicopter will probably
have to come back from Glasgow and fly around with a
searchlight and loudspeaker. Anyway, it will all be above
me. You follow me? If he's considering some sort of stand
against the police, to satisfy his public, some sort of Waco
style stand-off, he might just get it.'

'So you want me to talk to him?'

'It's worth a try.'

'So perhaps you can tell me a bit more.'

'A bit more of what?'

'What you've found; what evidence against Shem? Why
were you there? Why did he run?'

'As I said, we went to collect forensic samples.'

'But you need a reason to do that. You don't collect samples from everyone. You're not allowed to. I know why you're going to take a sample from me. Because you know I was at the manse. How do you know Shem was at the manse?'

Maclean shook his head. 'This is an open case Eamon. There are rules.'

'And one of them is that you get armed officers and a helicopter down here.'

Maclean was silent for a while. 'He was seen,' he said. 'Several times.'

'Let me guess; by Mrs Murray?'

'That doesn't matter. The witness is reliable.'

'Seen doing what?'

'Going into the manse. Several times, at night.'

'Why?' said Eamon but the wide blue eyes of Shem Murachar, the blonde hair and fresh strength appeared to him, again, like a shaft of sunlight through the trees. 'He was visiting?'

'That's right.'

'But that doesn't mean he killed them. Why would he?'

'For the same reason he killed himself, perhaps.'

Maclean let the answer hang in the air for a minute before asking if Eamon needed to get a jacket. Receiving a shake of the head in reply he started the car and drove in the direction of the croft.

'So what are you looking for now?' said Eamon. 'You have all the forensic samples you need. You have a witness that says he was a regular visitor. What about on the night of the murders?'

Maclean stared at the road rolling towards them.

'You might as well tell me the rest John.'

'Yes, he was there on the evening of the murders. But we don't have the weapon.'

'Which is?'

'A club of some kind.'

'And?'

'And we need to conduct interviews, with his parents, his brothers and sisters, everyone that knew him in fact, to find out if they know anything about his relationship to David or Kosma. And we need to see if there is any other evidence, for example, any written material, anything on his computer, that establishes this relationship.'

'He won't have a computer. Or a phone.'

Maclean looked at him.

'It's common knowledge. Johnny has a computer. He must have, to do his blog, but no-one else on the croft is allowed anything like that.'

'Well, a diary, for example.'

Eamon did not reply. There would be DNA from Shem at the manse, and a murder weapon that presumably would carry both his DNA and the victim's, somewhere at the croft. Someone would know or would have suspected

that he was having a relationship with David. And of
course, if they found a diary or a letter, something that
said, 'I love David,' or 'I love Kosma,' that would make
sense. Perfect sense. Straightforward sense. Because the
motivation was all there, all over his father's blog. Enough
hate for him to hate his lover, and plenty left over for him
to hate himself.

In the end there was no confrontation, no armed
officers, no helicopter hovering like a giant rushing heart
and scorching the croft with a searchlight. In the end
there was only an old, tall woman with a tear-stained
face marching up to the gate with a long stride, and the
only violence was when she was unlocking the gate and a
young man carrying a bat stepped up to say something to
her and she slapped him hard across the ear. He slunk off
to one side and she looked at the others standing there, a
half dozen of them, inviting another challenge. Johnny
himself did not appear. Mrs Murachar, for it was she,
shook John Maclean's hand, and wiped tears from her face
as she asked him to follow her. Eamon hung back as the
cars went in, knowing too well all that would follow; the
hours of tedious police-work that had nothing to do with
him, and he walked out, down the hill towards Loch Nish
and along the shore, in the darkness, listening to the soft
pull of a weed-filled tide on the stones as he followed the
ribbon of moonlit road.

Chapter 9

In the morning Eamon got up without waking Rona.
In the study he called the landline number he had for
Endpoint House but there was no answer. He drove down
to the shore of Loch Nish and tried to remember the
route of the path to the west that he had last walked as a
teenager. It led up through Murachar's croft to the top of
the hill, then along the spine of the peninsula. There was
no other way because the shoreline after the croft was
rocky and the forest went as far as the water's edge. It was
a walk that would take the whole day. If he went by water
however, it would take an hour. He called Stevie and
asked for Malky Scallops' number.

'I want to borrow his boat,' he explained.

'I haven't seen him for a week,' said Stevie.

'Where will he be?'

'He sometimes goes out clamming for a week at a time, and sometimes he goes to his mum's in Kilmarnock.'

Eamon called the number but got no answer. He turned the car and drove back to Duncul, turned to the south and went up over the hill to Loch Houn. Malky's boat was at the pier. As the road levelled off parallel to the shore a dirt-track turn-off led down to the old boathouse. Malky's black converted ambulance and a white van were parked half-way down in a passing-place.

There was no smoke rising from the ambulance stovepipe. Eamon knocked on the rear door and looked through the window. A piece of blanket obscured his view. He called Malky's name and tried the door. It swung open. The interior was dim and smelled of patchouli and woodsmoke, and it had been torn apart. The floor was covered in clothes and bedding and the contents of the cupboards; tins and jars and packets of food. The pot-bellied stove lay on its side. Eamon called into the ambulance and out to the bright day and the loch, then he walked along the shore to the boathouse.

The boathouse was his own, and still contained a rowing boat, the *Jessica*. Someone had been in here too, opening the lockers and tossing out ropes and lifejackets. Eamon went back to his car and drove on to the pier. The chains at the bow and stern of Malky's boat were fastened with big padlocks, and the engine attached to the hull

with a thick cable. He called Stevie and told him what he
had seen.

'Check the back of the van for diving gear,' said Stevie.
'I'll meet you there in half an hour.'

Eamon drove back to the ambulance and looked in
the white van. It was not locked and was loaded with air
tanks, a dry-suit and a compressor. He sat on a rock and
stared out at the barge above the wreck of the *Eloise* in the
middle of the loch and at the purple hills beyond, until a
battered pickup arrived.

'What are you up to *bruv*?' said Stevie.

'I want to pay a visit to Denis Nyst and tell him to lay
off Murachar. Do you have a number for Malky's mum?'

Stevie shook his head.

'Where else could he be?'

'The Clachan at Inverish?'

'You got a number for that?'

Stevie took out his phone. 'No signal.'

'You got anything in the pickup that'll cut a chain?'

'Yep.'

'You think he'll mind if we borrow his boat?'

'Nope.'

It took them fifteen minutes to reach the pub. Stevie held
the boat at the jetty while Eamon went ashore.

The door was open. A blonde woman was seated at a
table in the corner staring at a phone.

'I'm looking for Malky Macleod,' said Eamon. The woman looked up from her phone, but her face was still in shadow.

'Not here,' she said, shaking her head.

'When was the last time he was here?' asked Eamon, stepping into the room. The woman held up her hand to stop him.

'We're closed,' she said abruptly. 'Haven't seen him for a week, at least. We're closed.' Eamon nodded and left.

'Not a very friendly barmaid,' he told Stevie as he untied the boat. Eamon pointed the boat to the west and the end of Ardven.

'You know who that is?'

'No.'

'Eilidh Murachar. Shem's big sister.'

'Shit,' said Eamon. He opened the throttle and they motored without speaking in a roar of wind and waves. 'Do you think we should call the cops.' he shouted. Stevie shrugged. 'Call the cops?' Eamon repeated.

'Malky hates cops,' shouted Stevie, and a while later: 'He does stuff on his own. Lives on his own. Dives on his own. Deals with shit on his own. And he sells weed. He won't appreciate it if the cops come sniffing around his van.' Eamon stared at the sun beginning its descent towards the sea, a burning iron about to be cooled. He slowed as they approached the forested shore beginning its turn to the north and they saw the long, low white lodge, Endpoint, built right down on the shore so that you could walk from the front door straight out onto the jetty.

Eamon remembered visiting, at least twenty years ago, before Denis Nyst, before the wolves and the long, drawn-out battle with the council and Scottish Natural Heritage. He had followed the story for years, but had lost interest. He had no objection to wolves and re-wilding. He did not think they would escape from the peninsula, and he didn't believe they would eat hill-walkers, but the locals did not want them, and the council did not want them. He did not see how these obstacles could be overcome. Nyst was wasting his time.

He slowed the boat to a crawl as they skirted the rocks that fingered out towards the Atlantic and the falling sun. In the quiet, as the engine calmed to a low hum, he heard a cry from the forest that reminded him of the night spent on Murachar's croft. Then he saw a tall, thin figure, dressed in black jeans and hoody, standing by the trunk of a pine, watching the boat, speaking into a phone. Eamon waved but the man did not wave back. As they slid against the jetty three more thin figures appeared between themselves and the house. Again, Eamon waved. The figures disappeared into the trees and a man with short blonde hair came out of the house and walked out along the jetty to meet them.

'This is private property,' said Pik.

'Yes, of course,' said Eamon. 'I thought I might be able to speak to Mr Nyst. Denis. Is he here?'

'You can call him.'

'I did try, but there was no answer.'

'Try again,' said Pik. 'You are trespassing if you step onto the jetty.'

Eamon stepped onto the jetty while Stevie tied up the boat. 'This is Scotland, not the Transvaal. Eamon Ansgar,' said Eamon, offering his hand.

'If you don't get off the jetty I'm going to throw you off,' said Pik.

Stevie stepped off the boat and stood behind his brother. 'You really want to try?'

Pik curled his lip and whistled. The three thin figures re-emerged from the trees at the back of the house and began walking towards them. Stevie eyed the boathook, but a grey-haired man wearing an ankle-length tunic came out of the house waving his arms above his head. Pik sighed and gestured to the three in black. They stopped. Denis Nyst walked along the jetty until he stood behind Pik.

'Mr Nyst?' said Eamon. 'We've never met. Remiss on my part. I'm your neighbour, Eamon Ansgar, from Duncul. This is my brother Steven.'

Nyst nodded in reply. 'What do you want?'

'Is there somewhere we could talk?' said Eamon.

Nyst rubbed his hands over his face. 'You can come in,' he said, and turned back towards the house. Pik stood aside to let them follow.

He led them into a conservatory. The floor was thick with dust. There were old newspapers lying on sun-faded cushions and sun-loungers with broken wickerwork. Eamon recognised the furniture. It had not changed since he had visited as a boy, when the Wills had had this house. Nyst was a billionaire, but had not had the place re-decorated. It looked like he didn't even employ a cleaner. Nyst invited them to sit and looked at them with pale, watery eyes.

'Did you hear about Shem Murachar?' said Eamon.

'Who is Shem Murachar?'

'Johnny Murachar's son. He killed himself yesterday, in the woods above Glen Feshie.' Nyst leant forward and placed his hands beneath his chin. 'I was there the other night, at the croft,' said Eamon. 'You need to stop what you are doing.'

Nyst smiled. 'I offered him a million pounds for his croft. I would have happily given more.'

'But even if he leaves, you still need the council's permission to release wolves. It doesn't solve your problem.'

'He started it! He has grazing rights! He knows people on the council! Every bit of trouble I have was started by Johnny Murachar! How can you defend this man? He is the worst kind of man! He is a bigot! He is an oppressor of women! Do you know how many children he has?'

'I think six.'

'Six! Do you understand what would happen to the world if we all had six children? He and people like him are killing this planet! Choking it to death with the refuse and effluent, and filth, and plastics, and poisons, and heavy metals! And his domestic animals! Killing the land! Destroying nature!'

'I think he has grazing for twenty sheep.'

'It doesn't matter the numbers! It is the whole philosophy! The principle! He exploits! He is Biblical! "Go forth and multiply!" Naming all the animals! Ruling over the planet like it is a thing to be squeezed dry!' Nyst's lips grew wet as he spoke, and flecks of spittle balled on the dust on the floor. Eamon and Stevie sat still in the warm light that filtered through the dirty windows.

'His son died yesterday. You should give him time to bury him,' said Eamon.

'Should I? Why? It is not my fault his son kills himself!'

'I didn't say it was your fault. I am asking you to stop, to think, to call of your dogs.'

'My dogs? Hah! That is funny!'

'There have been two murders, and now a suicide. There is a police investigation. These protestors are only making things worse.'

'Worse? They are making things better! They are
purifying my land! They are cleansing it of Johnny
Murachar!'

'Do you have any children of your own?'

'No! Not human children. My children don't poison the
planet. My children are *of* this planet, living in harmony
with it.'

'You mean your wolves.'

'Yes, I mean my wolves. You will see. They will run
free! You will see Eamon Ansgar, ye of little faith!'

'They will shoot them. You do realise that Mr Nyst?
If you let wolves out onto the peninsula the council, the
authorities, will shoot them.'

'They will not!' said Nyst, his face an expression of
apoplectic rage. 'They will never!'

Eamon and Stevie got up. 'What you are doing to
Johnny is wrong Mr Nyst,' said Eamon. 'I am asking you
in the name of simple human kindness…'

'Kindness? Well maybe what we need is a new kind of
kindness, eh? A kindness to the planet.' Eamon offered
his hand but Nyst did not take it. 'What you have to
understand, Mr Ansgar, is that this, all this,' he gestured
around the filthy conservatory, 'is necessary! What I am
doing here is necessary!'

'I understand,' said Eamon. He and Stevie let
themselves out.

'He's crazier than I thought,' said Stevie. 'Shit!' he said, as he looked towards the jetty. They turned back to the conservatory where Pik was standing in the doorway. 'Where's the boat?'

'Are you sure you tied up properly?' Pik grinned. 'The tide is very strong here. Don't worry, I can show you the path.'

'No need,' said Eamon. He led Stevie to the back of the house, across the stretch of knee-high lawn and through the steading. A girl dressed in black was sitting on the roof of one of the barns eating an apple and there were two men standing by a gate. One blew kisses as they passed.

'Have a nice walk!' said the other. 'Watch out for faeries in the woods! And whatever you do, don't stray from the path!' The apple core bounced on the ground at Stevie's feet.

'Nyst's as mad as Murachar,' said Stevie when they were walking along the track by the shore.

'Yep.'

'Maybe madder.'

They followed the track for half a mile until it ended at the gate. The sun was kissing the sea beyond the mouth of Loch Nish and the branches of the fir trees were lit like embers.

'Malky's going to be pissed off about his boat,' said Stevie as they climbed up the firebreak into the forest.

'Yep.'

By the time they reached the first cairn it was almost dark in the shadow of the pines. Eamon peered at the stone cup on top of the pile of rocks. He took out his phone and switched on the torch.

'What is that?' said Stevie.

'I recognise this,' said Eamon. 'There was one like it in the manse.' He looked into the bowl of the cup. It was half-full with the heads of dandelions and daisies. A daisy chain had been arranged around its base.

'What do you mean?'

'There were two cups like this with all the stuff David and Kosma were collecting.'

'What is it for?'

'No idea.' Eamon took a photograph of the cup and the cairn. Ten minutes later they came to a second cairn. Eamon took another picture. It was dark enough for the camera to flash and in the moment of light Stevie saw a figure in the trees beyond. He switched on the phone-torch and turned and swung the light as they heard a twig snap behind them. An owl called.

'Let's keep moving,' said Eamon, 'before they start throwing shit at us.'

Chapter 10

For five days the laird of Duncul Castle attended to
his domestic duties. He took the mother-in-law to
physiotherapy and his son for vaccinations in Inverness.
He inspected the renovations of the cottage in the Ash
woods, discussed the cutting of a plantation of Scots pine,
took note of all the caveats the Piggots wanted included
in the lease for Burnum farm, made plans for the sale of
Rona's cattle when they came off the hill in the autumn,
took up smoking, gave it up again, and wore the rug in
the upstairs sitting room thin with pacing. Every day he
chopped and cut wood with Mike in the Ash Wood. It
was only there, in the shade from the fierce sun, amid the
flies and midges, close to the giant, that he forgot for brief
moments the deaths of David, Kosma and Shem. They

both stripped to the waist, as unselfconscious as when
they had swum naked in the Ash as boys. Eamon thought
of this eternal chore, storing fuel for the winter, and
watched the sweat running rivulets through the grime
on Mike's torso. Mike was as solid and dependable as the
castle itself. More permanent even, more loyal. The castle
could be sold, and its loyalty transferred to some Sheikh
or hedge-funder with the flick of a pen. Mike's loyalty was
to him, and his descendants and his ancestors. He tried
to bring up the subject of Mike's brother Finlay, and his
illness. Kirsty had told him that he was in a locked ward.
Mike said nothing but swung harder, sending slivers of
beechwood into the air.

Eamon called Maclean every day but Maclean only
picked up on the Friday afternoon.

'We're about to do a press conference. It'll be on the
Scottish News. You can hear everything you want to know
from that.'

'I doubt it,' said Eamon. Maclean sighed.

'It is all as we thought. We found a baseball bat that
matched the injuries. We found Shem's DNA on the bat.
We found Shem's DNA and blood and other forensic
evidence at the scene. We have a witness who saw him
going in and out on a regular basis…'

'What other forensic evidence?'

Maclean sighed again. 'Semen on and in David's body
and at the scene. Shem's semen. We found a diary.'

'Saying what?'

'Confirming his relationship with David Smart. Confirming he was thinking of killing himself.'

'And them? Confirming he was thinking of killing David and Kosma?'

Maclean sighed again. 'Neither David nor Kosma was what you would call discreet.'

'So he killed them because he thought his father would find out he was gay? That's what you're going with? That is 'straightforward' to you? There is something you don't know. Stevie and I were up at Endpoint House. We had to walk back, through the woods and over the hill. These protesters have set up cairns in the woods, with these cups, chalices, set up, like altars. I saw two of these cups in David and Kosma's room when I was at the manse, before they were killed. They must have stolen them from the cairns.'

'Eamon, please. What does that mean?'

'It means David and Kosma had crossed the protesters. They had stolen from them. These *Autonomass* are violent. Violent like Shem Murachar was never violent. They hit me with a bat. A bat! John?'

'You have an alternative theory. That they were killed for stealing a cup?'

'You found other DNA at the manse didn't you?'

'We found a lot of DNA at the manse.'

'You should be taking samples from these protesters at Endpoint.'

'That's not going to happen Eamon.'

'It doesn't make sense!'

'It doesn't have to make sense to you. It makes sense to the Procurator Fiscal. It makes sense to me, and my boss. And we have *all* the evidence.'

'All the evidence? What is it that you aren't telling me?'

'I have told you more than you need to know. This is a terrible thing, but it is not a mysterious thing. It has happened. We bury the dead. We move on.'

'Move on?' Eamon repeated. Maclean ended the call. Eamon switched on the television. A policeman in a braided hat was sitting at a little blue table. There were flashes from cameras. Eamon switched it off. He was sitting with his head in his hands when Rona and Kirsty came into the room.

'Mike says that a TV crew wants to know if they can park in the grounds,' said Kirsty. 'To get off the road.'

'Why are they here?'

'Have you forgotten about the conference?' said Rona, 'The Acturus McBean show?'

'Tell them no,' said Eamon. He looked out of the window to beyond the gates at the van with a satellite dish protruding from its roof. As he watched another van arrived. 'And if anyone asks no-one is available for a bloody interview.'

'It doesn't make sense,' he said, when Kirsty had gone.

'What doesn't make sense?' said Rona.

'It doesn't add up. Maclean is not telling me the whole story. "Move on," he said. That sounded so odd coming from him.'

'You think the police are covering something up?'

'I don't know. I know that they've stopped digging. They're not asking; "Why the hell were David and Kosma here?"'

'But I thought Mrs Murray's friend explained that.'

'He didn't though! He palmed me off, in the name of "discretion" and consideration for the family! Then there is the Asian guy I saw in the hills.'

'You said he was probably a hillwalker.'

'I thought that. But he saw me and Shem. He may even have seen Shem hang himself. What kind of a hillwalker walks away from that without coming to help? He just walked off, in a hurry, into the middle of nowhere! Who does that?'

'If he walked to Mallaig, maybe you can track him down.'

'How? Drive to Mallaig and ask if anyone has seen a hillwalker?'

'You said he was a Muslim. There aren't that many Muslim hillwalkers.'

'I don't even know if he went to Mallaig.'

'You said he was going in that direction.'

'It's fifty miles. I looked at the map. He was heading towards Halan.'

'What's Halan?'

'It's a building in the hills, miles from anywhere. It was a seminary.'

'A seminary? For priests?'

'When priests were illegal and outlawed they had a secret seminary back there. It was kept in order right up until the war, not used, but there used to be a pilgrimage to it once a year. I never went, but my mother did. It took a day to walk in and a day to walk out. But it must be a ruin now.'

'So go take a look.'

'No! It's a day in and a day out. What about you and Harry?'

'I have a baby, I'm not an invalid. Whose ground is it on? Yours?'

'Not by miles. It's Mahoud's. The seminary belongs to the Sheikh.'

'So, he's a Muslim. Maybe he knows something about a Muslim hillwalker on his ground. Call him.'

'You can't just call Mohammed Mahoud. He runs Dubai or something.'

'Qatar. He's Qatari.'

'You can't just call him. He's generally in a private jet for starters. You get one of his secretaries. He has about fifteen secretaries.'

'So call one.' They smiled weakly at each other. A faint cry came from the open door to the passage and she left.

Eamon took out his phone and found the number for the Glen Doe Estate office. There was no reply.

At the end of a busy evening in the Clachan at Inverish, with the chatter and laughter ringing in her ears, Eilidh welcomed the silence of her room. Solly had his eyes closed and she was looking down on his face, her own eyes reddened and swollen. As she spoke it seemed as if the words were coming from deep within her, from the child itself, like bubbles rising to the surface, pushing through the membrane that surrounded its world.

'I came back here because of my brothers,' she said. 'I thought I could help them. I couldn't go back to the croft. I never could. I didn't care about my mother and father, but I thought my brothers could visit me. They have never come here. Not once; not one of them. They were forbidden. I kept hoping one day Shem would walk into the pub.'

'Why did you leave?' said Solly.

She shrugged. 'I had a boyfriend. I used to walk from the croft to Duncul in the night to see him. I was caught. They began locking me up at night. One day, when I was sixteen, I just walked to Duncul and took a bus to Fort William and got a job. I used to try to visit my brothers but it got worse. My dad forbid me from coming near the place. Do you have preachers like that in South Africa?'

'For sure.'

'But not in your family. It's different when it is in your family. It's poison.'

'My Mum goes to church. She is in the choir.'

'I hated them too much, for what they did to us. I hated them. I shouldn't have hated them so much. Shem was the gentlest kid. He never fought like the others. Dad was always suspicious of that, because he was gentle. Now he's supposed to be a murderer?' The tears flowed and she wiped her nose. Solly drew her too him.

'I'm pregnant,' she said through the sobs. He gave a small smile but did not open his eyes. 'Did you hear that, Zulu boy?'

'I know,' he whispered. He buried his face in her neck, breathing in the scent of bath salts and sweat. 'Now we have a problem.'

'What problem?' she felt the chords tighten in her throat, and the membrane defeating the child.

'We have to think of a name.' He was laughing, his nose snorting and rubbing against her neck, moving down towards the top of her breast. 'And according to my culture…' the sentence was broken with his laughter, and they rocked into each other as she was caught by a wave of giggles and tears, 'according to my, culture…' he took a deep breath, 'I have to present your father with a cow!'

In the morning Eamon drove north along the south side of Loch Cul, then up the hill to Glen Doe House which looks out over the loch. It was a two-storey lodge, an older version of the house at Endpoint, like hundreds throughout the Highlands, built for entertaining shooting parties. It had never been a particularly extravagant example, and even though the Sheikh had spent millions, the improvement had been slight. The same planning committee that had stymied Nyst had stymied Mahoud. The gold taps in the bathroom had been permitted, but not the four-storey glass and steel extension.

'If I could, I would build a palace here,' Mahoud had told Eamon. 'But you Scottish don't want palaces. You want everyone to be humble. So I am humble. I am a humble man in Scotland, just like you. It is good for me. I walk among my deer and my sheep and go fishing in the river. I find God in nature.'

Eamon parked at the front of the house and rang the bell. He had rung it three times and had turned back to the car when he heard a click. The door opened a few inches to reveal a thin face and moustache.

'Yes?' said the man.

Eamon began to explain that he wished to speak to the Sheikh, and that he had tried to call. The door opened a little more and the man cut him off.

'The Sheikh is in Quatar,' he said. 'What is it about?'

Eamon hesitated. 'It's a delicate matter,' he said. 'I would rather speak in person. He does know me. We have met.'

'You must tell me what is the matter. I am unable to call the Sheikh without this information.'

'I saw a man, on the estate, a few days ago. A Muslim. I am curious about him.'

'What does he look like?' Eamon described the man in the black anorak.

'How do you know he is a Muslim? Because his skin is brown?'

'No. He prayed, with a prayer cap, on a mat, towards Mecca.'

'Excuse me please,' said the man and closed the door.

Eamon waited for a minute before the door opened and the man led him through the porch into a vast living room. The interior was typical Highland Shooting Lodge Edwardian Pastiche, except for the Koran verses on the walls, and the lack of paintings of dogs, horses and birds.

'Please be seated,' said the man, showing him an armchair. Eamon sat and studied the verses. The man returned with a small table. He left the room and re-entered with a laptop which he placed on the table, then he retreated to stand against the opposite wall. The face of Mohammed Mahoud appeared on the screen; clean shaven, bland and thin lipped, with the faintest trace of a smile.

'Eamon.'

'Sheikh.'

'I hear you are having good weather. When the sun is shining Glen Cul is close to Paradise.'

'Not quite.'

'I am sorry. That was clumsy of me. You have had some ugliness. I know of this also. I also hear you have come across my nephew.'

'Nephew?'

'Yes. His name is Tariq. He is my nephew.'

'And he is staying here at Glen Doe?'

'Yes. But also at Halan. Do you know Halan?'

'Yes. But it's a ruin now isn't it?'

'I had it renovated.'

'I apologise for the intrusion. I saw him on the hill.'

'Do not apologise. You saw a Muslim in the hills. I grant you that it was unusual. You are protective. I understand this. Tell me, where did you see him? What were the circumstances?'

Eamon told him about Shem.

'That is terrible news. I must apologise on my nephew's behalf. I can see that his behaviour appears callous. But I have to explain that he is recovering from some problems. He is a fragile and nervous person. He needs to be alone. He would not have wanted to be involved, especially to have to have been interviewed by the police. Let us say he is on a retreat. He has had some trouble in his personal life. He is recovering by walking in the hills. He is, shall we say, healing.'

'Of course, I understand.' There was a long silence.

'If there is anything I can do, to help, please speak to the man that met you at the door. His name is Hamid. He will give you his personal number.' Mahoud nodded to someone to end the call.

'Thank you,' said Eamon to the blank screen.

Mo, wearing a dry suit, leant on the rail of the *Sea Wolf*, finishing a cigarette. The sea was a silky skin stretched towards Ardven glowing in sunlight in the distance. Solly and Qualin had gone to forty metres and were taking their time to come back up. They would be hanging on the anchor chain at ten metres for the next half hour at least. The Germans were in the cabin. In a week they had said less than ten words to him. If they were going to be on the boat together every day for a month, they would have to talk. The atmosphere was becoming unpleasant. He had even thought that at some point it wouldn't be worth the money. But not yet. He flicked the cigarette butt into the water.

'You shouldn't do that,' said Brigitta.

Mo was surprised to see her leaning on the rail next to him. She was probably not much more than twenty; not much older than his own daughter. Only a month, he reminded himself. A month of this *kak* and then he was going to say goodbye to Pik and *alles*.

'You don't care, do you?' said Brigitta.

'About a *stompie* in the sea? Not much.'

'It poisons the sea.'

Mo looked out across the shifting depths. 'Sea can probably handle it.' He lit another cigarette. 'How old are you?'

'Why does that matter?' She was staring into his eyes.

'I'm just wondering about you. Why so hostile?' he smiled.

'You want to put a number on me. You think if you know facts about me I will make sense. I know what you want me to be.'

'What is that?'

'A woman. A girl. A thing. Sexy. Not Sexy. Good to eat. Not good to eat. I am a thing. Not a person.'

Mo let silence settle between them before he replied. 'I know what you mean. Among my people I am a person, but not here. Here I am a Muslim. But not all the time. People let their guard down and then I become a person. People have prejudices. They have ideas, but they can't keep them up all the time. I don't need to ask you questions to understand you. I know what you want. You see all the shit in the world and you want to cure the world, to make it better, and your method is to put a little more poison into it. Like suicide bombers, you want to make it better with poison. They think they are like chemotherapy.'

'What does The Koran say about respecting the planet?'

'What I was taught was respect your elders, don't beat your wife, take care of the poor, work hard. To be honest nothing about the "environment."'

'Why do your women wear the scarf? *The hijab*?'

Mo smiled as he thought of his own daughter with long dark hair and jeans, telling him about the latest night-club in London. He shrugged. 'Tradition.'

'Yes but why this tradition? What is the cause of it?'

'Protection. So not every man gets to see your beauty. So they can't eat you with their eyes.'

'So a woman needs protection from a man.'

'I guess.'

'In case he eats her.'

Mo shrugged. 'Where I come from, South Africa, women need protection from men. Maybe not so much here.' She was silent for a while, and he watched the sunlight on her face.

'I want you to go to stand at the other side, to look out the other side,' she said.

'Why?'

'I want to go swimming, like a Muslim woman, without being seen.'

He shrugged and moved to the other rail, and listened to her gasps and splashes as she entered the water. He

waited several minutes before he looked over his shoulder.
She was fifty yards out from the boat, a head bobbing in
the flat calm, looking away from him towards the hills.
He turned his head before she saw him watching. He
had time for two more cigarettes and was looking at his
watch, expecting Solly and Qualin to surface, before he
heard her feet padding on the deck. When she had dressed
she came to the rail and stood next to him. Her face was
glowing, warm and pink. They watched a seal disturbing
the surface in the distance. He finished his cigarette and
ground it out on the rail.

'I don't have pockets,' he said. She held out her hand
to take the butt. He was sure the corner of her mouth
turned up, a millimetre. 'What are we looking for
Brigitta?'

'AUV.' The mouth was a flat line, the eyes cold as the
sea.

'OK. Cool. AUV.' He turned to go aft and check on
Solly and Qualin's progress.

Brigitta looked at the butt in the palm of her hand.
'*Chemotherapie*' she said, and flicked it into the water.

On the fifth floor of Duncul Castle Harriet held out
her arm to let her daughter put on her shirt. Harry was
wriggling his legs on the bed and cooing in the back of his
throat. He was happy for the moment, but it would not

last long. He would want to be picked up in about sixty seconds.

'Where has Eamon gone now?' said Harriet.

'He went up to Glen Doe,' said Rona.

'Why?'

'Estate business.'

'Yes, well, there is a lot of that now, isn't there?' said Harriet.

Rona knelt in front of her mother and began to do up her shirt buttons. How did she imply so much with such a simple line? What was she implying? It wasn't even worth thinking about, she told herself. She began to rush and fumbled with the buttons. She was becoming familiar with the feeling that she had to get out. It had been her own decision not to have a nanny, but she was regretting it. She had to get out and she couldn't leave Harry with her mother. Her mother could hardly hold him, let alone pick him up or change him. Harry began to cry.

'I want to go downstairs,' said Harriet.

'You can't until Eamon gets back.'

'You could call Mike.'

'Mike's in the Ash Wood'

'I don't want to stay here.'

'I'll be back soon.' Rona scooped up her son and almost ran from the room. As she put on his suit and strapped on the baby-carrier in the hall she found herself breathless, heart racing, hands hot and quivering.

'Panic Attacks,' the doctor had said. 'Not unusual for first time mothers. Nothing to worry about.'

She strapped Harry to her chest and his blue eyes looked up at hers.

As soon as she was outside she began to worry he was going to get too hot in the suit. She took down the hood and let the breeze move the wisps of hair. He smiled. He was fine. She had a nappy in her jacket pocket and two breasts full of milk. She walked.

She passed the two TV vans on the verge at the castle gates with a long, strong stride. She had not thought of a route, she just had to get away from her mother. She hesitated at the crossroads in the village, thinking about the shore at Loch Nish, but turned past Tarr Bow and over the Tarr burn, up the hill towards the manse, and beyond the manse to Mrs Murray's house.

Mrs Murray was in her garden, with her back to Rona, doing something with shears. Rona paused at the gate and was about to carry on towards the path that entered the woods at the end of the avenue when the old woman turned.

'Rona,' she said, and a wide smile ensued as she noticed the baby and came towards them. She reached out with a frail hand to caress Harry's scalp. 'He should be wearing a hat in this sun.'

'It's a bit hot for a hat.'

'Come into the house, into the shade. You'll have a cup of tea.'

'I'm sorry about Eamon asking you questions,' said Rona when she had unstrapped Harry and lain him on a crocheted blanket on the floor.

Mrs Murray came through from the kitchen with tea and pancakes. Her smile fell at mention of Eamon, but soon recovered as she contemplated the boy, who was kicking his thick legs.

'It's no bother,' she said. 'He was upset.' She poured tea and smiled at Harry. 'I remember David when he was this size.'

'You knew him when he was a baby?'

Mrs Murray looked up at her. 'You mustn't say anything. It's not important now anyway.' She cooed at the child. 'Yes, as a baby, and as a boy, and as a young man.'

'I didn't know that. Is that why he came here? Because he knew you?'

'Yes,' she said, and because Rona did not ask again, she went on. 'He was very troubled. A very sick young man. They tried to help him. His parents, and others. They tried everything they could. We tried everything we could.'

'What do you mean, "sick"?'

'It is a sickness you know. It can be cured. Nobody wants to say that now, but it is true. Dr Simmonds tried his best, but David would not be helped.'

'"Dr" Simmonds?'

'I'm sorry dear. I've said too much. Perhaps you should go.' She began to clear away the teacups.

'You tried to cure him? Of what?'

'You should go dear.'

'Yes, I should.' She picked up Harry and strapped him in. He began to wail. She had to walk. 'Thank you, for the tea.' Mrs Murray held the door for her. 'Mrs Murray, I don't think you can cure someone, of that.'

'Well my dear, Dr Simmonds had many successes.'

Rona stepped out into the sun and scent of rhododendrons.

'One more thing. Did you know Kosma when he was a child too? Did Dr Simmonds try to cure them both?'

'I never set eyes on Kosma before he turned up here. He made everything worse. Goodbye dear.' She closed the door.

Rona could feel the heart rising and the breath falling away from her as she walked down the path with the gaping, howling mouth beneath her chin. At the bottom of the hill she turned right at the crossroads and set out along the road that wound along the Ash on its way to Loch Nish.

In half-a-mile Harry was asleep. She pulled up his hood for shade. She lengthened her pace and breathed in the coconut-scent of gorse. The Ash slid by like an endless, warm, brown serpent, its transparent belly full of stones. She felt like running beneath the perfect sky, raising her arms and shouting, becoming a madwoman running towards the sea, but she only kept up a stiff pace. She was a mother now. She was a serious person. She felt like throwing off her clothes and jumping naked into the Ash and letting the ice-cold course through her. She felt like buying a packet of fags and a half-bottle and getting pissed on the shore, but she strode on, a little faster than was dignified for a mother, she thought. It was not long before she reached the beach.

The tide was out and she walked beyond the pebbles and the band of weed onto the sand, leaving a trail of boot-prints through the worm-casts and cockle-shells. The sea fizzed up and retreated, as if it couldn't make up its mind about something. She walked the full length of the beach, to the north, and then turned back, at last beginning to feel tired. It was as she was walking back that she saw the body.

She knew what it was as soon as she saw it, although there was no detail that made it a body. It was a shapeless black lump moving at the border of the listless sea. As she approached she realised that on her way up the beach, it must have been just beneath the surface, and she had

walked within yards of it. It was dressed in a black t-shirt
and jeans, and one black sock, and all these things were
wrapped tight around the limbs and torso, as the body
had swollen, so that it bulged at the belly above the
waistband of the jeans and beyond the sleeves of the shirt.
It was lying face down, with the knees slightly bent, and
the arms outstretched; a man prostrate, as if in prayer.
Her instinct was to wrinkle her nose, but there was no
smell beyond the subtle stench and the weed rotting
further up the beach. She supposed it was a man. He had
close-cropped hair and earrings. The t-shirt was rumpled
up above the swollen belly and back and although the skin
had darkened a thicket of tattoos was visible. The index
finger of the left hand ended at the second knuckle in a
ring of flesh around white bone. Rona walked into the
sea, around the body, getting her feet wet. She thought
about dragging it further up out of the water but did not
want to touch it. She looked around for something to pull
or prod it out and saw a heavy piece of driftwood further
up the beach, but she had a sleeping, softly-breathing baby
strapped to her chest. She took out her phone.

Eamon was on his way back from Glen Doe. 'I can be
there in ten minutes,' he said. 'But you should call the
police.'

Chapter 11

In the darkened study at Endpoint House the only light came from a flickering screen. Nyst sat hunched in an armchair. The interviewer was excited to be talking to Acturus McBean.

'On the face of it this seems to me to be a strange hill to die on. Denis Nyst is an obscure figure. He hasn't been seen in public for years. He minds his own business. He wants to release wolves onto his estate, and the government won't let him. Surely there are other things that the public wants to hear about? Jobs, housing, immigration, constitutional issues?'

'But I do talk about all of these things. And you are right, Denis Nyst is an obscure figure. But here is this billionaire, in the shadows, pulling the strings.

The mainstream media wants to talk about "dark money". Denis Nyst is the living, breathing epitome of dark money! Dark money with an inhuman, callous, ideological agenda! Yes, you might say this is an obscure battle in an obscure corner of this great country, but it matters that a foreign billionaire can foist his ideology into a traditional crofting community. A community that has maintained its traditions for centuries unchanged! People like Johnny Murachar are the backbone of this great country! Yes, you and your ilk in the media, the hummus-eating classes, might not like the un-house-trained Murachar's of this world, but he speaks for the common man! The man who just wants to get on with his life, within his own culture and traditions, without interference from the likes of Denis Nyst! What you've got to understand is that Denis Nyst is fake! He is a wolf in sheep's clothing! What masquerades as an attempt to re-introduce wolves into the Highlands is the thin end of the wedge!'

'If you knew that Denis Nyst was watching right now, what would you say to him?'

'I would say go home Mr Nyst! Go back to Holland, or wherever it is you come from, and foist your dangerous ideas on your own people!'

'That's a very anti-immigration message.'

'I am not anti-immigration. I am all for the right sort of immigrants. That is why, on the fifteenth of this month we will be welcoming delegates from all over the world to Johnny Murachar's croft…'

Denis Nyst rubbed his face with his hands.

Eamon and Rona sat on a rock at the top of the beach at Loch Nish, looking at the dark lump at the water's edge. Eamon had called Stevie and in ten minutes his pickup drew up at the end of the road. He went to look at the body before approaching Eamon and Rona.

'It's Malky,' he said. 'If you don't believe me you can ask his tattooist.'

'I believe you.'

'That explains.'

'Explains what?'

'A lot of phone calls. He's got unhappy clients. Wee shit. He owed me money. The tide is going to turn. We'd better pull him up the beach.'

Eamon suggested a rope but Stevie insisted that that would be undignified.

'We could wait until the police get here,' said Eamon. Stevie walked into the sea and took hold of a foot, swung the body around and began to pull. Eamon wrapped his hands around the other ankle and felt the deep cold of the dead.

He expected Maclean, but after an hour only uniformed officers arrived. After moving the body further up the beach and the giving of statements it was evening by the time Eamon and Rona arrived back at the castle. Kirsty came into the study wearing her coat.

'Your mother has been quite upset today,' she said.

'I'm sure she has,' said Rona, laying Harry on the couch to undress him.

'She wanted to be taken down to the sitting room.'

'I'm sure she did.'

'I'll let her know you are back before I go.'

'Please don't. I will go myself shortly. 'Kirsty, how long has Justin Simmonds been with us?'

'Oh, a couple of years now. Not long. He came at the same time as Mrs Murray.'

'And is he a doctor?'

'I don't know. He was never a doctor here.'

'And he's involved with the church?'

'No, not really. He has prayer meetings in his house. Nothing to do with The Kirk.'

'What kind of prayer meetings?'

'I don't go myself,' she said. There was a pause.

'Kirsty,' said Eamon.

'Yes?'

'The photograph you showed me, on your phone…'

'It's deleted.'

'Good,' he said. Seeing that there were no more questions Kirsty shuffled out of the door.

Rona was looking at her phone. 'Here he is. That's him. "Dr Justin Simmonds PhD. Omni Psychotherapy."

But the page isn't there when you click. I'll google Omni Psychotherapy. Here we go: "Omni Psychotherapy," address and telephone. Peterborough. I could call the number. Hold on, here's something else. Someone's blog.

"Omni Psychotherapy is the worst kind of shit." That's the actual title. "Quack Psychotherapy that damages kids. Omni is one of the last practices offering so-called "conversion therapy" for gay teens in Britain. Only this time it comes with a twist; this is not Christian Shit, offering to purge young people of their very soul in the name of Jesus, but New Age Shit of the highest order, offering to extract the hard-earned cash of gullible parents that hope they can "pursue a programme of spiritual cleansing that will facilitate the ordering of the psychosexual self in relation to age-old archetypes." That's a messed-up way of saying, "we'll chase away the gay!" Under the direction of "Dr" Justin Simmonds Omni has been operating in the Peterborough area for ten years, and get this; all parents and clients have to sign non-disclosure agreements about their practices. Is this even legal? We intend to find out…" They tried to "cure" David,' said Rona.

'In Peterborough. He said he was from Peterborough. His parents are from there.'

'They tried to stop him being gay, when he was a kid. There's more here. This blogger started a campaign. They got it into the local press. It looks like they closed them down.

"Good riddance Omni Psychotherapy. I have one message for Dr Justin Simmonds and his secretary Mrs Edwina Murray for their imminent retirement. Go far away and die soon, you evil cunts."

"Far away",' said Rona. 'That's here I suppose. But why did David come here? I mean, why would he want to?'

'Maybe he didn't want to.'

'How so?'

'If you think about it,' said Eamon, 'All the nicking stuff. It was as if he was trying to make himself annoying, trying to embarrass someone. Maybe he was here under duress?'

'And Kosma? Mrs Murray said she didn't know anything about him. She had never seen him before. She didn't seem to like him.'

'Well he wasn't exactly helping the "curing" process, was he?'

'But what has this got to do with their deaths?' said Rona.

'Perhaps nothing. Perhaps neither has Shem Murachar.'

'But the police are sure.'

'Shem Murachar wasn't violent. Yes, he was in love, or lust, with David. That much is sure. Yes, he was ashamed. He was ashamed enough to kill himself because he knew the police would expose everything.'

'But the evidence…'

'What evidence? He was seen there, he was there, let's assume he made love there. But the only evidence that he killed them is the bat that was found on the croft. The protesters are throwing things over the fence every night, and I'm witness to the fact they like to use a bat!'

'You think *they* killed David and Kosma?'

'Think about it. They're violent. They didn't think twice about attacking me. I've seen them up close, these guys are nuts!'

'Yes, but why? Why kill them?'

'They want to discredit Johnny Murachar and his bigotry. They've succeeded in that.'

'But murder? Two murders?'

'I know. It seems incredible, but there is something else. I saw those cups, or whatever they are; chalices, in the woods behind Endpoint. I saw the same in the manse. The boys had stolen them. They are something to do with the protesters. What if David or Kosma stole them and the protesters came to get them back? I need to find out from Maclean if there were any of those cups in the house when the bodies were found. And I need to know how Malky died. Is that something to do with the protesters too?'

Harry started to cry. Rona picked him up. 'I have to go and see mother,' she said.

Eamon called Maclean and got voicemail. He called the police HQ in Inverness. He was put through two secretaries and a full minute of Vivaldi's *Four Seasons* before he was answered by a female voice.

'I'm afraid Detective Superintendent Maclean is no longer with us,' she said.

Eamon felt his breathing stop. 'He's…'

'Retired,' said the voice.

Eamon breathed. 'When?'

'At the end of the month. He's on leave until then.'

'Why?' said Eamon, without thinking. He could tell the woman was smiling as she replied.

'Same reason as everyone else. He's getting old.'

'Who's taken over the case? The double murder in Duncul?' There was a pause.

'I'll put you through.'

There was a click, then a man's voice. 'Yes?'

'I want to talk to someone about the murders in Duncul.'

'Yes?'

'To whom am I speaking?'

'This is DS Troy.'

'Are you in charge of the investigation now?'

'It's no longer an investigation.'

'But what if there is new information?'

'You have new information?'

'No. Maybe. I was wondering…'

'Yes?'

'Is there any way I could find out what was found at the murder scene?'

'I'm sorry?'

'At the murder scene, there were things that David and Kosma had stolen. Perhaps I could look at some photographs.'

'Could you give me your name please?'

Eamon gave it.

'And what is your interest in the case?'

'I don't think Shem Murachar did it.' There was a pause.

'And who do you think did?'

'I don't know. I think you should be investigating further.' Another pause.

'We'll call you back Mr Ansgar.' The phone clicked.

Solly was leaning out of the window of the flat above the Clachan, blowing smoke into the cool morning air and tapping into his phone. Eilidh was making the bed.

'But I am not a Muslim,' he said.

'I know.'

'I am a Pentecostal. We have to pretend to be Muslims, for the job. The boss is a racist...'

'I know.' She straightened and smoothed the duvet.

'Soon I can leave the job. I will have enough money.'

'But then your work permit will not be valid.'

'We can work it out.' He stubbed out his cigarette on the windowsill and turned to her. She looked at him, framed in the bright square. Thinking about him was like running her hand over velvet. Solly and Eilidh, merging into each other, and she carrying that knot of love in her stomach. But beyond him, also framed in the window, she could see the hills of Ardven; five siblings and a mother and a father. You can leave a family, but can you do that to your child? Deprive them of their family, history, everything that would be passed down? Aunties, uncles, cousins, grandmother, grandfather?

'We could go to South Africa,' she said.

'We could,' he grinned.

'The Rainbow Nation.'

'It is.' Solly's phone buzzed, and he frowned as he stared at the screen.

'What is it?'

'It's Malky.'

'Malky Macleod?'

'He's dead.'

Eamon was in the kitchen when Richard Blackwell called on the landline. Even on a phone his lawyer's voice resonated as if he was in some cavernous hall.

'I'm up at Ben Breckie! Catching trout! I will bring for luncheon!'

Eamon spent the rest of the morning chopping logs with Mike among the beeches and saw the little car filled with RB as it crunched up the drive.

'Mercy! Mercy!' he grinned as Eamon approached, sweating, with an axe swinging by his side. RB emerged swathed in tent-sized tweed and plus-fours. He held up a supermarket bag darkened with blood. 'We come in peace!' Eamon shook the thick hand and grinned in return.

'To what do I owe the honour?'

'Oh you know, in the area and all that.' They ambled the short distance to the front door in silence. Eamon led him to the kitchen and set about frying the fish. RB sat at the table, looking up at the vaulted ceiling and down at his restless fingers. Eamon placed a bottle of Chablis and glasses on the table. RB stopped gazing at the ceiling, drank one glass straight down and settled into sipping the second.

'Who were you visiting?' said Eamon.

'Ewan McIver. You remember McIver?'

'No.'

'I was at school with him.'

'You were at school with a lot of people.' Eamon set out plates and cutlery.

'I was indeed. He went into the civil service. Big cheese now. *Un Grande Formaggio.*' Eamon adorned the plates with small brown trout, skins crisped in butter, four for himself and six for RB.

'You are too kind.' RB blessed his plate and refilled his glass as he waited for Eamon to sit. Eamon watched his lawyer shovel forkfuls between enormous teeth.

RB stopped shovelling and chewed. 'Can't beat it eh? Fresh this morning. You look suspicious. Ask me about McIver.'

'Which civil service is he a big cheese in? English or Scottish?'

'Well both, sort of, actually. They do cooperate you know, the auld enemies. He's in charge of cops.'

'Police Scotland?'

'Not exactly. But in a way, sort of.'

'Come off it RB.' RB stuffed in half a trout and washed it down.

'You have had a tragedy. Two tragedies. It is a shock. It is awful. And you want to know how, or why. And once you know you want to do more than know, you want to understand. Am I right?'

'Yes.'

'But Evil, my boy, defies understanding. You are staring into the abyss, and all you will see is clouds and mist and darkness.'

'What did McIver say?'

'He asked me to ask you to leave it alone. They have the murderer. The case is for all intents and purposes closed.'

'Shem Murachar's family have to live with that forever. Their son killed two people then killed himself. Forever. It's like a sentence. In Hell.'

'Johnny Murachar is a poisonous bigot. Maybe he deserves a bit of Hell. He certainly wishes it on the rest of us.'

'What if it is not true? Isn't it wrong for Shem to be remembered like that? He killed himself; that is awful. But a murderer? What if it isn't true Richard? McIver and the government want it to go away. Why?'

'Perhaps you should consider that they may have a good reason.'

'Willingly, if you'll let me know what it is.'

'When was the last time there was a homophobic murder in Scotland?'

'I don't know.'

'It was more than a decade ago. Before that, nineteen-ninety-five. It is rare.'

'So?'

'The Scottish Government has made tremendous efforts to prevent such crimes. We are one of the most gay-friendly nations in the world.'

'You're saying it is a reputation-saving exercise? To save face?'

'If Shem Murachar did kill David and Kosma it is a *crime de passion*. He loves David, David loves Kosma, or something like that. Shem snaps, there's a fight,

Shem wins. But if anyone else has killed them, it's a homophobic murder. Two overtly gay men living in a remote Highland village, beaten to death. It's a hate crime. Acturus and his merry crew are coming to town. I see the TV people have arrived. The last thing anyone wants is a homophobic murder, including the SIC and their ilk. You could say there is a homophobia phobia, at the highest level. Shem Murachar makes that all go away.'

'But there are pictures, of the crime scene with writing on the wall. "Kill the Gays' etc." Why would Shem write that?'

'Sadly, self hate.'

'I don't believe he did it!'

'You believe someone else did it.'

'Yes!'

'You believe it was the German anarchist deep-green climate-heroes that are trying to get Johnny off his croft.'

'Yes!'

'And you are going to do your damnedest to prove it, and go out of your way to kick up as much fuss as possible until you get the police to pay attention.'

'Yes!'

'And turn over every rock to see what is under it and poke your stick in every hornet's nest you can find until something is done.'

'Yes!'

'And nothing I say is going to stop you?'

'No.' RB leaned back from his empty plate. Even the
bones had gone.

'You are very like your father, you know. Once you
get the bit between the teeth, you won't stop. And your
grandfather too, who had a bit more heart. You are the
best of both.' He smiled. 'I am going to be very rude now
and depart. My services are required elsewhere.' He got
up and Eamon walked him to his car, which rocked on
its springs as RB eased himself into the driver's seat. He
wound down the window.

'I do have a solution for you. What you seek, my boy,
is peace of mind. The stress, you know, of becoming a
father, and now this trouble in the village, and so on.
What you need to do is go on retreat.'

'Don't be ridiculous.'

'I'm serious. Everything will become clear when
the mind is at rest. You need to go away to a house of
prayer. Make a pilgrimage.' He started the engine. 'Make
sure you choose the right one though. I can make a
recommendation. Somewhere beautiful, peaceful, in the
hills, away from it all.' He reversed the car.

'What are you talking about?'

'You should make a pilgrimage!' And before Eamon
could think of a reply the little car was half-way down the
drive.

The *Sea Wolf* was north of Raasay, heading towards the first dive site of the day. There was a strong breeze and light and spray flicking from the tops of short waves. Mo saw the navy boat first, twenty metres of grey boxes on a sleek hull. It was moving fast, and soon it was alongside, sounding an alarm, and a smart voice over a loudspeaker was telling them to 'stop all engines'. Mo cut the outboards and the RIB drifted to a stop against a wall of steel. Two men wearing boiler-suits appeared above them.

'Do you have a radio on board?' said one.

Mo nodded.

'You need to switch it on. The emergency channel is sixteen,' said the man.

Mo nodded.

'This is a test day. You need to leave the area immediately.'

'What area?'

'Do you have a chart?'

'Yes.'

'Do you ever look at it?'

'Yes.'

'It's marked with a red line, and the letters, B U T E C. This is a naval torpedo testing range. You need to head due west now, and get out. Today and tomorrow are scheduled test days. There's a notice in every harbour on the west coast. Where have you come from?'

Mo opened his mouth but Brigitta spoke. 'Oban,' she said.

'Then you should be aware of the schedule,' said the man. 'Your boat can be confiscated. Start your engine and head due west.'

Mo went into the cabin to start the engine. As the navy boat receded towards the coast he looked at the red outline on the chart-plotter. It formed a rectangle running north to south between Raasay and Applecross. There were two dive sites inside the rectangle.

'We can't do these until later on in the week,' he told Brigitta, and pointed to where they would dive instead, at a site closer to the Skye coast. 'We can do this dive and maybe another on the way home. Find that torpedo!' It was a joke that he made three or four times throughout the day; a weak joke, but he repeated it because each time it made her smile.

'Come on!' he said as Solly and Qualin got ready for the second dive. 'Let's find that thing before the navy finds it!'

When they arrived back at the barge the sun was easing itself into a calming sea. They were taking off their dry-suits in the deckhouse when Brigitta, Horst and the other three men came in and stood in a row between the divers and the door. Horst was holding a length of steel bar.

'You must give us your phones,' said Brigitta.

Mo looked at Solly. Qualin looked at Mo.

'What?' said Mo, his brow lowered.

'You must give us your phones and you must stay on the barge.'

'Stay on the barge?'

'*Ja.*'

'Is this a joke?'

'Give the phones please.'

'Fuck you!' said Mo. Horst stepped forward and swung the steel underarm, catching him on the shin. Mo fell back onto the bench behind him, clutching his leg, his mind swamped with pain. Horst grinned and moved closer.

'OK, OK!' said Mo. The three divers handed over their phones.

'We will bring you food,' said Brigitta. Horst and the others followed her out and locked the door behind them. Mo inspected the ugly welt on his shin. His face had gone pale.

'What just happened?' said Solly.

'We just got locked on the barge, my *bru*,' said Qualin.

'Why?'

Qualin did not answer but tried the door and looked through one of the portholes as an outboard started outside. 'They're taking both boats,' he said. 'Hey! Hey!' he shouted, slapping the steel walls. He turned to Mo, who was rocking back and forth on the bench, holding his leg. 'What?'

'It's a torpedo,' whispered Mo, taking sharp breaths between each word, 'They're. Looking. For. A. Torpedo.'

Chapter 12

Eamon and Rona were in their bedroom, Eamon in his pyjamas and Harry lying on the bed naked and glowing after his bath.

'That's crazy!' said Rona. 'You would think the government would want to root out homophobia. Don't they?'

'It's to do with Acturus McBean and that lot, coming here.'

'But the government hates Acturus McBean. Why would they protect his reputation?'

'Once you get into politics anything is possible. Perhaps it's not his reputation they're protecting but the reputation of the country. McBean tarnishes us all. He's gaining support. They have spent the last twenty years portraying us as a non-racist, non-sexist, non-homophobic country. A homophobic killing is simply not good for the brand.'

Rona had managed to button the wriggling child into the baby-grow and was pushing his face to her breast. He kept lifting back his head and smiling.

'We know about David, but we know nothing about Kosma. Milosz is a Polish name. I googled him. There is nothing. Not even Facebook. Isn't that weird?'

'I'm not on Facebook.'

'Yes, but you're old, and anti-social.'

'What if you google Kosma Milosz and David Smart, together?'

'Nothing.'

Eamon lay back on the bed.

'So who knows him? Who knew anything about him? *Were* he and David partners? David was having a relationship with Shem. Shem was seen visiting the manse, but was anyone else?'

'Mrs Murray would know.' Eamon closed his eyes.

'Richard Blackwell says I need to go on retreat, to get away from it all.'

'He wants you to stop.'

'He was very insistent. Said I need to go on a pilgrimage.' Eamon pulled the duvet up to his chin. 'Malky had lost a finger. How? How long had he been in the water? I'm not a pathologist. I'm a landlord. I need to speak to the police again. You should go and speak to Mrs Murray again, see if anyone else was going to the manse.'

'Mrs Murray gives me the creeps.'

'But she likes you because you have a baby. She doesn't like me. Malky didn't fall off his boat and drown. His boat was at the pier when he was in the water. He didn't drown while he was out diving. What the police gonna' say 'bout that?' Images swam up from somewhere beneath his mind. Malky's body caressed by the waves on the grey sand. The green and purple hills of Ardven towering over him like an immense wave. Shouts and points of light in a forest; the metal grid of the fence close to his face. Then he was floating above the bright land, feeling the light in his limbs, looking down on indecipherable twists of heather, rock, paths, streams; a small figure, wearing a prayer cap, walking along a path, a toy figure from this high up, wending a way to the south-west, up hill and down dale to… 'Halan!' He heard the word like a clanging bell, and it jolted him awake. 'Halan!' he said and jerked himself upright in the bed.

'Shush!' said Rona. She was reading a book as she fed Harry.

'He was dropping a very obvious hint. Halan. He was telling me to go to Halan. "Go on pilgrimage," and all that.'

'RB?'

'Yes!'

'Why would he do that?'

'RB has been told by his old-boys network to stop me looking into this. But he's a friend. He's a friend of my father's, my mother's. He knew my grandfather. He's a friend of Duncul. Perhaps that counts for more than the old-boy's network? He wants me to go to Halan, to meet…' he struggled to remember the name, 'Tariq. Mahoud's nephew. The man on the hill. Because there was something very odd that he did. He saw Shem Murachar hang himself, or at least saw him hanging, and he did nothing. He walked away. Why would you do that? If you are a hillwalker, if you came across Shem, you would intervene and help. Anyone would, if they knew nothing about what was going on. This guy, Tariq, he must have known what was going on. His action is the action of someone who knows. Am I right?'

'But why didn't RB just say: "Go to Halan"?'

'Because plausible deniability. He's not allowed to say it.'

Rona put her finger to her lips and put the sleeping boy against her shoulder. She nodded and kissed her husband goodnight.

After the slamming and locking of the door to the deckhouse of *The Kelpie*, the late-night delivery of sleeping bags and pizzas folded in half so they could fit through the port-hole, then the night on the creaking barge, which by morning had impregnated their bones with its hard, damp nature, by morning Mo, Solly and Qualin felt a year older.

They had talked about what they should or could do. Mo, nursing his bruised shin, did not want to admit that he had little idea, beyond promising not to tell anyone about the torpedo. The only leverage he had was that they could refuse to dive. But it nagged him that he could not believe that Brigitta had not thought of that. Qualin had wanted to talk about fighting their way out. Solly had been silent. He would not speak until there was something worth saying.

They had been awoken by aching bones as the first tepid sun came through the portholes, illuminating rust streaked walls, hanging dry-suits, piles of tanks and crates of tangled belts and webbing in a humiliating light. It was the same light that comes after a night of hard drinking, when all the imperfections of the world leap out and claim your responsibility. They had lain unspeaking for hours, listening to the slap of waves on the hull, anticipating the sounds of motors, and at last had heard the low hum from across the loch. There was a moment when they all thought of some kind of fight; of scuffles and bruises, someone throwing an air tank; something like all the other fights they had witnessed or been part of in their years in a rough business in a rough country. They thought of something undignified and even painful, that entailed a certain denial of risk, a lot of shouting, flecks of spittle, even blood, and then a resolution and a de-brief in a bar. They thought of something that in the end would not be truly serious, with few repercussions; something that had always been a kind of game. But none of their hearts were in it. All three of them had been locked in police cells, but never imprisoned by people who were not the police. All of them had come up against serious people, with guns; gangs and mafias, in the course of their work in South Africa. But somehow, without even a gun being brandished, they sensed that what Brigitta and her men had done, and what they could do, was worse. Perhaps it was because any kind of normal fight was always about honour, money or a woman and whatever Brigitta was thinking about, it was none of these.

They listened without comment to the squeaking of the *Sea Wolf* against the side of the barge, the clatter of footsteps on the decks and the wrenching of the lever on the door to the deck-house. They could refuse to dive, Mo thought again as the door opened. No-one could force someone to dive. He had expected Brigitta and an imperious, deadpan speech. He had expected Horst, the steel bar, and the joy he got out of swinging it. He got an anonymous minion handing Solly a scrap of paper and Solly's incredulous look. The paper was three inches square. It showed blurred white shapes, fading to grey. The minion exited without a word and left the deckhouse door unlocked. Solly stared at the paper. Mo looked over his shoulder, at the curlicues, shadows and impregnated light. It was little more than a thumb-print in a triangle of darkness, a little snow-storm in the cavernous night, and stamped and dated with some numbers in the top right, and in the top left a name in clumsy font: 'Elidh Murachar.' It was a print from an ultrasound scan, a photograph of the beginnings of a Zulu.

'What does this mean?' shouted Solly, and received only the echo of deck-house walls in reply.

It was not long after sunrise when Eamon parked at the Loch Houn pier. It would have been far faster to travel by sea to Inverish, and from there head due south to Halan, but he lacked Malky's boat. He set off at a fast pace, following a path marked on a cloth-backed map he had found in the library, because he knew at a certain distance from the loch his phone would be useless.

It was mid-afternoon before he saw a white, two-storey building with small windows in the distance. The seminary had been built to be unseen, nestled in a corrie surrounded on three sides by steep hill, the source of the Halan Burn, which entered the sea at Inverish. Eamon lay down in the heather and took out his binoculars.

The building stood out against a little field of sheep-cropped grass. It had been newly painted and new windows and doors installed. There was no road to Halan. Eamon imagined tradesmen descending from helicopters.

He scoured the hillsides and seeing no-one crept up the steep glen of the Halan Burn. There were no trees around the building and it could not be approached without being seen. He thought about waiting until dark, but the dark would not come until an hour before midnight. So he walked up to the front door and knocked loudly, then tried the handle. The door was locked. He looked through the windows. The ground floor rooms were carpeted, newly painted and without furniture. Eamon called 'Tariq!' at the windows, several times, then sat on the grass before the front door. By a quirk of the lay of the land he could see the tip of the Ardven peninsula, six miles distant, framed by the steep sides of the Halan Burn glen. He lay on his back and stared up at the few clouds that marred the blue. He almost fell asleep, breathing in the scent of sheep manure and heather as a breeze descended from the tops. RB had been right; this place was a balm to the soul. Eventually he walked around to the back of the building and tried the door and windows there. He found one of the windows open and after calling for Tariq again he climbed into an unfurnished room that smelled of fresh paint.

The room entered into a corridor. The ground floor rooms were empty, newly carpeted and painted. From the corridor he entered a narrow stairwell.

At the top of the stair he stepped into a room with a sleeping bag and mat in one corner, a cheap office chair

and a desk with thin metal legs supporting a lap-top and
something that looked like a router. A thick telescope
stood by the window, pointing towards Ardven. On the
wall behind the desk there was a whiteboard displaying a
row of photographs; three women and ten men. Eamon
recognised Denis Nyst and the South African, Pik, who
had met them at the pier at Endpoint House. There was
his brother Stevie, and Malky with the tattoos on his neck,
Kosma Milosz and himself, from the same photograph
that was in his passport. He recognised one of the
women. She had long blonde dreadlocks and a flattish
face. He had seen her in the woods behind Murachar's
croft. He took out his phone to call Rona, but there was
no signal. He was about to descend the stairs when he felt
the blow on the back of his neck.

It wasn't a heavy blow but it shocked him and he fell
first to his knees then onto his face. He tried to turn over
but there was a knee in his back and someone pulling up
his left arm causing pain that pulled at every nerve in his
body. He opened his mouth to yell but nothing came out.
A cable tie zipped around his wrists, then two around his
ankles. He recognised the sound because he had used
them to bind men himself. He tried to turn his head but
as he did a cloth sack was slipped over. His phone was
removed from his pocket. His feet were lifted and he was
pulled over the carpet onto a vinyl floor. His legs were
dropped, and he felt footsteps close to his head. He called

out, 'Tariq!' and the footsteps paused. Then the door slammed and a key turned in the lock. The cloth of the balaclava did not completely shut out the light. He could tell that in the room beyond the darkness was complete.

Chapter 13

It was afternoon by the time Rona had left the castle. She had awoken to the sound of her mother calling from her room, had half-dressed her, gone back to the awakened and hungry Harry, changed, dressed, fed Harry, returned to Mother with Harry, finished dressing Mother, found Mike, helped Mike help Mother down to the living room, fed Mother her breakfast, fed Harry for the second time, re-dressed Harry to go outside, settled Mother in front of the TV, got dressed herself and attached Harry with his ten straps.

She had considered a casual, 'just passing,' encounter with Mrs Murray but did not find her in her garden. Rona knocked on the door. Mrs Murray did not look pleased but smiled at the baby and led them through the dark corridor to the living room. Rona unpacked the infant and he cooed and wriggled on a blanket between them. Mrs Murray's eyes were red and swollen.

'Are you alright Edwina?' Rona's question was met with a sigh and a plaintive shake of the head. Mrs Murray took a sheet of paper from a side-table and handed it to her guest.

'Justin gave me this this morning.'

It was a print-out from a blog: 'New-Age Gay-Hate Hiding Out in Scottish Highlands,' ran the title.

'Well, surprise surprise! It seems like Omni Psychotherapy is not dead after all. Not dead and still causing death and destruction. I was informed of the terrible news of the murder of David Smart this morning, about which Police Scotland are saying "there is no evidence to suggest this is a hate-crime". Some of you will have fond memories of David from the college here in Peterborough and the local scene. He was a gentle soul, with many friends, but a fragile person. I tried to interview him about his experience as a boy with Omni Psychotherapy. He refused to talk about it and I did not pursue the subject because he was entitled to his privacy. But as it turned out my suspicion that he retained some kind of loyalty to Justin Simmonds, who if you remember was a personal friend of his parents, was justified. The name Duncul rang a bell, and so I had a dig around in the archive we keep on people like Justin Simmonds, or should I say "vermin". Where did Justin Simmonds go after we closed down Omni? It turns out the village of Duncul produced a search hit, about a year after he left here. Dr Justin Simmonds keeps a zero social media profile, but someone let slip that he is on the Scotland in Bloom committee for Duncul Community Council, arranging gay and trans hating flowers for the yokels, and it turns out still playing host to the vulnerable children he tortured for their sexuality, now grown into vulnerable adults. So, Dr Simmonds, who else is visiting? Is Omni still in business? And what do you have to do with poor David's death? One thing is for sure, we are going to be keeping a very close eye on the village of Duncul, and so is your local newspaper whether they like it or not, and so is every queer in our network. Say goodbye to a peaceful "retirement."!'

Rona handed the printout back and met Mrs Murray's haunted look with all the sympathy she could muster.

'Dr Simmonds will have to move. The hate-mail will start again, the phone-calls and the rumours.'

'And you? Will you go with him?'

'Yes.'

'Edwina, was anyone else visiting David and Kosma? Apart from Shem Murachar?'

'Is this you and your husband doing the police's work for them?' Rona did not reply but shook a rattle above

Harry's grasping hands. 'Are you on *their* side?' Mrs Murray pointed at the printout on the side-table.

'No,' said Rona. 'This is nothing to do with you or any of that. This is a family matter.'

'Oh, I see. You want to know if Stevie Van was selling them drugs?'

'Not Stevie. What about Malky Macleod?'

'What does he look like?'

'Small, shaven head, tattoos all up his neck and on his arms.'

'Yes. He used to come.'

'And you told the police this?'

'Yes.'

'When did he visit? Often?'

'He came about once a week. Dr Simmonds knew he was their drug dealer. He said he could smell it.'

'And Malky was there on the night of murders?'

'No, not that night, but the day before.'

'That was the evening they came to dinner at the castle.'

'Yes. He was here before they went to the castle.'

'You are sure of this? You were watching all the time?'

'Not all the time but keeping an eye out. You would be surprised how many visitors they had. People you would never think of.'

Harry's smile was beginning to fade. Rona picked him up and began to tighten straps.

'And on the night of the murders? You told the police you saw Shem Murachar?'

'Yes.'

'What time?'

'I've told the police.'

'Tell me.'

'About ten. As usual.'

'As usual?'

'He was there often. Sometimes later, sometimes earlier.'

'So that night about ten? And the bodies were discovered when?'

'I'm not the one who found them.'

'The Macdonald boys found them. That was not long after ten. Am I right?' Rona began to move around the room to keep Harry distracted. 'Did you see Shem leave?'

'No. I wasn't watching all the time.'

'But what it means is that Shem arrived at ten, killed them, smashed the whole place up, and then left before say half-ten. Really? And you didn't hear anything? No shouts, no fight?'

'No.' Harry was starting to kick his feet.

'Who else was visiting?'

'Shem. The tattooed young man. Reverend Farrawell visited, for pastoral reasons. The hippies. Your man Mike Mack, working on the big tree at the back.'

'The hippies? You mean the protesters from Ardven?'

'I don't know. Dr Simmonds calls them hippies.'

'And were they here the night of the murders?'

'I didn't see them that night.' Harry opened his mouth wide and howled.

Eamon could not tell how much time had passed before light filtered through the knit of the mask and footsteps padded past his head. He heard the legs of a chair scrape, then hands under his arms. 'Up!' said a voice, and he was helped to the chair. The man left the room, then returned. Eamon could hear his breathing, close, somewhere in front of him. He could hear his breathing. Eamon was about to speak when the ski-mask was taken off. The man was sitting not a foot away from him, leaning forward with his elbows on his knees. He was cupping his chin in one hand. In the other he held a pair of wire-cutters.

'Tariq?' said Eamon. The man nodded. The brown eyes were wide and bulbous. Eamon had thought he had seen a young man on the hill, but now he wasn't sure. There were fine wrinkles around the eyes, and the expression was one that Eamon had become to recognise in Afghanistan; the cold, tired look of a man who is familiar with cruelty. Eamon leaned back in his chair.

'Eamon Ansgar I presume?' said Tariq. Eamon brought his head forward with all his strength and felt a satisfying, wet crunch as his forehead caught the bridge of Tariq's nose. Tariq catapulted backwards and his head made a hollow sound as it hit the floor. Eamon's eyes followed the wire-cutters as they flew up from Tariq's hand and clattered to the floor on the other side of the room. Eamon estimated he had five seconds before Tariq recovered. In one he had jumped to the cutters, in two he had them in his hands and by five he had placed the jaws over the cable ties and snipped. In another three seconds he had cut the ties on his ankles. Eight seconds passed before he looked at Tariq. He need not have hurried. The only thing moving was the blood trickling from the man's nose. Eamon ran his hands over him and took an automatic pistol from a shoulder holster. He checked the pistol for rounds and put it in his waistband. He went into the room with the desk. There was a backpack in the corner and in one of the side pockets he found cable ties. In another he found a roll of tissue. He noticed the neat row of pieces of his own dismantled phone on the desk. He clipped it back together and put it in his pocket.

Back in the other room he cabled Tariq's hands together, then he staunched the bloody nose. The flesh around the eyes was already swollen and purple. Tariq began to stir. He muttered something unintelligible and spat blood. Eamon helped him sit on the chair he had been sitting on five minutes before.

Tariq grimaced. 'You didn't have to do that.' His accent was British public-school tainted by American.

'Why not start by telling me who you are and what you are doing here?' said Eamon. There was a long moment of silence.

'You can keep calling me Tariq.'

'And what are you doing here?'

'I'm not authorised to tell you more than that,' he said.

Eamon felt the words like solid things landing in the bare room. He did not want to pick them up. 'You're government?' he said.

'I'm not authorised to tell you that either.'

Eamon sat on the other chair. 'What are you authorised to tell me?'

'You've just broken my nose.'

'You tied me to a chair and put a hood over my head.'

'I didn't recognise you at first.'

'And if you had? What would you have done?'

'Probably the same.'

'Why am I here? Why did RB send me?'

'RB?'

'Richard Blackwell, my lawyer.'

'Your lawyer sent you here? I know nothing about that.'

Eamon went through to the room with the desk and took the photographs from the white-board.

'You have my picture. No doubt you've done your research and you know what my job was in Afghan?'

'Is that a threat?'

'Me, my brother, Malky, Kosma Milosz. Denis Nyst.
I recognise this guy, he works for Nyst. Who are the
others?' Eamon stared at him and Tariq stared back with
eyes reduced to slits behind the swelling. Fifty questions
swirled in Eamon's head, but he was aware of a sense
of calm; the ease that a professional feels as he sits at his
desk. It occurred to him that he had been successful at
two professions in his life; extracting rent and extracting
information.

'I knew Kosma and David,' he said. 'I knew Malky
Macleod.' But Tariq was professional too, he thought.
So he would not talk. 'It's not the same for you. You
will go and do something somewhere else.' Tariq was
a professional, and he had a reputation to protect. 'But
for me this is different. It's personal. This is my…'
Eamon paused, unsure of the word. What was it? Patch?
Neighbourhood? Territory? Was he really going to say
that? This is my land? My kingdom? This is the place
where I extract rent. Extracting rent and extracting
information. It was the same method, in the end; the
threat of increased cost. The threat of some kind of
violence. 'I can get you to Inverish in a couple of hours,
even if I have to carry you. From there I can get you
to Duncul by boat. There are at least three TV vans at
Duncul, full of bored journalists.' The slits within the
swelling widened. 'As soon as I get a signal I can start

making calls. What will your government think about you becoming a celebrity?'

'I am not your enemy,' said Tariq.

'If that is true I am not yours either.'

'No, you are merely an inconvenience.'

'How so?'

'You ask too many questions.'

'Try this for starters. Why are you here?'

'I work for the Quatari government.' Tariq took a long time to lift his eyes and hold Eamon's gaze. 'And you are going to regret everything I say.'

'I will be the judge of that.'

'I am here because your government is lazy, incompetent and afraid.'

'Tell me something I don't know.'

'I am here because of Malky Macleod.' He almost smiled. 'And now it seems, because of Brigitta Neilsen.'

'I'm listening.'

'About three months ago Malky was diving in the Minch and he found something that no-one was ever supposed to find. A torpedo. A torpedo with a nuclear warhead. Missing since 1965.'

Eamon waited. 'A test torpedo?'

'No. Not even your navy was stupid enough to test torpedoes with real warheads. No, it was a real-live warhead, but not armed. It was dropped from a fighter-bomber that was about to crash. Jettisoned, as per procedure in an emergency. The possible search area was huge. They were not even sure if it had been dropped beyond the Hebrides or in The Minch, and they couldn't find it, so they covered it up. I guess they reasoned that if they couldn't find it nobody else could. They buried the accident, so well and for so long that eventually even they didn't know it had been lost. Then along comes Malcolm Donald-John Macleod, diving for scallops. He found it and raised it. Then he did something really, really stupid. He put it on Ebay.'

'Ebay?'

'Not Ebay Ebay. Ebay for drugs, child pornography, weapons. You've heard of Pirate Bay?'

'No.'

'Well, like Pirate Bay, but not. The Dark Web.'

'He tried to sell it?'

'He tried to sell it.'

'To whom?'

'To the highest bidder. Ultimately, he tried to sell it to terrorists. Who else would be interested?'

'And?'

'He tried to sell it, for approximately five minutes. Then he changed his mind. He took down the ad.'

'Why?'

'He had a change of heart, we believe. He is, was, a man unable to stick to his guns. My personal theory is that he simply smoked to much marijuana.'

'But you saw the ad.'

'We saw it, and as far as we know, we were the only ones. As far as we knew. Now we are not so sure. I need some water. There is a kitchen on the other side of that room.' He indicated with a nod of the head.

Eamon went through the room with the desk to the kitchen. The sun was setting behind the tip of the peninsula in the distance and the sea firing beams at a sky glowing like a forge. He returned with the water and held the cup to Tariq's blood encrusted lips.

'We identified the weapon and we told your government. Your government is comical. It tries to be inscrutable, but it is not very good at it. There are layers upon layers of denial and obfuscation, just like the Middle East, but here their hearts aren't in it. They lack conviction, a bit like Malky. In the end we got an admission that they knew what we were talking about, although even this was unofficial and deniable. Then they wanted our help. They wanted a foreign intelligence agency to look for a weapon they had never lost and then give it back to them. I am not sure how they managed to persuade us but we agreed.'

'So Malky found it. Put it up on Pirate Ebay and took it down. Then about a week ago he was killed. Am I right?' Tariq only stared at him. 'By you? By who? How did you know the torpedo was here in Duncul?'

'We didn't. All we knew was it was put up for sale on a computer in a caravan that belongs to your brother.'

'Stevie's computer?'

'We traced the computer. Of course we thought of Stevie to begin with, but we watched, and saw who came and went to the caravan. Quite a lot of people. Malky was the only diver. Kosma made contact.'

'Kosma was working for you?' said Eamon. Tariq nodded. 'And David?'

'Not David.'

'How was David involved?'

'He wasn't.'

'But he was living with Kosma.'

'Yes. He was a cover for Kosma. He advertised on Facebook for a flat-mate, to share the rent. We were looking for a way for Kosma to be on the ground in the village. It was a good fit.'

'So he wasn't David's lover, or boyfriend?'

Tariq shrugged. 'They became friends. Kosma has, had, a special talent for friendship.' Eamon looked into his eyes and saw an inkling of regret. Tariq looked down at his knees and up again. 'Kosma's brief was to befriend Malky. He made a very good job of it. Perhaps too good.'

'How so?'

'Malky became devoted to him, to the point of obsession. He had his face tattooed on his arm.'

'And he told Kosma where the torpedo was hidden?'

Tariq shook his head. 'Kosma was sure he was about to, but as you are aware Kosma, and David were killed.'

'By who? Why?'

'I don't know.'

'The *Autonomass*?'

'That's possible.'

'And they managed to implicate Shem Murachar.'

'They had been to the manse before. David was a kleptomaniac. He had a problem. He had a thing for garden ornaments. And he was walking all over the place, on the Ardven peninsula, within the fence. He stole two cups, sort of chalices. He took them back to the house. We don't know how they found out, but they did, and they came to get them. They came with baseball bats. They took back the cups. That was last month. It is possible that David stole something else, perhaps the cups again, perhaps something more valuable, and they came again.'

'If you know this, why not tell the police? Why not arrest the *Autonomass*?'

'You have to understand I have no permission even to be in the country. I work for a foreign government. I certainly have no permission to arrest anyone. Nothing is going to go to court. Our job is to find the torpedo. We don't care about a homophobic murder or a murder committed out of jealousy or a murder committed because of a theft. We don't even care whether Malky is dead or alive. My job is to find the torpedo, that is all. I need to pee. The bathroom is beyond the kitchen. May I?' Eamon nodded and Tariq stood up unsteadily. Eamon reached out to steady him, saw the wire-cutters in his hands, and in the moment that he realised that Tariq had cut the cable-ties when he had been in the kitchen fetching a glass of water Eamon felt a blow on his temple and there was a blank space before he looked up from the floor. Then he felt the foot on his jaw and his head was knocked back and a wave of nausea swept up from his stomach. Tariq rolled Eamon over, pulled the gun from his waistband and pointed it at his head.

'I told you you would regret everything I said,' he said. Tariq's finger tightened on the trigger. It was the steady squeeze of a trained hand, and the windowless room faded to black.

Chapter 14

Eamon swept his hand before him through the darkness.
He felt the steel of the gun against the back of his hand
and the muzzle flash against the back of his eyeballs.
The round went off like a kick hitting somewhere inside
his head. He caught and pulled the wrist so that the gun
was above his own head. There was another shot which
lit up Tariq's face inches from his own. Eamon lunged
forward and Tariq fell back. Eamon took hold of the gun
hand with both of his own and felt the grip relax as he
twisted and Tariq grunted in pain. He swung through the
darkness with the pistol-grip but hit nothing; he swung
again and again, and heard the door slam followed by
footsteps in the room beyond. He scrabbled in his pocket
for his phone, switched on the torch and aimed it with

the gun. He tried the light-switch but it did not work.
As he was about to open the door he stopped to listen.
Beyond his own breathing he heard footsteps running
down the stairs, then an angry shout, thuds, the sound
of something hard hitting flesh. He opened the door to
the room with the desk. The window framed a fat moon
disappearing behind a cloud. Torchlight was ascending
the stairwell. Voices whispered in German. *'Ruhr!* Quiet!'
A stair complained under the weight of a foot. Eamon
fired at the doorway and in the flash from the round saw
wood splinter from the frame. Footsteps thumped down
the stairs and a door slammed. He crept on his belly
towards the stairwell. A slumped figure was lying at the
bottom. There was a cry like a bird from outside, then in
answer the long cry of a wolf. A man imitating a wolf. A
good imitation. There was a sound of a window breaking
on the ground floor, then the one behind him shattered,
showering glass onto the carpet. Cold air followed the
shards into the room. Eamon cursed and crawled over
the glass into the shelter of the stairwell. He checked the
pistol's magazine and counted seven rounds. He slid down
the stairwell to the figure slouched at the bottom, keeping
the pistol aimed at the head. It was Tariq, solid and heavy;
a dead weight. Another window shattered. Eamon felt
sticky blood in Tariq's hair. The wolf-howler howled again
and was answered by laughter. Rocks thudded against

the roof and walls. Eamon switched off the torch, crept towards the back door and ran out into the night.

There was barely enough light to see the ground. He saw half silhouettes to his right and left and fired off two shots then ran towards the hill. Whistles and shouts came out of the darkness. He ran, keeping his head down, up-hill, stumbling, falling, scrabbling into the heather. He thought he heard someone nearby and he twisted, falling backwards, swinging the gun at the dark, but saw only the shape of the house against the moonlight. A powerful torch shone in his face. He stumbled backwards, swung the gun, fired two shots into the light and regretted it, counting his rounds. The torch-beam swung, and for a moment lit up a thin woman, with long dreadlocks and a flat face. Eamon ran on, smelling the lengthening heather, feeling the cooler air on his face, forcing his legs to take long strides that launched him into the darkness. When he had put height and distance between himself and the house he turned and watched the flailing torch-beam.

The *Autonomass* were on the flat ground around the house. He listened to whistles, calls and the ridiculous wolf howl. The torch beam swung over him and to the side. They were talking but he could not make out the words. Someone began shouting off to his left, then a reply came from his right. He moved further up the hill, into the safety of its vastness. Then he lay down and listened as the shouts diminished, until the beam was

switched off, and silence returned to the black mass of the
house against the less black sky. In the distance there was
a single light at Inverish or Endpoint. It was only when he
stood again that he flinched at the pain in his ankle. He
lay down again, felt the swelling, and took out his phone.
There was one percent of the battery left, but three bars
of signal. He called Stevie.

'Where are you?'

'Halan,' said Eamon, 'with a sprained ankle.'

'I can come up the glen, but it'll take me 'til morning,
even if I take a boat to Inverish.'

'No, don't come by Inverish or the Halan Burn. Come
along the top of Ben Briagh. They saw me! Tell Rona to
stay in. Lock the doors! Lock all the doors!' There was no
answer. The battery was dead.

Solly, wearing a dry suit, was leaning on the rail of the
Sea Wolf. A fine rain was falling and from somewhere
above the small isles a golden orb, muted by mist, was
beginning to warm the morning. Solly stared at the scrap
of paper, the photograph of a Zulu. There was no way
of telling if it was a boy or girl. It was a person. It was
amaZulu, People of the Sky. Like him, a Zulu; like Eilidh,
a Highlander. He had never spent much time thinking
about History. But there was a feeling in his chest,
something like a pain, as if a bullet or a blade had entered
and was settled there, and it was making him think about

things that he had never thought about but had always
known.

The Zulus had a bad reputation, from before when
the *Boere* arrived. The Zulus had lived for fighting. Men
like himself had longed for war, for killing, for blood,
for tearing out and devouring the gallbladders of their
enemies. He had never been proud of that history, unlike
many of his friends. He had never been involved in what
passed for 'politics' in Natal; marches where shields and
spears were brandished, and the chanting of war songs;
the constant edging towards violence. His attitude had
always been the same as Mo's; let them get on with it;
there is work to be done, money to be made, and then,
when there is enough money, relax and enjoy it. Not
that there was not violence in his life. He had once shot
a man, but only in the thigh, and he had shot at men
several times. But that was not the same kind of violence
as political violence. It was violence with no meaning
beyond the moment. It was a reaction to someone
stealing, or attacking; nothing more important. The guy
he had shot in the leg had been coming at Mo with a
panga. Afterwards they had bought him a bottle of brandy
to calm his nerves before dropping him off at the hospital.
Solly Matobela had never *thought* about violence. He had
never premeditated it. But now he was thinking about
it constantly, and remembering that he was a Zulu, and
his enemies were close by. They were in the cabin behind

him, smoking roll-ups and cracking jokes in German.
They were thin boys, like him, and they had no weapons.
He thought about cutting out their hearts with the diving
knife strapped to his leg, '*Usuthu! Usuthu!*' and throwing
them over the side. He thought about the blood pinking
as it mixed with the saltwater, and sharks eating flesh.
He didn't want to think about these things. He tried to
think about other things: lying on her bed in the room
above the pub, stroking her belly; smoking weed with
Mo and Qualin, on a beach on the Natal North Coast, or
up in the hills, drinking *uMquomboti* with his cousins and
listening to their stupid jokes. But as soon as he thought
about the cousins he remembered that they were the
ones who liked to dress up and dance around with spears,
and he thought again about killing every single one of
these Nazis, including the sinister little witch in charge.
He looked at the image, the scrap of a thing on a scrap
of paper, fluttering in the breeze that was coming from
the direction of the sun. He held it above the sea that was
rising and falling like a great chest breathing, raising the
boat and the Germans behind him and lowering them
down towards the sea floor. He could cut their throats in
two seconds he was sure, but Mo and Qualin were twenty
metres below and he would have to wait for them, and
even if they got to Inverish without Brigitta finding out,
what if they had taken Eilidh somewhere else? They had
already talked about this for hours in the deckhouse of

The Kelpie. Mo and Qualin had tried to calm him down, had said he should just wait; a few more dives and it would be over. But that feeling in the chest wasn't going away; it was getting worse.

'Thou shalt not kill, Solomon Matobela!' That was what his mother would have said, and his father too, if his father had ever said anything. 'Love thine enemy, turn the other cheek!' And they were both proud Zulu's. Jesus Mo, if you two don't hurry up and surface I'm going to *slag* these *wit o's now now*, God help me!

Dawn came to Eamon on a hill-top enclosed in mist. His ankle had swollen in the night so that he had had to take the boot off, but he had kept walking. He heard the growling of the Argo amplified through the damp air long before he saw it. The sound at first came from in front of him, to the East, from Glen Feshie and the forestry plantations, and then by some trick of the echoes from behind, from the glen of the Halan Burn, from shorewards, from the space above Loch Houn, and then from the bare mountains to the south. He was walking on a track along the backbone of the long, undistinguished mound that was Ben Briagh. The mist began to thin as the sun rose, and eventually Stevie emerged at full throttle, making the eight-wheeled machine bounce. He slid to a stop in front of Eamon.

'Did you tell Rona to lock the doors?' Eamon tossed his boot into the back of the Argo and lowered himself backwards, leaving his swollen foot dangling over the side.

Stevie nodded. 'Mike's there. I told him to watch for anyone in the grounds. What happened?'

'Have you got your phone?'

Stevie took it out. 'No signal. We have to go back down. What happened?'

'They killed Tariq.'

'Who's Tariq?'

'We need to call the cops.'

'Eamon, who? Who killed who?'

'The *Autonomass*! They killed Tariq, at Halan, because he was a spy! They've got a nuclear bomb!'

'What?'

'Just drive.' Stevie gunned the engine and spun the machine, churning sods of peat into the air.

Chapter 15

It was late morning by the time Eamon and Stevie arrived at the pier at Loch Houn and afternoon before they got back to the castle.

Both doors were indeed locked. Eamon looked over at the figure filling the doorway in the south wall. Mike was carrying an axe handle in one hand. He raised the other to wave.

Rona came down to the tower door when he rang the bell. 'Mum tripped on the rug next to her bed last night. Nothing broken, but she bruised her hip. Kirsty and I are putting her into a bath right now.'

'Can you leave her for now? Come down to the study. We need to think. I'm going to call the police.' In the study he called the police station at Aberfashie, but there

was only a message instructing him to call one zero one
or triple nine. Kirsty came into the room.

'I saw some people in the woods on the other side of
the Ash,' she said. 'But I wasn't close enough to make
them out. The village is full of strangers. All kinds of
people are here for the convention at Johnny Murachar's.
Everyone is on the Airbnb. Mary Ellice has got ten
Nigerians in her house. And there is a man with a swastika
on his neck renting Maggie Maclellan's shed.'

Eamon hesitated, then called triple nine. 'I want to
report a murder,' he said. He was asked for his name,
address, and number by a woman's voice and transferred
to a man's voice.

'Where did this take place?'

'At Halan. It's a house in the hills above Inverish.'

'Halan?

'H A L A N.'

'What's the postcode?'

'No postcode.'

'You don't have a postcode?'

'A man was killed for God's sake! He's lying up there
now, and no, I don't know the postcode!'

'If a man was killed, we're going to have to go to
the house. We need a postcode in order to locate the
building.'

'Do you know what a map is? Halan is about six miles south of Inverish. Follow the Halan Burn. You'll need a helicopter. There is no road.'

'Inverish? Do you have a postcode for that?' Eamon closed his eyes and bit his lip. Stevie typed something into his phone and showed Eamon the postcode. Eamon read it out.

'Do you know the name of the individual who was attacked?' asked the officer.

'His name was Tariq. I don't have a surname.'

'How do you spell that?'

'I've no idea. However you like.' There was a long silence. 'Write this down, or record it, or whatever you do,' said Eamon. 'There is a body of a man who went by the name Tariq lying at the bottom of the stairs in Halan House, six miles south of Inverish. No postcodes. He was beaten to death by men who are part of a group called *Autonomass* A U T O N O M A S S who are living at Endpoint House on Ardven Peninsula. You will need a helicopter to get to Halan, and at least a boat to get to Endpoint. Tariq is a Qatari citizen who was working for Qatari Intelligence Services, so you might want to notify the Qatari embassy. Meanwhile you should put me through to whatever organisation you have dealing with terrorist activities as I have information about a nuclear device.'

'I'm sorry? A nuclear device?'

'A bomb. A nuclear bomb. Who deals with that kind of thing?' There was another long pause.

'I'm going to put you on hold.' Vivaldi. Four Seasons. It was a long time before a female voice answered.

'Mr Eamon Ansgar?'

'Yes.'

'Can I call you Eamon?' Eamon closed his eyes and took a long, slow breath.

'You can call me whatever you like.'

'OK Eamon. My colleague says you have information about a nuclear bomb? Is that right?'

'Yes. No. A torpedo. A torpedo with a nuclear warhead. It went missing in the sea off the coast here, about fifty, sixty years ago. Someone has found it. It's here. Now, in Duncul, or somewhere near here.'

'OK.' The woman took a deep breath. 'How do you know about this Eamon?'

'Tariq told me. He's an agent, a spy, for the Qatari government. He told me last night. He's been killed. His body is at Halan. I've already told the police. They are on their way to Halan. You'll find him at the bottom of the stairs. They beat him to death with bats.'

'OK. With bats. Who is "they"?'

'The *Autonomass*. A U T O N O M A S S. They're a group of anarchist protesters. They're working for Denis Nyst, at Endpoint House. Ardven. You've heard of the re-wilding guy? The guy that is trying to release wolves?'

'No, I can't say I have. Do the *Autonomass* have the nuclear device?'

'I don't know. All I know is they killed Tariq, and three other people. And they are probably going to try and kill me.'

'You think these people are going to try to kill you?'

'Yes. I don't know. I wouldn't be surprised.'

'Can you tell me your location now?'

'I'm at home. Duncul Castle. Duncul. PV40 8DN.'

'You live in a castle?'

'Yes.'

'And these other murders, are the police aware of them?'

'Yes. But they think Johnny Murachar's son did it. They got the wrong man, and he killed himself. But it was *Autonomass*.'

'Johnny Murachar?'

'He's the guy that hates gay people. You must have heard of him. He's on the internet.'

'I'm going to put you on hold right now Eamon.' Vivaldi. *Four Seasons*.

'She doesn't believe me,' said Eamon, 'She doesn't believe a word I say.' There was time to smoke a whole cigarette before the woman's voice returned.

'Hi Eamon. Sorry for making you wait there. Is this the best number to get you on?'

'Yes, but…'

'Eamon, someone is going to call you back. Thank you for that information. This is very important information, OK? And I'm going to get the right person to call you back as soon as possible.' She ended the call.

'Call Richard Blackwell,' said Rona. There was a faint cry from upstairs. 'That's Harry,' she said, and left the room.

Eamon dialled Richard's number but got voicemail. 'Eamon here. I did as you said. I went to Halan. I met Tariq and he told me about the torpedo. They killed him, Richard. Get back to me as soon as possible.'

Rona came back into the room carrying Harry and followed by Kirsty. 'You need something to eat,' she said. 'When was the last time you ate?'

'I'll make him his porridge,' said Kirsty.

'I don't need damn porridge!' Kirsty gave him a grave look and left. Eamon lit another cigarette and limped up and down the room.

'You should sit down Eamon,' said Rona. 'Calm down.'

'Rona!' a voice sounded from somewhere above them.

'Coming Mother!' shouted Rona. 'You need to tell us what happened. What do you mean a nuclear bomb?' But Eamon had limped out of the room.

He went up the spiral staircase to the next floor and opened the door of the back-bathroom. Harriet McColl was sitting upright in the bathtub, gazing at her feet.

'You have to wait Harriet. She's busy right now. Perhaps you might try to get yourself out of the bath.' He slammed the door, returned to the study and told all that he had learned from Tariq to Rona and Stevie.

'They killed Tariq. They killed David and Kosma, and Malky. Because of the torpedo.'

'Does that mean they have the torpedo?' said Stevie.

'I don't know.'

'Or does it mean they are looking for it?'

'I don't know.'

'What do they want it for?' said Stevie. There was a moment of silence.

'Whatever the reason, it's not going to be good.'

'What can they do with it? They can't set it off, surely?' said Stevie. They looked at each other.

'But are these guys terrorists? I thought they were environmentalists?'

'They're anarchists above all. They hate authority, police, army, neo-Nazis, fascists, the far-right. Johnny Murachar. Acturus McBean. These kinds of people.'

Eamon, Stevie and Rona moved to the bay window and looked out over the lawn towards the gate and the TV vans. On the low mound just beyond the gates to the castle at the crossroads that marked the centre of the village a woman in a red skirt was interviewing a man with blonde hair. He swiped his straight fringe away from his face and gesticulated. Eamon switched on the TV and scrolled through the channels.

'Wonderful!' said Acturus McBean. 'Everything is wonderful! The weather is wonderful! The people of Duncul have been remarkably hospitable to all these strange people from all over the world. It shows Scotland at its best! I think there is so much support for us here. The silent majority, the political demographic that dare not speak its name is welcoming us with open arms. As a Scot, I am proud of the people of Duncul!'

'But you have had some dissent, have you not? You have had a protest, and I believe the police were called.'

'Unfortunately yes. Some very unpleasant people broke into the venue this morning.'

'We can show that now…' The image cut to mobile phone footage of the inside of an enormous marquee. A woman brandishing a length of rope was running through chairs and tables, knocking them over, throwing placards and paperwork into the air and lashing out at catering staff.

'Nazi Scum! Off our streets! Nazi scum! Off our streets!' she called as she was wrestled to the ground by two bodybuilders in suits. The camera was knocked over and switched off.

The TV cut back to Acturus, wearing a frown. 'Very unfortunate. Apparently this woman had false ID and was impersonating a delegate. We have had to tighten security,

and it just goes to show the lengths these so called,
"tolerant" people will go to disrupt a peaceful gathering
of like minds from around the world, most of whom are
Christian based organisations. An ambulance has been
called to take care of the injured.'

'Are you anticipating more protests? More violence?'

'Yes, we are prepared for more intimidation. There have
been bomb threats. We have had sniffer dogs patrolling
the perimeter fence and checking all the equipment
coming into the compound. And we have been working
closely with Police Scotland, who have been wonderful
defenders of law and order in this picturesque, delightful
glen!' He gestured around himself.

'And you have the opposition of the owner of the
Ardven Peninsula, Denis Nyst. Are you anticipating some
sort of intervention from Denis Nyst?'

'Denis Nyst is the local landowner and has of course
been invited as an honoured guest! His name is on the
list, as are the names of all the local landowners. We want
them to come and see what we are about. Denis Nyst,
if you are watching, please come and meet some of our
delegates, you might be pleasantly surprised. Who knows,
you might join the movement!'

'So you heard it here first,' said the woman in the red
skirt to the camera. 'Denis Nyst invited to the Alt-Scot
Convention! I wonder if he'll turn up? Well, thank you
Acturus, for talking to us.'

'Thank you, Penny, always a pleasure.'

The image narrowed to include only Penny. 'Now we are going to talk to some of the local inhabitants of Duncul to see what they think about all this.' The camera zoomed out to include the space that had encompassed Acturus McBean. He had been replaced by a frail old woman and a short man with a shaven head and an earring.

'That's Mary McKay,' said Stevie, 'and the postman, Bill Withers.'

'We have Mary here and Bill, both local residents. Mary, you've lived here all your life? Is that right?' She held out the microphone.

'Yes, that's right.'

'And how old are you now?'

'Eighty-two last week.'

'Wow! Well done you! Congratulations!'

'Thank you.'

'Now, have you ever seen anything like this happen in Duncul?'

'No.'

'So this is a really big event for Duncul. I have to say, we really are in the middle of nowhere here. It's what, fifty miles to Inverness?'

'Fifty-two,' said Mary.

'Wow! That's a long way to go for your groceries!'

'Well we have the Tesco Van now.'

'So that makes everything a lot easier for you, that's great! Now tell me Mary, do you follow politics?'

'Yes.'

'And what do you think about this convention and the kind of organisations that are being represented here this week?'

'Well, I think Acturus McBean is a wonderful man, and he is standing up for what is right in this country, and we've got too many foreigners, so I am in favour of that.'

Penny turned to camera. 'Now we have Bill, who I believe is not so supportive.'

'He's a fascist,' said Bill. 'They're all fascists. This entire thing is fascism!'

'And you don't think they are doing any good for your community? Boosting the local economy?'

'They can take their money and shove it up their collective arse.'

'Ooh! Might need a bit of editing there! Apologies to viewers with children! Have you been involved in any of the protest incidents?'

'I've got a job to do. I don't have the time to go on protests. But I wish the protesters well. If I had my way this kind of thing wouldn't be allowed to happen. They're nothing but bigots and they're all in it for the money.'

'So, there you have it!' the camera zoomed in on Penny. 'Trenchant opposition from Bill, and a passionate defence of the convention from Mary. We have a community divided here in Duncul, and we wait to see how deep and lasting these divisions become in the days ahead. Over to you in the studio Andrew.' The screen displayed a bright studio and a man in a suit before a towering screen. As he gestured at the screen, blocks of colour swirled and overlaid each other.

'Let's have a look at the kind of organisations that are included in the umbrella term, "Alt-Scot",' said Andrew. 'And let me tell you, there is quite a variety!'

Eamon switched off the TV.

'If I was an anarchist with a nuclear bomb, I know what I would do with it,' said Stevie. Eamon picked up the phone and dialled Richard Blackwell again. There was no answer. Kirsty came into the room with a bowl of porridge.

'You need to eat,' said Rona.

'Rona!' her mother's voice came from upstairs.

Eamon lit another cigarette and limped up and down the room. He called the police on one oh one and asked if they had arrived at Halan yet. He was put on hold, then the line went dead.

'I'm putting you to bed, you need to put that foot up,' said Rona. 'Now.' Eamon stubbed out the cigarette and followed her and the bowl of porridge from the room.

Stevie poured himself another whisky and sat in the window seat, gazing out across the park. A bus was disgorging passengers by the crossroads as another pulled up. People with little suitcases on wheels were filtering out into the village guided by their mobile phones. His own phone buzzed.

'Hi, this is Raymon Salamanca. I'm your Airbnb guest for tonight.'

'Hi there Raymon. This is Stevie. Aye, the caravan is open. You can let yourself in. I'll be along in a wee while. Help yourself to a beer.'

Chapter 16

Sergeant Peters had never been keen on helicopters.
He could only just cope with the aeroplane when he
was going on holiday with the family. He had been up
twice in a chopper, both times for work, and the whole
contraption just seemed *unlikely*. The only thing that
had consoled him on these trips had been the confidence
of the pilot. That morning in Aberfashie, as the blades
whipped grass cuttings from the school field into a blue
sky, he sought re-assurance in the face of the pilot, and
was rewarded with a weak jaw, no smile, and watery eyes.
But he buckled up and slammed the door as he was told
to, because he was a cop, and a man, and apparently there
was a body in a house in the hills beyond Inverish.

The chopper wasn't even the police chopper, because that was based in Glasgow and was busy somewhere in Ayrshire. It was a private hire from Inverness and Peters was sure that that made it more likely to fall out of the sky into Loch Cul, or Loch Nish, or the Ardven Peninsula, or Loch Houn or somewhere into the boulder-strewn green and purple wilderness beyond Inverish; onto the steep sides of the Halan Burn's narrow glen, or onto the roof of the neat white house set in the smooth field, which thanks to a God who became quite real whenever Peters was in an aircraft, was perfect for a smooth landing.

The brief was straightforward. There had been a report of an assault and the death of a man named Tariq in this house. There was a question mark over the veracity of the report and they been unable to make contact with the owner. The report had to be checked out.

Peters walked towards the house as the blades slowed and paused to call headquarters but neither radio nor mobile could get a signal. He noticed that all the windows on the upper floor were broken. He found the back door open and entered the hall. There was a distinct smell of urine.

There was no body at the bottom of the stairwell. He went through all the rooms. The only furniture in the whole place was a desk and a chair in an upstairs room. Two more windows had been broken on the ground floor of the house. The rest of the building clean apart from the large living room on the ground floor. Here there were crushed beer cans, a broken vodka bottle, cigarette butts that had been stubbed out on the carpet. There were three condoms and their torn packets. The smell of urine was coming from a corner of this room.

Peters went through the house twice, and into the boiler room that abutted the west wall, looking for signs of a struggle or blood. He returned to the living room and the word emerged from his mouth involuntarily. 'Kids.' He took photographs of the cans, glass, cigarette butts, urine stains and condoms, and then the broken windows from the inside and out. He circled the house several times looking just in front of his feet into the grass but found nothing. He looked at his phone again but found no signal. He contemplated the helicopter.

The weak-eyed pilot was standing leaning against the nose, looking up at the sky and smoking, comically like a fashion model. Peters took a deep breath and approached the machine. It was bearable when it wasn't switched on, but still ominous, like a holstered gun. Years of Health and Safety training had instilled an infallible instinct, but he stopped himself from saying something about smoking next to an aircraft full of fuel.

'All done?' said the pilot with an English accent and a half smile. Peters' throat resisted speech. He nodded and opened the door. The pilot took his time about finishing the cigarette and flicked the butt into the grass.

As soon as they were above the house the signal icon appeared on Peters' phone, but there was no way he could talk above the noise. He sent the photographs and typed a message out with his thumbs.

'No body at Halan. Broken windows. Looks like kids from Inverish had a party. Who reported body?'

'Eamon Ansgar, Duncul Castle,' came the reply.

'Definitely no body,' he typed. Soon he was looking down with a frown at the red sandstone of Duncul castle set among yellow lawns and the bright tracery of beech trees. There were TV vans at the gate. There were two buses parked on the road up to the manse. There were a lot more cars than usual. He thought about what he was supposed to be thinking about which was how he was going to police the conference at Murachar's croft. The chain-link fence would help, and he wanted to prevent anyone but delegates from taking the road along the shore of Loch Nish, but there was a debate about whether this was a public road. In five minutes they were at the playing fields in Aberfashie and he was waiting for the signal from the pilot to open the door. He walked quickly away from the noise and was surprised by the pilot's voice just behind his shoulder as he was halfway to his car. Health and Safety again; surely this guy wasn't allowed to leave his machine until the blades had stopped?

'I wasn't going to say, not my business and all that, but...' the pilot hesitated. 'I don't know if it matters and I don't want to be telling you how to do your job...'

'What?' said Peters, sounding more irritated than he meant to.

'We weren't the only ones there today.'

'What do you mean?'

'There was another aircraft there, within the last few hours.'

'A chopper?'

'Yes.'

'How do you know?'

'The footprint of the landing gear, in the grass.' The pilot was reaching for the cigarettes in his shirt pocket.

Peters stared into the watery eyes. 'You're sure?' The pilot nodded. 'Thanks,' said Peters, and turned towards his car. 'Thanks a lot,' he muttered as the sound of the blades faded behind him.

It was dark and hot in the study at Endpoint House. The printer buzzed and hummed on the table, scenting the thick air with a high, sweet smell. Nyst scratched himself and smiled at the form taking shape. He crossed to the window and peered through the curtains, letting bright rays flicker across the room. He smiled as he pressed a button on his phone.

'Pik? Where are you now?'

'I'm checking the fence, like you said.'

'OK. I will see you when you get back.' He touched the screen and took a key from the small cupboard behind the desk. Then he picked up a sock from the floor next to the bed and put it in the pocket of his tunic.

He crossed the steading yard with his head down, staring at his socks-in-sandals, entered a door in the steading and climbed a stairway to a locked door which the key opened. The small room contained a bed, a chest of drawers, a wardrobe and a gun cabinet. There was a military neatness and lack of ornament. The top of the chest of drawers displayed a coiled belt, a wallet, a picture of a blonde child and a small wooden box, all placed in a straight line. The bed was made up with blankets and finished with a turned over sheet and hospital corners. Nyst tried the handle of the gun cabinet. He began to whistle an aimless tune through his teeth as he searched the room for a key. He opened the drawers and found folded clothes. He went through the pockets of several anoraks and camouflage jackets and a dress jacket in the wardrobe. He found the small key he wanted in the box on top of the chest of drawers, along with a pair of gold cufflinks and a tiepin.

There were three rifles and three shotguns in the cabinet and several boxes of shotgun cartridges and rifle rounds. He studied the labels of the boxes, then took one round from the box marked with two twos. He put the

round in the pocket in the front of his tunic, closed the
cabinet and stopped whistling and jerked his head around
suddenly as he heard a sound in the yard.

Nyst put the key back in the box and left the room.
He paused at the top of the stairs to listen the buzz
of an engine starting and fading into the distance. At
the bottom of the stairs he contemplated the row of
wellington and work-boots aligned by the mat. He slipped
off his sandals and tried a pair of green Hunters, found
they fit, and went out into the yard with his whistle
resumed.

There were two bikes and two quads in the shed. Nyst
regarded them from a distance, with a perplexed look,
before approaching and studying the dials, switches and
levers. It was several minutes before he mounted a quad
and pulled up his tunic to reveal bare knees. He started
the engine and reversed out of the shed.

Eamon awoke in his bedroom on the fifth floor of Duncul
Castle. A night-light cradled Rona and Harry in a pool of
yellow. He moved gently, winced as he put his sprained
foot down and limped out of the room.

In the study he looked at his phone. There was a missed
call from RB and he called him back.

'Eamon old chap! What an extraordinary message!
Cryptic! Exciting! What on earth are you talking about?'

'Stop it Richard. You know exactly what I'm talking about. I went to Halan, as you suggested…'

'Whoa there boyo! "I suggested" what? Halan?'

'To go on retreat, you told me to go on retreat.'

'Some misunderstanding here old boy. I suggested you go on retreat, that much is true. You looked exhausted. I was thinking of Pluscarden Abbey. Wonderful place! Caters even for infidels like meself. I never said anything about Halan. As far as I remember that's the old secret seminary up in the hills beyond Inverish, on Mahoud's ground. Am I right?'

'Yes, you're right,' Eamon felt himself deflate.

'And you went there, ostensibly on my suggestion. To seek peace and quiet?'

'No. Richard, you have to be honest with me. Do you know about the torpedo? Yes or no.' There was a long pause.

'What torpedo?'

'Stop it Richard!'

'Stop what?'

'What did McIver say to you? Why did you visit me? What was the message?'

'I thought it was pretty obvious. They want the whole thing left alone.'

'And nothing more?'.

'Nothing more. Who is Tariq?'

'Tariq was killed there last night. And before he died, he told me some stuff. Richard, I have the feeling that we are running out of time. I need you to speak to McIver, and for McIver to speak to whoever he knows. I need to speak to someone who will admit to it. And I need you to vouch for me. To vouch that I am not an idiot, and I am not mentally ill. Can you do that? Can you tell me now that you trust me?'

'Of course.'

'I need you to pass on a message that might seem ridiculous to you, and then the person you tell it to will tell you it is ridiculous and then even the person above that, but you have to persevere, for my sake, for Rona, for Harry, for the sake of everyone in Duncul.' He went through everything that Tariq had told him, and when he had finished and answered all of RB's questions and had been re-assured of his efforts, he put the phone down on the desk and noticed a shadow moving on a chair in the corner of the room. A lighter flashed and he smelled tobacco.

'When did you get here?' said Eamon.

'Just now,' replied Stevie. 'My couch is uncomfortable and Ramon snores.'

'What?'

'Nothing, it's hardly pertinent, given what you've got going on.'

'Not me. Us.'

'Exactly.'

'We need to work some stuff out. We need to think.'
Eamon moved to the desk and took out a notepad and
pencil. Rona came into the room in her dressing gown.
'We need to think about Malky.' He wrote his name.
'Malky finds a torpedo, by accident. Who does he tell?'

'He didn't tell me,' said Stevie.

'He put it up for sale on your computer.'

'That's possible. He was on it for hours when I wasn't
there. Supposedly playing *Call of Duty*.'

'He came and went as he pleased?'

'Pretty much.'

'He has a key to your caravan?'

'No key. I don't even have a key.'

'Who else is his friend? Partner? Dive buddy?'

'I don't know. He wasn't very talkative. He doesn't
have a girlfriend. Never has had. Lives on his own in his
ambulance. Dives alone. He's an odd guy, but not in a
bad way. People say now, "on the spectrum". I would say
that's a pretty accurate description of Malky. He could fix
anything. He could take apart that fifty-horse engine on
his boat down to the last screw and put it back together
again. He could dive for longer than anyone on the West
Coast, something to do with slowing down his heart
rate and his breathing, but he never talked much, at all. I
suppose he talked about politics a few times.'

'What politics?'

'He was against organised religion, and capitalism. Nothing unusual.'

'What about family?' said Rona. 'He wasn't from here.'

'Kilmarnock; mother in Kilmarnock. I think. But he was brought up in the Highlands.'

'That's all we know? Seriously? He's been here for years. Boyfriend?'

'Never got that impression.'

'Hobbies? Did all he do was dive and play computer games?'

'Smoked weed. Like I told you, he supplied a few people.'

'We need to know who those people are.'

'I don't know all of them. I know about David and Kosma, because I'd seen him go there. He told me about the three Muslim guys in Inverish.'

'Why?'

'I don't know, I suppose it was unusual, up here. And I think he liked them.'

'Anyone else? The *Autonomass*, the anarchists. They smoke weed? Right?'

'I don't know. You'd be surprised who does and who doesn't. But if Malky was selling to them, I wouldn't necessarily know.'

'If he was selling to them he could have told them about the torpedo. Right?'

'Possibly.'

'Anyone else? Doesn't he have any *friends*?'

'Oswald.'

'Who?'

'Oswald, the tattooist. He spent a lot of time getting tatts. In Aberfashie. Malky had literally hundreds of tattoos. He was running out of space. Most of them were done by Oswald. You spend a lot of time getting tatts, pretty intimate time. Malky had tattoos and piercings in places that were pretty unorthodox.'

'And Oswald lives in Aberfashie?'

'Above the tattoo shop.'

Eamon paced and limped and lit another cigarette. His phone rang.

'Richard.'

'Eamon dear boy. I have had some very strange conversations on your behalf, I have to say. Like talking to clouds. Everyone is either completely stupid, or disingenuous, or downright rude. McIver was good enough to put me onto a chap I was at prep-school with, Binty. Haven't seen him in fifty years. Didn't even know he was at the MOD.'

'And?'

'Nobody knows what you are talking about, and you are completely mad. Nobody has heard of the mysterious Tariq, and the idea that the Qatari intelligence services are working for us is preposterous. The British Navy has never lost a nuclear warhead.'

'Richard…'

'I know. Hang on. I'm reading between the lines, dear chap! Peering through the clouds. I used the hypothetical, "asking for a friend". I'm a damn good lawyer, and should have been an advocate but for my mis-spent youth. "What if, in theory, my client were to come across a nuclear warhead, to come into possession. What is the procedure? Should he contact the press, who happen to be in throngs in the locus of Duncul *a ce moment*? That cut poor old Binty dead in his tracks and he had to go and be silent for a while stage-left. When he came back he had a changed tone, all stiff, like he'd been on the receiving end of twice six.'

'And?'

'Still denies all knowledge. But it's the tone that counts! It's like using an echo sounder, ping, ping, ping and then PING! Something resonates, somewhere in the bowels of Whitehall. I am sure of it.'

'But that's not enough RB.'

'That's all I have.'

'It's not enough.'

Chapter 17

Mo was diving, alone. Deep, with the weight of all the dark seas above him. He was walking on the bottom, on grey mud, over a seabed as empty as the surface of the moon. He was walking with slow strides as if through treacle towards the edge of a drop-off. Silt was rising from his feet and the air was hissing in and out of the regulator. His feet felt like lead and a sense of dread was filling him. He was sure that something hideous was going to lunge out of the darkness. He looked down at his feet and saw he was wearing expensive work-boots with steel toecaps and they were filled with gold Krugerrands. He tried to bend to take them off, but his suit was too bulky. Something was moving in the dark beyond the drop-off. He tried to shake off the boots, and gold coins fell into the mud. He fell backward, trying to raise the feet, but they remained stuck in the mud. He knew he was dreaming. The shape moved in the dark, emerging from the nothing, becoming real. The only way to stop it was to take off his face mask. He pulled at the mask, felt the water fill his lungs, and woke up, sweating and shivering in the deckhouse, feeling the cold steel under his back. They had made four dives the day before, which was too many to be safe. The RIB had arrived and the *Autonomass* were on the deck outside.

'I want to speak to Brigitta,' he told the thin youth that opened the door.

'She doesn't want to speak to you.'

'Tell her I know where it is.' The kid took a long look at Mo, then went out.

'What you trying to do Mo?' said Qualin, sitting up in his sleeping bag. Mo did not look at him. He pulled on damp socks. Solly kept his eyes closed, trying to preserve the last remnants of a sleep that had brought the warmth of Eilidh's body curved into his own. Mo stood and dressed in silence. He took a bite of last night's pizza and was chewing when the door re-opened and the kid held out a phone.

'I know where it is,' said Mo into the phone. 'Hundred percent. Close to here. When you get it you let us go. And we get paid for all the dives, including the five we haven't done. I check my bank account before I show you.' He handed the phone back. The youth left and slammed the door.

'What Mo?' said Qualin.

'Getting paid. You know how much five times three times thirty-five is?'

'Thirty-four. It's thirty-four dives. And it's touching one million rand, depending on the rate.'

'Thirty-five.'

'Thirty-four. They said thirty-four. You can check the satnav.'

'I did. I checked the satnav when we started. There were thirty-five. These Nazis can't count. Thirty-five. You ever play roulette?'

'No. Roulette is for idiots. I play black-jack.'

'Thirty-five numbers in roulette. Thirty-five to one. I deleted the thirty-fifth. When no-one was looking.' Qualin only looked at him with a frown. 'These guys must be stupid,' said Mo. 'I thought. These plots are all over the place, out above Skye, in the Small Isles, here in Loch Houn, in Loch Nish. All in the sea. And what do we find when we dive?'

'Nothing.'

'Not nothing. Scallops. Sometimes a lot, sometimes not many. Because wherever they got this chart from, it's a scallop diver's chart, and he's marking scallop beds. That's all he's interested in. They are all scallop beds. Apart from one.'

'Which one?'

'The one I deleted.'

'Why?'

'Because thirty-four, thirty-five dives, is a million rand. I'm not going to find the AUV or torpedo or whatever on the first day, am I? Thirty-five. They think there is thirty-four, so I placed my chips on the one it has to be. The one that is not in seawater. Scallops live in seawater. Why does he have a location in fresh water?'

'Where?'

'In the river, where it flows into this loch. You can see it when the tide is low, the track of the river. He put a marker there. There could never be scallops there.'

'What if you are wrong?' said Qualin.

Mo shrugged. 'It's roulette. Sometimes you lose.'

'Russian Roulette maybe.' Qualin shook Solly. 'Anyway, it proves one thing. You are definitely a full Muslim. There is nothing half about you. Only a full Muslim can get paid for being kidnapped.' The door banged open again.

'You wait now,' said the kid. 'Boat is going back for Brigitta.'

Stevie drove Rona to Aberfashie and explained on the way that she should interrogate Oswald the Tattooist. 'There's stuff, in the past, between me and Ozzie.'

'What stuff?'

'Just stuff,' he said, and did not offer anything more.

They stopped on the main street, which was also the only street. He looked out of the window as she breast-fed Harry, and looked back at her when the boy's belly was full and she was strapping him back into the harness against her chest.

'You taking him with you?'

'Who else is going to look after him?'

The tattooist studio in Aberfashie was in an alleyway off the main street, two steps down from the road, through a doorway low enough to crack half the skulls that entered. On the lintel at skull level ran the hand-painted legend, 'Rebel Hearts. Body Art and Piercings.'

Skulls were a big theme in Oswald's work. In the front window there were skulls above cross bones, skulls with snakes piercing eye-sockets, skulls on the bodies of voluptuous women, skulls with pentagrams on their foreheads, skulls smoking joints, skulls grinning, scowling, screaming and skulls expressionless, as if contemplating their own mortality. Rona opened the door to the ringing of a tinny bell, quaintly announcing her to a room with a counter and a thousand photographs of tattoos arranged in plastic folders on the walls. A doorway behind the counter led into a fluorescence lit chamber that emitted the sharp note of anti-sceptic and the buzzing of a needle. Rona had a rose on her left ankle, and remembered the scent of transgression, the titillating not-so-painful pain, the sinister dentist's chair, the crossing of a threshold. It had been done on her first trip to London without her parents, age seventeen.

The rose had been chosen almost at random, urged upon her by a gang of school-friends. It had been chosen as a tattoo, *per se*, because her mother would be outraged, shocked and saddened. Then she had kept it hidden for half a decade, until she hadn't, after a morning's walk escorting Harriet with her two walking sticks down to the Ash, listening to a litany of slanders about a neighbour, then some disingenuous sneer about her soon-to-be-dead father. Rona had stopped listening to stare into the golden, flowing tendrils of currents that swam above smooth rocks, and had felt the welling of the river inside her, enough to drown in. She had thrown off jacket, jumper, shirt, wellies, socks and jeans, before her mother could think of telling her not to, and had dove into a deep pool. At the bottom she held onto a rock and opened her eyes to see the silver underside of the surface, until her lungs ached. When she had come up she had swam about, playing with the current, and then thrown herself, freezing, onto the warm grass of the bank, spreading her arms and legs to invite the sun. She had thought that she had seen an almost-smile from her mother, standing above her on the path; a smile at her child, grown woman, casting adulthood to the wind and laughing into the water, but when she looked again she saw it was a sneer.

The voice was clear and precise above the mumbling of the river

'Is that a tattoo?'

Rona had stared through squinted lids into the sun, thinking about how that same sun shone right now on distant lands, on different lives, and succeeded in imagining for less than a second that one of those lives was her own, and this undefinable burden that was and was not her mother, her father and Burnum Farm and thirty head of cattle, and that feeling of carrying a knot within her chest of the intertwined strands of guilt, shame, sadness and fear, had vanished like a bubble of air popping up to the surface of the Ash, for less than one second.

'Yes mother.'

'Uugh!' said Harriet. Rona had forced a flattened smile, dried herself with her shirt, wriggled into her jeans and let her mother lean and stumble against her for the long walk back over the fields towards the house.

'You can never get rid of it you know. When I was young only sailors had tattoos. Prostitutes get them, I suppose.'

The bell and Rona's tentative steps were answered by a shout from the back room; a Southern English accent.

'With you in a minute!'

Rona rocked on her hips to encourage Harry's sleep and perused the photographs. There were hearts in scrolls, knives entwined with snakes, Chinese characters and Latin mottos, sleeves of fish scales, Maori patterns, oriental dragons, eagles across shoulder blades, wolves in the moonlight, skeletons on Harley Davidsons, eyes on pyramids, hieroglyphics, flowers, dolphins, nymphs, magic mushrooms, marijuana leaves and lists of children, living and dead. There were tombstones and crucifixes, Buddhas and elephant gods, and the endless varieties of skulls; in short, all the standard designs. Where Oswald individuated was displayed in one corner near the counter. These were Highland Landscapes; lochs, glens, shrouded in mists, bearing the occasional stag, but more often a simple view of the hills, with delicate, subtle colours, groves of Scots pine, oak and alder, nestled in a rocky glen, as if a watercolour had been painted on the skin. They were, in contrast to the hyperbole of the others, quite beautiful, and Rona was staring at them when Oswald emerged behind the counter, his long goatee and nose-bolt moving vigorously up and down to the demands of chewing-gum.

'Can't be done,' he said.

'Beg your pardon?'

'I get asked a lot.'

'Asked for what?'

'No tattoos on a baby. I don't make the rules.' Rona
assured him she did not want Harry tattooed. A young
woman with her bloodied arm wrapped in cling-film
came out of the back room and said goodbye. The last
note of the doorbell took an age to fade.

'I'm not here for a tattoo at all,' said Rona. Oswald
took hold of the hoop in his ear and tugged. Rona shook
her head. 'I understand you knew Malky.' She watched
Oswald's face grow pale and his eyes soften.

'Yeah. I already gave a statement.'

'I'm not the police.'

'What then?'

'I just wanted to know, who is this?' She pointed to a
photograph of a tattoo on the wall. It was a finely drawn,
beautiful male face, with large black eyes, surrounded by
ringlets of black hair and a fuzzy halo.

'That's one of Malky's. How did you know?'

'I know who it is. Do you?'

'That's Jesus.'

'But you did it from a photograph, didn't you?'

'How do you know that?'

'Can we sit somewhere?' He showed her into the back
room and gestured to a worn couch.

'I told the police everything I knew.'

'What did you tell them?'

Oswald shrugged, 'They wanted to know if Malky was
depressed. I said yeah, he was always depressed. That

didn't mean he would kill himself. They wanted to know
if he owed anyone money, for drugs. I said no, he had
plenty of money. He made wads of cash on the scallops
and didn't have anything to spend it on. He sent most of it
to his mum.'

'In Kilmarnock?'

'Yeah. They wanted to know if he visited her, and I said
I had no idea. They asked who his friends were, and I said
maybe Stevie Van.'

'And you.'

'Yeah, I 'spose. I did all his tatts.'

'All? How many?'

'A hundred, something like that. A lot.'

Rona tried to think of what to say next. It was difficult
to lead up to the question, 'Did he tell you what he did
with the nuclear torpedo?' Instead, she asked him if he
had photographs of Malky's other tattoos.

'Yeah. I've got a folder just for him.' He took a fat file
from a shelf and turned the plastic sleeves for her. At the
beginning there were two photographs of Malky, naked,
with his arms in the air, back and front. He was tattooed
from chin to toes. 'There was no overall plan with him.
He just built up. It would have been better if he'd had a
plan. We were just filling in gaps towards the end. He was
thinking about getting the face done, and he was getting
into piercings, and other stuff.'

'What's other stuff?'

Oswald produced a vaporiser, adjusted the current and blew out a thick cloud of strawberry shortcake. 'Stuff that I'm not allowed to talk about.' Rona quizzed him with a frown. He studied her and let out a smoky sigh. 'There's been a case. Down in England. Guy lost his shop, almost went to jail.'

'A tattooist?'

'Yeah. You can do tattoos, and piercings, but the other stuff is illegal.'

'What?'

'Implants. Amputations.'

'Amputations?'

'Somebody wants an ear removed, or a nipple, that's an amputation. Your supposed to have that done by a surgeon, in a hospital.'

'And implants?'

'Horns are the most popular. You put a plastic implant under the scalp, two of them, here and here, and it looks like horns.'

'People want that?'

'And tongue splitting. So your tongue looks like a snake's tongue. That's a grey area.'

'And Malky wanted horns and his ears removed?'

'Horns. He was thinking about horns, but it was a big step, even for him. Then he changed his mind when he met Jesus.'

'You mean Kosma? The guy in the tattoo?'

'Yeah. He stopped talking about getting his face done. He started talking about Jesus.'

'You mean about Kosma.'

'No, Jesus Jesus. He started talking about the Bible and repentance and salvation. Proper Jesus. Kosma, the guy in the tattoo, was like Jesus, was Jesus, but not Jesus Jesus. Malky was a Christian, all of a sudden.'

'Oh.'

'Yeah. Exactly. I was relieved actually. He stopped talking about politics. I'm a kind of Christian too.'

'Oh. So then he didn't want the horns and he stopped getting tattoos?'

'No, not tattoos. He was still getting tattoos. He still had space on his back. He didn't want any more implants after he got chipped.'

'Chipped? Like a dog?'

'Kind of. He got chipped in his back. And a tattoo there, in one of his last spaces.' He turned the pages of the folder to a large picture. It was one of Oswald's specialities: a Highland landscape of hills rising, ridge after ridge, a river snaking between boulders into a loch; a line of trees along the shore running into a wooded glen, and above all these faded blues, subtle purples and greens, the fiery orange and yellow of a mushroom cloud. It was Armageddon in the Glens. 'Quite proud of this one actually,' said Oswald, puffing and nodding. 'Nice.'

'Where's the chip?'

'Right there, under that rock.' He pointed to a boulder directly beneath the mushroom cloud. Rona's pulse quickened, but she tried to keep her voice steady.

'What was on the chip?'

'No idea. It's just a chip, bio-sealed of course.'

'But what do people have on their chips?'

'Varies. Sometimes it's like personal data. Sometimes people have them put in the wrist, and they can open doors and stuff. He didn't say. We respect people's privacy here.'

'He didn't say anything about it?'

Oswald thought for a moment, and puffed, and shook his head. 'He was talking about Jesus at the time. He said that was the end of the world. The End Times. The End Times is coming and all that, and Jesus was going to separate the wheat from the chaff and the lambs from the goats. All that stuff.'

'Jesus Jesus, or Kosma Jesus?'

'Jesus Jesus, I think.'

Harry opened his eyes and let out a long howl. Rona stood up.

Chapter 18

Rona undid the straps and began exposing her right
breast. 'We need to speak to the police. We need to call
them now. Call Eamon.'

Stevie looked out of the pickup window. 'Which?' he
said.

Rona tried to put her nipple in the wailing, puckering
mouth. 'Eamon. Call Eamon. Shit. Need to change him.
Need to go in the back.' Stevie got out of the pickup to
let down the tailgate. Rona pulled down her fleece and
brought Harry round. She lay him on the plywood floor
and began to unbutton. 'The police. The police will have
done an autopsy. They need to check his body for a chip.
He had a chip put in his back.'

'A what?' Stevie averted his gaze from the spectacle of Harry's nappy.

'Shit.'

'You can say that again.'

'I left the wipes in front. Get me the wipes. A computer chip or something. Something with something on it.'

'What?'

'I don't know exactly! A bag. Can I use this bag?' She picked up a rubbish-filled plastic bag.

'Be my guest. A chip. What makes you think it's important?'

'The nuclear explosion thingy, mushroom cloud, that he had tattooed above it.'

'Oh.'

Rona handed him the plastic bag containing nappy and soiled wipes. 'Get rid of that. Come on. We have to phone Eamon.'

Eamon was lying on his back on a couch in the study. His ankle had been smeared with ibuprofen and wrapped in a packet of frozen peas but he had risen every ten minutes to limp to the window and back again. Earlier Mike had come in to tell him that he had seen men dressed in black in the Ash woods.

'What do you want me to do?' he had asked.

Eamon had watched him clasp and unclasp his massive hands. 'Don't go near them. Stay in the woods, keep watch.'

Eamon had already called the police three times that morning. He had tried to obtain a home number for John Maclean, but had been told that it was against the policy of Police Scotland to give out personal numbers. He had eventually succeeded in receiving a call-back from DS Troy.

'How can I help, Mr Ansgar?'

'It's about Malky Macleod.'

'Malky Macleod. Remind me.'

'The body that was washed up on the shore of Loch Nish last week.'

'Ah Yes. Malcolm Macleod. The drowning.'

'The drowning? You think he drowned?' There was a long pause. 'Hello?'

'Malcolm Macleod drowned, according to the pathologist.'

'You don't think he was murdered?'

'What makes you think that?'

'His finger was missing. Why was his finger missing?'

'Mr Ansgar, his finger isn't missing.'

'But I saw his hand, there was a missing finger.'

'Missing from his hand, yes. But we have the finger. It was found caught in the anchor-chain of his boat, which was found drifting at the mouth of Loch Nish.'

'But that's not possible,' said Eamon. Malky had gone
missing on Monday. Then he and Stevie had seen his boat
at the pier on Loch Houn. Which day was that? Then
they had taken his boat to Endpoint House. There the
Autonomass had stolen it while they had been talking to
Nyst. Had he and Stevie used the anchor? He tried to
remember. Not at the pier at Loch Houn. It had been
moored to the pier. Not at Endpoint. They had tied up
at the jetty. Could there have been a severed finger in the
anchor chain all the way from the pier to Endpoint and
they hadn't noticed? Yes, but then Malky had moored the
boat at the pier. Without a finger? Tied it up and coiled
the ropes, all the time with a missing finger and the finger
caught in the chain? And then he had drowned? Possible,
if he had fallen out of the boat at the Loch Houn pier,
but then his body would have had to have drifted up Loch
Houn, around Ardven, and back into Loch Nish, to arrive
at the beach. Was that possible? Would tide and current
do that?

'Are you still there? Mr Ansgar?'

'Yes.'

'Do you have something you want to tell me?'

Eamon took a deep breath. 'No.'

When he had ended the call he lay back on the couch
and gazed up at the ceiling. He tried to call RB again, but
the phone went straight to voicemail. Then his phone
buzzed and Rona's name appeared. When she had told

him about the tattoo he dialled the police number again
and asked for DS Troy. He was put on hold, and then told
that DS Troy was 'on training' for the rest of the day and
would not be available until the following afternoon. He
was informed that, 'If it is an emergency you should dial
triple nine.' Eamon thanked them for this information,
ended the call, and threw the phone across the room in
the direction of the waste-paper basket. It missed and
broke into pieces on the floor. He stood up, winced,
limped crossed the room, and put the pieces back together
again. He thought about dialling the emergency number
and imagined the conversation. They would consider it a
declaration of insanity.

'There's a body lying in a mortuary in Inverness and if
you look at the back you will see a tattoo. It is a picture
of a nuclear explosion above a highland glen, and at the
base of the nuclear explosion you will find a rock. If
you make an incision around the image of the rock and
remove a half centimetre of flesh you will discover some
sort of microchip. Somehow gain access to the chip. This
will give you information as to the location of a nuclear
torpedo that was lost by the Royal Navy off the West
Coast of Scotland fifty years ago. You had better do this
quickly, because if you don't, the *Autonomass*, which
is a bunch of crazy environmentalist fundamentalist
anarchists from Germany, are going to get hold of the

nuclear torpedo first, and do something with it, but I don't know what.'

Eamon lay back down on the couch and closed his eyes. Images of Malky's tattooed limbs and torso floated through his mind. Images of Shem hanging from a tree. Then images of David lying face down on the floor of the manse living room, surrounded by broken ornaments and furniture. What did Malky's death have to do with David's? Were they connected at all? Or as the police thought, nothing to do with each other? He tried to see the picture taken through the window of the manse in his mind's eye. The body and smashed up room. Had the cups from the forest altars been there, lying on the floor? He tried to see the writing on the walls. Why would Shem have written those things? They only incriminated him and his family. He could not see the writing on the walls. He had never seen it, he remembered. Yet it had been there. Was that because he had not wanted to see it? Because, like the Scottish Government, he did not want to believe that the murder was homophobic? He had wanted Kirsty to delete the photo from her phone. The police had made everyone, everywhere delete the photos. Delete the evidence. And now he needed to see. He cursed.

Denis Nyst stopped the quad while still on the hill-top above Johnny Murachar's croft and walked the last mile down into the woods. He whistled most of the way, and

the stumbles he made among the thigh-high heather and
chest-high bracken did not interrupt his smile. When
he was still far from the fence he could hear and feel
the vibration of generators. As he got closer there were
shouts, hammer blows and the whine of power tools; the
sounds of men putting up a venue in time for a deadline.
He made for the top of the croft, as far from the noise as
he could get, and for the last fifty yards he crept on his
belly.

When he reached the fence he peered through the
chain-link and could see the whole croft below him. In the
centre, before the platform that supported the cross, an
enormous marquee had been set up, and around it were
smaller tents and a row of port-a-loos. Nyst grinned and
dug into his pocket to take out the cartridge and the sock.
He wrapped the cartridge in the sock and stuffed the sock
into the chain-link about six inches above the ground,
then he took a bracken stem and wove it into the fence
above, over and under the wires. He watched the activity
on the croft for a while, then crept on is belly back into
the trees.

It took two hours for Brigitta to arrive back at *The Kelpie*
and have the door opened for her so that she could stand
silhouetted against the square of light formed by the
sea and sky. Mo, Qualin and Solly looked up from their
sleeping bags.

'You have been playing us,' said Brigitta. 'Where is it?'

Mo raised himself on an elbow so that he could reach
for a packet of cigarettes. 'Money in the account, then we
tell you.'

'Maybe we just give Eilidh some pills, then you tell us,'
said Brigitta.

Mo shrugged. 'Then everybody loses. What do you
care about the money? It's not yours. You put the money
in the account. You give me my phone so I can check, you
give Solly his phone so he can call Eilidh, then we take
you right there. It's not far. Half an hour, and you can
have your torpedo.'

'AUV.'

'Whatever.'

Brigitta remained motionless against the swaying
light, then waved a hand at a shadow beyond a porthole.
A thin man brought in the phones and Mo opened his
bank account. Nine hundred and eighty thousand, eight
hundred and sixty-seven ZAR. The boots were well
and truly filled. Solly retreated to a far corner of the
deckhouse, apologising and uttering soothing words into
his phone. Mo watched him and received a nod.

'Let's go now,' said Mo, looking at his watch. 'The tide
is right.'

There was a light breeze playing in the birch trees on the
south bank of the loch as the *Sea Wolf*, with her engine

just above tick-over, followed the low-tide stream of the river Feshie. To the east the river completed its escape from the glens, at last gaining respite from the rock-bed it had flowed over all its life, and slowed for the last quarter-mile through a meadow of rushes. From there it flowed into that undecided zone of short, thick grass and purple flowers, between salt and freshwater, and took its ease, beginning to weave. At high tide it would squirm along a hidden track beneath the black surface, but at low its weaving was visible, and stretched from the pier to the southern shore, to languidly approach the bank of shimmering birch, then turn and snake out again, through the grey sand exposed by the retreated sea, back to the pier and back to the bank, nonchalant before its inevitable fate, the sea, which would at first sully its Highland freshness with salt, then obliviate its being.

The *Sea Wolf* worked its way up the oscillations, only inches from the banks of the channel. Mo was only half concerned about the narrowness because the *Sea Wolf* was not much bigger than Malky's boat, and he stood at the bow, an impassive figurehead, gaze fixed on the first turn of the river beneath the overhanging birches and steep hill. As they approached the bend he lit a cigarette and called a halt with the smoking hand.

The channel was deeper on the outside of the curve, deep enough to be dark, and darkened by an overhang of the hill's rock, and the shade of the trees which caught the sunlight and flicked it back into Mo's eyes. He held one hand over his brow, gestured with the cigarette to Qualin to cut the engine and moved the hand from brow to rock to stop the last momentum of the boat, so that they stood silent in the stream. He leant over the side, close enough to the water to smell it, and saw his own face, pale against the gloom with a bright white *kufi*, and saw Brigitta's face next to him. In the shadows it was ugly; not just flat and plain, but as if the half-light revealed previously unseen undulations. A dreadlock fell from behind an ear and disturbed the image as it hit the water and something about the hair in the clear water made Mo feel ill. Through the ripples he saw an ominously straight line, curving and meeting another at a point two metres below; something sleek and solid and alien to the riverbed; after these weeks of searching, something other than sand, worm casts and scallops, something that could only have been made by a human mind.

The torpedo was half silted over, but he judged in a moment what it would take to raise it. It would take a man with a snorkel, two straps, and the little derrick crane amidships of the *Sea Wolf*. There would have to be some balancing of the boat, and anchors laid out to port to stop her listing, and they would have to be quick, before the tide caused trouble, but it was not a diving job. He looked about him, at the strip of sand before the hillside, at the sand stretching west for a mile along the southern shore

of Loch Houn, at the sheep paths on the hillside leading
through the heather towards Inverish, and he made a two-
note whistle through his teeth that made Solly and Qualin
look up in surprise. It was a sound they had not heard for
a year, but a familiar signal; when a job is going wrong,
when someone is approaching, when there is danger, this
simple sign, long since agreed, which means that no-one
asks a question or hesitates a moment, and no-one runs
but all leave together, and tools are let lie where they fall.
Mo stood up and stepped off the starboard bow onto
the land and pulled the gunwale towards him so that his
partners could step off from the stern.

'Hey! Hey! Hey! Where are you going?' said Horst,
grabbing the wheel that Qualin had let go. But in reply
the three Muslims only left a trail of footprints across the
glistening sand.

'Hey Mo,' said Qualin, when they had gone a hundred
yards. 'Why are we leaving?'

Mo ignored the question and turned to Solly. 'Eilidh is
safe yeah?'

'*Ja*, she is with her friend in Mallaig.'

'Why we walking Mo?' asked Qualin.

Mo took out his phone. 'Jobs over. Call Eilidh and tell
her to buy tickets for Joburg, for the next flight. How long
from here to Glasgow? Four hours? Next flight will be
tomorrow afternoon. We need to be on it. She needs to be
on it. Business class if necessary. I'm paying.'

'What's the hurry?'

'We have to go. You ask too many questions.' The three were silent for a while.

'Mo, this torpedo,' said Qualin. 'How did you know which marker to delete?'

'I told you. The one in freshwater can't be marking a scallop bed.'

'But how did you know the others were marking scallop beds? Before we started Mo, before we had done any dives, you deleted that one, and you knew the others were marking scallop beds. How? You knew it was Malky's chart plotter, *neh*?'

'Too many questions *bru*.'

'I've got more.'

'Sometimes better not to ask.' They walked on in silence.

'Jobs over yeah?' said Qualin.

'*Ja,*'

'Can we take off these damn hats now, eh?'

Mo stretched out his hand to receive the two *kufis*, folded them carefully and put them in a pocket.

Chapter 19

The gel he had applied to his leg and the ticking of the ormolu clock on the mantelpiece had made Eamon drowsy and he had fallen into a disturbed sleep on the couch in the study. He dreamt of men in NBC suits, remembering training at Sandhurst; of restricted vision through the facemask, the smell of neoprene and rubber, misting up glass, muffled curses and suffocating heat. Then he was in the room at the manse looking through the visor, the sound of his own breathing filling his head. He was in the photograph of body and broken furniture, glass crunching under his feet. There were stone chalices amid the debris and graffiti on the walls but as he turned they disappeared. He looked down at his own hands and saw he carried a bloodied bat, then he looked towards the back window, saw his own face looking in, and woke up with a shout, breathless but did not get up. He felt relief in laying still on the couch, his body locked into a pleasurable immobility, his mind in a half-dream state. Then he became aware through half-closed eyes of a presence in the room.

There was a grey shape somewhere on the edge of his field of vision. If it had been Kirsty or Mike he would have known, perhaps by some scent or particular detail of dress, or sound of their breathing that consciously he would not have recognised, but which his deeper mind would note. He knew Kirsty, the woman who had held him in her arms against that same blue overall, whose scent was a milk that had nourished him as much as his mother's. He knew Mike as well as he knew the gardens he had walked through his entire life, knew him as a boy whose limbs had tangled with his own as they wrestled on the lawns; knew him as a teenager who had shared his first beers; knew him as a man with whom he had shared the loads of tree trunks on his shoulders. This person was a complete stranger, and then he saw it was Harriet McColl, mysteriously younger, taller, blonder, with her hair down over her shoulders. She was standing at the end of the couch, erect, holding her head up, steadying herself with only one walking stick. Eamon was so startled he almost spoke and would have sat upright and greeted her had not his sensation of paralysis made him hesitate. She

was standing with her back to him, but he could make out
the line of her jaw behind strands of hair, and the tip of
her nose beyond the rise of her cheek. It was enough for
him to see what she was staring at.

Behind the desk of walnut veneer, pen-stand and lamp
emerging from a Chinese vase, on the dull red wall,
elevated to survey the entire room, still master of this
domain long after his demise, hung the full-length portrait
of his father, Asgard Ansgar. He was wearing a tweed suit,
standing on an imaginary hill to the west of Duncul with
the Castle diminished in the distance, on a woodless plane
that also did not exist, with Loch Cul in the background.
The artist had flattered him, Eamon had always
thought. He had caught his father before alcoholism and
belligerence had set in, clogging the arteries and damming
up blood in the face. He had caught him on the cusp
between youth and seriousness, still with a smile, not the
grimace Eamon had come to know. He had caught him
before Eamon's mother's death.

Harriet McColl gazed up at the portrait for several
minutes while the sleep-state seeped from Eamon's
arms and legs and was replaced with the impulse to rise.
Then he stirred, by sighing and moving his feet stiffly
to the floor and only after rubbing his face and clearing
his throat did he stand and prepare to meet her with an
expression of surprise. His surprise was genuine when he
saw that the room was empty, void of even the memory

of her presence, leaving the possibility that he had dreamt her. It was only several minutes later, when he had lit a cigarette and poured himself a whisky, that he looked up at his father's face, and found reassurance that she had indeed been present.

When Rona and Stevie returned to the study, they began going over the visit to Oswald the Tattooist, re-vivifying the details of their discovery, puzzling over the whereabouts of Malky's body and the location drawn on its back. Eamon listened and replied but was absorbed by the memory of Harriet.

She had only stared at the portrait. There was nothing remarkable in that. He realised that the striking image was simply her; the realisation that it was her, after the initial non-recognition; the moment that she had become herself. She had been no-one, and then some-one. 'Because she did not look like her.' He tried out this idea, almost sounding the words out with a draught of smoke from mouth and nostrils, and then, as he drew in air with a sip of whisky, he revised the thought; it was not that she did not look like her; it was that she looked *more* like her; a her that was not decrepit, hunched over, old, sour. She had looked years younger, for perhaps a minute. Her hair had shone. Or perhaps between the moment of non-recognition and recognition, while his half-sleeping mind had imposed no comment, he had seen her unaffected by the insidious impatience and resentment that always accompanied their meetings, had seen her as she truly was? He felt a rush of sympathy towards his mother-in-law, so that when the harsh call came echoing down the spiral stairway, 'Rona!' from the rooms above, and Rona raised her head from her suckling charge, Eamon put down his glass, stubbed out his cigarette and told her he would go.

He climbed one storey and knocked on the door of her bedroom. It was ajar, and he pushed it open when she did not reply. He was shocked by the difference between the woman who was sitting on the crumpled bed and the woman who had stood before the portrait minutes before. Again, he considered whether he had been dreaming. Harriet McColl was as she had always been: hunched over, lank hair in an untidy bun, frail, grey, wearing a cotton dress and a cardigan. Harriet McColl was an old, sick woman who could barely stand, who carried with her perpetually, as precious as a cupped candle flame, some unfathomable grievance, whether at her illness, or her daughter, or himself, he had never managed to discern. He spoke to her as he had always spoken, with as much politeness as he could muster, but letting slip his irritation.

'What is it, Harriet?'

'I need to use the lavatory.'

Eamon turned to go but paused with his heart thumping. 'She's feeding Harry. You were in the study just now, on your own.' The look she gave him chilled all the anger out of him. The sunken eyes darkened and the mouth set into a lipless line. He held her gaze until the line split in two, and grey teeth and a hiss emerged. Eamon did not move until she hissed again, causing her head to jut forward on protruding tendons. He closed the door and returned to the study with the instruction, and was left holding his son, who was replete with milk and thankfully in a giggling mood.

When Rona returned Eamon called RB.

'We have more information, Richard.'

'Jolly good! What?'

'We have a map, of sorts.'

'Tremendous! Of what sorts?'

'A tattoo, on a man's back. We think it might show the location of the missing device.'

'Fascinating. Where is this chap?'

'He's dead. He drowned. The police have his body.'

'Oh.'

'And there is a chip, a computer chip of some sort, implanted into the map.'

'Good God!'

'The trouble is the police don't believe me. They must still have the body in the Inverness mortuary I presume. We need to get access to it. To look at the tattoo and if it's possible to remove the chip.'

'And you are wondering if I can help?'

'Perhaps, if you know anyone who works, I don't know, in Inverness, with the…' Eamon tried to think of the name of the office that dealt with dead bodies. He knew that RB knew a procurator fiscal in Inverness, or at least had done.

'Eamon, really? You can't expect me to know someone in a position of authority in every part of the civil service in every part of the country whenever you have need! We are not Edwardians for God's sake! They don't all dine at the same club and they didn't all go to school with me! There are procedures that have to be followed; protocols, channels. There are rules goddammit! You think I can get you permission to cut a hole in a corpse that's in police custody? What are you hoping for? You want a pass to go into the mortuary, hand a tenner to the night-watchman and go at it with your scout-knife?'

'No of course not,' said Eamon, as he realised that that was precisely what he had had in mind. 'What do you suggest?' He heard RB sigh. 'Where are you?'

'I'm in Edinburgh, chez moi, about to tuck into Waitrose's finest microwave meals for one. What of it?'

'Did you manage to get anywhere? Speak to anyone, about the situation?'

'As I said, I didn't go to school with everyone. Above a certain level that doesn't count anyway, believe it or not. I fagged for the head of MI5. Cleaned his rugby boots and warmed his toilet seat, but it doesn't count a fig. And the other thing, half the whole caboodle is run by women.'

'So?'

'So, I didn't go to school with any women, ever! Hardly spoke to one at Uni, and rarely since, unless you count my sister. And then there are whole cohorts of *professionals*, you know, the sort of fellow who takes the whole procedure and protocol thing *tres seriousement*. I've got simply no leverage with these people, no kudos, no *cachet*. In fact, I have to say, I am beginning to get the distinct impression that a lot of them don't like me at all. Half of them think I'm mad and the other half have me condemned as a presumptuous anachronism, white, "cis", male and all that. I'm banging my head against a brick wall. I can keep banging, for your sake, but I have to be honest about the prospects.'

'You have to keep trying Richard.' Eamon ended the call. 'We have to warn them,' he said to Rona and Stevie.

'Warn who?'

'The conference. Acturus McBean.'

Witness to the raising of the (M) Type 45 nuclear torpedo lost at latitude -57.9907 longitude -5.9997 on the fifth July 1963: one heather covered hillside, one brilliant orb swallowing one soundless sky, one shining sand-flat about to be chilled by the incoming tide, one empty pier at the head of Loch Houn, six German anarchists.

The torpedo had a presence as forceful as the sea, sand, sun and sky. The five men and one woman peering over the side of the RIB into the river saw only the tip and the beginning of the body, but were filled with an un-nameable force, as if the churning, glistening waters turned within them. Mouths hung slightly open; hands shivered as they grasped ropes; pupils dilated, and every sound in this still corner of the world seemed to resonate from the metal tube, as if the contents spoke through birdsong, the whisper of birch leaves, the lapping of wavelets against a rubber hull, occasional words in German and English and the far-high scream of an eagle over Ben Briagh.

Malky Macleod had moved the weapon by strapping it to the hull of his RIB, and had intended to take it further up-river. He had approached the mouth of the Feshie at high-tide, by the light of a full-moon, but the torpedo had bumped against the first boulders in the shallows, and in spite of Malky's definite technical knowledge that nothing in the world could induce the thing to explode after fifty years submerged, there remained the superstition that we all suffer in the presence of a bomb. He wasn't going to drag it over rocks. He retreated, chastened, with the hollow sound that the metal casing had made on the riverbed echoing somewhere in his bowels. He had motored back out towards the southern shore, far from any chance of being seen or heard, and had sat in the dark for half the night, smoking the weed that turns time in upon itself, pondering the squirming surface and tentacles of sound that curled upwards from his hull. It was the retreating waters themselves that offered the plan, as they revealed the serpentine track of the river, the hairpin bend beneath the hill, and the deep pool.

In the months that had passed the sea had tended with diligence to one of her many arts, which is to entomb, swathe, circumscribe or bury anything in sand she finds within her realm. She had done her work gracefully and draped about the tube a sheet of particles that clutched it hard, as if she loved it.

'You must go in,' said Brigitta, to no-one in particular. Her crew knew how cold the water was. Horst tore his gaze away from the shape and looked over his shoulder at the dry-suit lying on the deck. He had never worn one but had watched Mo and his partners don and doff the clumsy things daily. Horst was too tall to fit the suit, which had been made for Mo. A smaller, younger man was ordered to wear it. When he entered the water he floated, a wrinkled bag with head and flailing arms, like an unshelled turtle. They hauled him back on-board.

Horst suggested weights. The weight belt was tied around the youth's waist. It too had been designed for Mo, who carried a comfortable coating of fat. The young man was a life-long vegan. He rolled backwards off the RIB and sank with proverbial efficiency. Through the

clear water his friends saw him stir up a cloud of sand
that obscured waving arms and panic-stricken face. They
waited almost a minute, in silent shock until the diver
succeeded in making a calculation in his cortisol-drenched
brain, pulled the clip that released the belt, and catapulted
to the surface, where the spittle from his curses joined
the spray and bubbles. They hauled him up and unzipped
him. Horst disrobed, without discussion, put on the
facemask, took the end of a rope and dove. He put a hand
under the nose of the torpedo to hold himself down.
For a moment he paused, feeling as if he had reached
through the surface of the world, experiencing an electric
current of horror. But he recovered himself and smiled
as he slipped the rope beneath, tied a naïve knot, and
returned shivering to the boat. He felt like a man who has
harpooned a whale. But the leviathan sulked in its lair.
As he rubbed his white flesh dry the rope was pulled and
slipped off the end of the casing. He spat a curse into the
face of those who had pulled.

Horst dove again. He tied a firmer knot. He returned to
the boat, and the noose slipped over the nosecone again.

On his third dive, after two surfacings for air, he
succeeded in making two firm loops about the casing.
The boys on the deck hauled, but only succeeded in
moving the inflatable gunwale of the *Sea Wolf* towards the
torpedo. Horst dressed and sat on the deck smoking with
the others while Brigitta made a phone call to Endpoint.

Then the silent sky, sun, sea, and hill saw the RIB
negotiate the channel towards the loch and hurtle down
the length of the peninsula.

The sun, sea, sand, sky and hill stood guard. A bird
returned to its nest in the birches above the pool but
fluttered out again as the boat returned carrying a winch
and tackle which the crew hooked up to the base of a
tree. Even then Horst had to make several dives to scratch
out the sand that was holding fast around the tube. Still, it
could not be raised onto the boat. It was simply too heavy.
They raised the nose to the surface hard up against the
bank. By this time the tide was in and the boat no longer
afloat in the river but on the sea that had covered it. The
torpedo was much larger than anyone had imagined.
Brigitta produced a diagram and smoothed it out on a
crate. After some discussion she ordered the nose to be
lowered beneath the surface while once more the boat
returned to Endpoint.

This time it returned with a grinder, and Horst set to
work on the metal casing. It took an hour to sever the
nosecone from the body, and the sparks became brighter
as the evening advanced. The body was allowed to
sink back to the floor; a decapitated monster, wires and
tendons of steel protruding from its severed neck. When
the head lay on the deck pointing at the sky there was a
moment when the crew, crouching, kneeling, exhausted,
soaked, paused, in silence and half-light as if before a body

or a shrine, until Brigitta issued an order that turned and raised the prow of the boat to fly over the water towards the portent of sunset above Ardven.

Chapter 20

Stevie and Mike followed Eamon up the spiral staircase to the top door. Eamon kicked at the base to open it outwards and was about to exit onto the roof of Duncul Castle when his brother touched his shoulder.

'Get down.'

They crawled to the parapet. Mike pointed out the Mercedes van with painted-over windows parked by the side of the road leading towards the Ash Bridge.

'There's three of them,' said Mike. 'They're sleeping in the van. I've seen them going to the shop and walking around the garden wall in the wood. They take turns.'

'And they haven't made any attempt to break in?' Mike shook his head. Eamon sat with his back against the parapet and lit a cigarette.

'They know that I met Tariq. If I were them I would want to know what I know. But they're just watching.'

'And waiting,' said Stevie.

Eamon looked towards the reddening sky above the village. 'For what?'

Stevie shrugged.

'Whatever it is the answer is at Endpoint,' said Eamon. 'With Nyst. We need to go back to Endpoint.'

'We'll need a boat.'

'Not by boat. They'll hear us and see us. We'll walk in.'

'On that leg?'

'It's a sprain. I'll take a pill.'

'We could get hold of a boat in the morning.'

'If we go now we can be there while they're still asleep. But these ones here can't see us leave. Mike, you'll have to distract them.' Mike looked puzzled. 'Knock on the van, with the tractor. Say sorry. Make it look like an accident. Don't hurt them. Call me when it's done.' Mike nodded.

In the study Eamon took a tobacco tin from the desk. Stevie watched him break a pill the size of a two-pence piece out of a silver wrapper.

'Codeine? You'll fall asleep half-way there.'

Eamon held up a blue capsule. 'These stop you falling asleep. Leftovers from Afghan.'

'Speed plus heroin? And I'm the one who's supposed to be a junkie.'

Eamon led Stevie down five floors to the basement. He retrieved a ladder from among the old mattresses, bikes, tea-chests and broken furniture and placed it beneath a window twenty feet above.

'This opens out into the bushes around the old kitchen wing.'

'What now?'

'We wait for Mike to call.'

Mike switched on the tractor's rotating orange light. As he trundled along the road, he let the steering wheel slip through his hands until the edge of the cab made contact with the side of the van and gouged in, making a long, slow screech, like finger-nails across a blackboard. He stopped the tractor before the cab was ripped off. Two young men in black hoodies emerged from the rear door of the van.

'*Was ist los*?' screamed the one with a sad face.

'Sorry!' said Mike.

The young man with a boyish face shouted and gesticulated in German. Mike started the engine and began to reverse. The corner of the cab dug in further and began to peel back the side of the van. There were more shouts and curses. Mike stopped, took out his phone and called Eamon.

'There's only two here.'

'You need to see the other one,' said Eamon. 'Leave the tractor. Check along the garden wall.'

Mike jumped down from the road side of the cab, and was turning to walk back in the direction of the castle when he felt a tap on his shoulder. As he turned he was hit on the jaw. When his eyes opened he saw the thin, hooded face of the sad one and swung at it. The sad one retreated with two delicate hands cupped over his nose. Mike turned towards a sound behind him and ducked as the boyish one swung a rake at his head, then slid down the bank into the wild garlic beneath the trees as the boyish one followed. The sad one slid down behind, talking into a phone. Mike backed away, then turned to run. When he was fifty yards into the wood he saw the third, tall young man, slide down the bank. The boyish one was only twenty yards away and the river Ash was ahead of him. He called Eamon.

'I've got three of them now, in the woods.' He ended the call and began to run in the direction of the river. Behind him the three paused to confer.

'How many?' said the tall one.

'One only. The gardener,' said the sad one. The tall one signed that they should follow Mike while he turned back at a jog in the direction of the van.

At the road he quickened his pace until he was fifty yards from the Duncul front gate. He turned onto the narrow path between the woods and the garden wall until he was out of sight of the road, then climbed an ancient ash to the first fork. It was almost dark but the tower door and the main door of the castle were illuminated. Two figures were running across the lawn from kitchen wing of the castle, making for the garden wall opposite. The tall one dropped down from the tree and continued jogging along the path behind the wall.

After a hundred yards he stopped at a fallen beech that was being sawn up for firewood. He picked up a heavy, short branch and felt the weight in his hands, then waited behind the trunk of another beech for the sound of feet running on the path. He timed his swing by ear alone. The branch caught Mike Mack on the forehead and made a popping sound, which was echoed by a duller thud as the back of his head hit the dry earth.

In the Old Schoolhouse Guesthouse at Inverish, Qualin H Bremner was throwing socks into a suitcase. Mo was lying on his back on the bed, blowing smoke at the ceiling. Solly was firing a laser at a walking tree.

'No smoking in the room,' said Qualin.

'We leaving tomorrow. What are they going to do?' said Mo.

Qualin shrugged. 'It's just respect, eh?'

'Turn that shit down man Solly!' said Mo. 'Give it a rest!'

'Level thirty-six coming up! I'm getting to level thirty-six.'

'What's so special about level thirty-six?'

'You get the nukes *bru*! Get to vaporise *alles*!'

Mo swung his legs to the floor and watched as Solly slew a mutilated dragon.

'Yeeeeesss!' As Solly spoke the screen filled with a glowing yellow trefoil and a fairy-tale bell rang out.

'You knew it was Malky's chart, before you deleted the marker in the river,' said Qualin.

'So?'

'So how did you know it was Malky's chart? From the beginning. From when they first showed us the chart-plotter?'

Mo lit another cigarette and moved to the window.

'Malky's dead,' said Qualin.

'They say he fell off his boat and drowned.'

'Malky's dead and Brigitta has his chart-plotter. You knew it was his chart-plotter, but you said nothing to us. When were you going to tell us *bru*?'

'Stop *narring* me man! Stop playing that shit Solly!' Solly paused the game. 'Malky tried to sell me that torpedo, months ago.'

'What?'

'He told me had a torpedo. One night we were smoking out there by the picnic bench. I was telling him about the scrap jobs we had done, like the train we found

in the river, and the tank in Mozambique. He tried to sell
me a torpedo.'

'And?'

'"A torpedo?" I says, "Where did you get a torpedo?"'

'"I found it," he says, "At the bottom of the sea." Eh
man! We laughed!'

'And?'

'I am forty years old *bru*. When I was twenty, yes.
Someone wants to sell me a torpedo, I would have bought
it without even thinking what I was going to do, just
for laughs! But now? I'm in a foreign country. I'm not
sure about all sorts of stuff, like what are we doing here
anyway? You know, getting paid for *mahala* by this Pik,
and not being exactly incognito. Being the only Muslims
in the glen and all that. I turned him down. "What am I
going to do with a torpedo?" I said. "What do I get out
of it? You think 'cos I am a Muslim I want to blow things
up? You know it's illegal to be Islamophobic." Malky
was laughing, with that crazy weed, you know? He was
laughing and I was laughing and I said he should try
sell to someone who actually would make use of it, like
those crazy German protest guys that were causing all
the trouble at Ardven. It was a joke. I didn't think about it
after that.'

'But then, you knew when Brigitta came on the boat
what she wanted. Why didn't you tell us?' said Qualin. Mo
looked at him, then away, out of the window.

'When she came on the boat with the chart-plotter I didn't know. It was a guess. As I said, I was playing roulette. If you knew and Solly knew then she might know that I knew. It was need to know! Nobody needed to know nothing! Do the job, get paid, get out!'

'You should have told us man. Now tell us, why we leaving in such a hurry?'

'Because crazy girl has a torpedo. You need another reason? Pack your socks!' He sat next to Solly and picked up a controller.

In her mother's bedroom at Duncul Castle Rona placed Harry on the bed and knelt before Harriet to undo the buttons at the neck of her dress. Harry wriggled until the fourth button but then decided to utter a howl that hurt his mother's ears. Rona let him cry as she finished. Harriet's face was impassive.

'I need my tonic,' she said.

'Where is it?'

'I don't know. Kirsty gave it to me this morning. She took it with her. Where has Eamon gone now? You know, he should be helping you more with the baby.'

Rona pulled off her mother's socks. 'It's not "the baby". His name is Harry. Can you say that? "Harry." Just for once?'

'It's not a name I would have chosen.'

Rona felt her heart in her throat. Her legs trembled as she stood. 'Why not mother? Why would you not have chosen it? What's wrong with that name?'

'You think he's a royal baby don't you?' Harriet's mouth was set in the familiar sneer.

'What are you talking about? We thought it was a nice name!'

'No need to get upset.'

'What is wrong with you? Why do you sneer at everything?'

'I don't sneer.'

'Yes! You do! And you won't help! You're supposed to help!' She picked up the child and rocked him against her breast. He calmed but kept breaking into tears as her voice rose.

'I'm an invalid,' said Harriet.

'You could still hold him! You could still pick him up! Why don't you hold your own grandson?'

'You don't want me to hold him. You don't trust me.' Rona closed her eyes, breathing in the scent of his hair.

'Mother, why don't you just tell me what is the matter? Is it Eamon? You don't like Eamon? You don't like living here? Is it something I've said? Or done?' She looked up at her mother's dress open to the waist, revealing her bra and wrinkled stomach.

'He gave us Burnum out of pity. Did you know that? Pity!' She lifted her head and laughed.

'What are you talking about?'

'Asgard!'

'Eamon's dad?'

'He was going to marry me! Me! He would still have married me. I was waiting for him. And when *she* died, he would have married me.'

'I don't understand. You had an affair?'

'Pfff! Nothing so tawdry.'

'Then what? What are you saying? He was going to marry you, then he changed his mind and married Eamon's mum. That's what you're upset about?'

'He got me pregnant!'

'Asgard?'

'Your father!' Harriet screamed. 'He was never meant to get me pregnant! Asgard would have come back to me if that hadn't happened!' Rona felt her embrace of Harry stiffen. 'And you know why he didn't marry me? Because we had no money. We. Had. No. Money. And she did!'

'But what about Dad?'

'Pfff! Your father got what *he* wanted!'

'Why are you so awful? Why are you such an awful, horrible person?' Rona did not wait for a reply, but ran from the room to her own, slamming the door behind her.

She busied herself with undressing, bathing and re-dressing Harry. He complained at her brusqueness. She got ready for bed, put out all the lights and tried to sleep but the argument would not leave her alone.

'Awful, horrible person!' She heard her own voice and saw her mother's scowling face. How could she say that? To her own mother? The two streams of remorse and anger merged and became a river too large for its banks. She got up, paced the room and thought of poor Harriet along the corridor; alone, half-dressed, unable to put herself to bed, and cursed her. She tried to read, but the words became meaningless runes. She fought the temptation to call Eamon and pour the pathetic argument down the phone to him as he was crossing the hill. She put out the light and calmed herself, with deep, long breaths, and fell into an anxious sleep, dreamed of her mother dying and awoke in shock to the sound of her son softly crying, it seemed from sadness rather than hunger. When she had fed him she looked at her phone to see the time and was surprised that most of the night had passed. Harry gurgled and smiled. There was no way he was going back to sleep. Rona dressed them both and exited by the low door in the corner of the room.

At the bottom of the tower the door was locked, and she turned the enormous key to let herself out into a still, warm night. At the south wall she found the door and went out into the woods and the true darkness beneath the trees. She stood still, staring into the vague shapes and shadows of leaves and branches, feeling the midges begin to tickle her face. Harry mewed and tried to rub his eyes. Seeing the big moon through the lattice work above she turned him to look up and he was stilled. Again she thought of her mother's face and tried to think her way through the why and what of it all, but all that came were sobs of anger and sorrow. Her father had taught her not to indulge one minute of self-pity, and she had practised resistance against it her whole life. The sensation her mother induced had become normal and Rona had got into the habit of thinking of her as a thing, not a person; like a piece of furniture or a building that could not be moved. Harriet was not going to change; she simply had to be lived with. Getting angry did not help. Rona took deep breaths. Her anger had been foolish. She would apologise, in the morning.

The figure detached itself from the darkness; it could have been the limb of a tree, only there was a thin white face on top. All the sobs were knocked out of her and where Harry had been, a warm ball of need between her hands, there was midge-filled air as she sprawled on the forest floor.

Chapter 21

Rona's mouth formed the beginning of a scream but her lungs could not force it out. She fought against hands on her arms and legs and felt duct-tape binding her. A bag went over her head and the material was forced against her mouth with tape. Still she screamed, stopping only when she heard a voice with a rasp next to her ear:

'Shut up now, or I hurt him! Shut up!'

She strained to interpret Harry's cries as she was lifted over a shoulder and felt the rhythm of walking. A man's voice cooed and shushed her son.

The tower door squeaked and groaned: she had not locked it. She heard bolts close and the shifting of feet on the tower steps and grunts as she was borne up. Her captors must have seen Eamon and Stevie leave. Where was Mike? Kirsty had gone home. Only her mother remained in the castle.

They carried her up, past the upstairs sitting room. She felt herself tipped onto a couch and recognised the warmth of the study. When she tried to speak someone slapped her. Harry could be heard, not crying but gurgling and cooing. Someone was making him happy. There was conversation in German, the sound of something being smashed, then the tape was unwrapped from her head and the sack pulled off.

There were three thin, young men in the room, wearing black jeans and hoodies. The tallest of the three, with a long face and nose and too many teeth, was standing over her, grinning. Behind him the one with full lips and rosy cheeks, a boyish face, was holding Harry, making faces and sounds to him, lightly bouncing him in his arms, and succeeding in making him smile. The third, with a sallow, sad face, stood by the fireplace. He was holding a baseball bat.

'Hallo *Principessa*!' said the tall one.

'My husband will be back soon,' said Rona.

'Good. The sooner the better!'

'What do you want?'

In reply the tall one grinned and gestured to the sad one, who handed him the baseball bat. The tall one gave some instructions in German and the sad one nodded and left the room. 'What I ask, you give. OK?'

The boyish young man began to dance around the room, loudly humming a waltz, holding the entranced Harry at arms-length and swinging him back and forth.

'He's just a baby,' said Rona 'Don't hurt him.'

'He is not a baby Rona,' said the tall one. 'He is, how do you say? *Ein kliene schwiene*. A piglet!'

Harriets voice came from above; screaming. Then shouts and a door slamming. The sad one pulled her into the room and pushed her towards the fireplace. Her limbs flailed as she fell into hearth and made an attempt to raise her head before resting it in the ashes.

'*Alte oma, total verrucht,*' said the sad one.

'Where has hubby gone?' said the tall one to Rona.

'I don't know.'

'Hubby don't tell you these things? He don't share with you? You just sit at home and feed the baby, cook and clean for him and when he comes home you lie back on the bed?'

'Pretty much. How do you know my life so well?'

The tall one showed his crooked teeth. 'Bring it here,' he said to the boyish one, gesturing to the sofa.

The boyish one laid Harry on the couch and put a finger to his lips. The tall one handed him the baseball bat. He swung the bat in a circle and took a step back. Rona began to speak but her breath vanished as the young man swung the bat over his head in an arc that ended with a loud smack against the cushion next to Harry's smiling face. The child stopped smiling and his eyes flicked from side to side before his brain caught up with the shock of the sound and a howl emerged. The boyish one put his finger to his lips and danced backwards and forwards to re-capture the child's attention.

The tall one smiled at Rona. 'OK. You get it? Now you answer. Where did he go?'

'To Ardven.'

'To Endpoint?'

'Yes.'

'Why?'

'To look, to see what he could find.'

The tall one paused, watching her. 'Where did he go out?'

'From the basement. From the window in the basement.'

'How do you get there?'

'Down the tower, keep going down.'

'*Gut*,' said the tall one. He turned to the boyish one and gave him some instructions. The young man left the room. 'How do you get to the top?' Rona nodded towards the door to the tower in the corner of the room. The tall one sent the sad one through it.

'Now tell me what the man in the hills said to hubby.'

'The man in the hills? I don't know what you mean.'

'Don't make me an *arschloch*. You know what I mean. The pig in the mountains. Your hubby met with him.'

'Yes, but I don't know what they talked about.'

The tall one took a buzzing phone from his pocket and answered in German. He stood up to listen and talk and walked over to the fireplace where Harriet lay. As he spoke he poked her with the toe of his boot. Harriet moved a hand slowly to where the toe touched her chest. The tall one moved away, deep in conversation. He drew the curtains and settled into a wing-back chair. Harry began to wail again and stuck his arms out rod-stiff, clenching his fists, making his face glow with anger. The tall one frowned at the child Rona then put the call on hold.

'He's hungry,' said Rona.

'Where is his milk?'

'It's in my breast.'

'Not that milk. Where is the bottle milk?'

'I don't have bottle milk. I have to feed him. You will have to undo my hands,' said Rona, raising her voice above Harry's screams.

'*Nein.*'

'He won't stop.'

'*Schiese!*' said the tall one. He picked up the child and held him at arms-length. Harry bellowed into his face.

'Please, undo my arms.'

'No.' He put the child back onto the couch and knelt on the floor before Rona. 'Which tittie?' Rona was silent. 'Which tittie must he suck?'

'The left.' The tall one raised her jumper above her breasts and unbuttoned her shirt. He paused when confronted with the bra.

'It opens,' said Rona with her mouth set in a straight line. 'There is a clip.' He undid the bra and her breast swelled towards him.

'So big!' He picked up Harry and held his face towards the nipple. Harry, smelling the milk and feeling the nipple against his cheek, turned and began to suck, oblivious to all else in the universe. The tall one watched intently and gradually his lips parted to reveal the crooked teeth.

'*Sehr gut*! Delicious milk!'

Rona watched her son's jaws settle into their familiar rhythm and wondered that even like this her milk should flow, even as she felt the course of hatred through her veins. Then she looked away towards her mother and their eyes met. Harriet's mouth that was set in a straight line like her own. Rona found her gaze holding the so recently reviled face as if she was drowning and reaching out for something solid and her mother kept her own eyes firm as she lifted her head and pushed with great effort against the floor to raise herself to sitting. Her face and hair were dusted with wood-ash from the grate. Harry drank, and the silence in the room was broken only by the sound of his lips on her flesh. A full ten minutes passed, until Harry spat the nipple out with his usual disdain and wailed at the pain in his stomach. The grin fell from the face of the tall one and he tried to force the mouth back to the source. Harry spat and wailed louder.

'You have to burp him,' said Rona.

'*Was*?'

'He has wind. Put him on your shoulder, rub his back.'

'Like this?'

'Higher up. Now rub, round and round, quite hard.'

'This is good?'

'Yes.'

'I make a good daddy, no?' His grin returned. Rona watched her son and willed his wailing to cease. The tall one's phone buzzed and he answered in German.

'Cover me,' said Rona, when he had finished talking.

'No. I like this breast. It is erotic for me, and besides, he might need to eat again.' He sat on the couch.

'And now?' said Rona.

'And now, we wait for Brigitta,' he grinned, rubbing Harry's back.

'Who is Brigitta?'

'You will see. Brigitta is the special one. *Die Auserwählte*. How do you say? The Chosen One.'

'Why? Why is she The Chosen One?'

'Because she is pure. She has not *Schuldkomplex*, how you say? She has no guilt.'

It had taken four men to lift the head of the monster into the house at Endpoint. They had carried it from the jetty suspended beneath two scaffolding poles, moving slowly, being careful of their footing on the planks in the half-light, and had been silent as they laid it on the carpet of the once-grand living-room. Two of the *Autonomass* spread out the diagram on the floor and set to work with screwdrivers and the grinder. Brigitta and Nyst watched. She wore no expression. He hummed and grinned at first but grew bored and returned to his study. The two with the screwdrivers consulted in whispers and took an hour to remove the first aluminum plate, so that they could peer inside with their phone torches.

Nyst returned at dawn. 'Get a move on!' he spat, 'We have a schedule!' One of the two held up a screwdriver.

'You want to try, old man?'

Chapter 22

Dawn glimmered on the backs of Eamon and Stevie descending towards the woods at the end of the Ardven peninsula. Eamon was limping but ahead of his brother, at times half running, then stopping to wait for Stevie, looking warily into the yellow light creeping into the sky behind them.

They had walked without pause for five hours and Eamon had taken two doses of amphetamines. The heather at his feet, the clouds above, the shadows beneath the branches of the pines ahead and the sound of Stevie's breathing and his own boots brushing against the heather, the soft air on his face and the sound of his own teeth rubbing between his gums all competed for attention in a stubborn cacophony, while the codeine carried him above everything, like a priest at an altar.

After parking Stevie's pickup at the beach at Loch Nish, they had walked up the hill before climbing the fence to avoid Murachar's croft, which was overflowing with white light and the hum of generators. They had emerged from the woods onto the top of the hill and had increased the pace, moving in silence save for the sound of a rising west wind. They had stopped only for cigarettes, twice, and each time Stevie had asked the portentous question; 'Are you alright?' while scrutinising Eamon's insistent gums and darting eyeballs.

'We used this stuff a lot,' Eamon explained, working his jaw. 'On night patrols in Afghan. I'm used to it.'

'At some point you are going to crash.'

'Not yet.'

For most of the walk it had seemed to Eamon that he could see through the night, further than the moon could show him. He could see the roots of the heather at his feet, and he could see far ahead, beyond the shapes of rocks and peat hags. He was sure he knew the path so well that he could run and Stevie had several times urged him to slow down. It had seemed to him that the pain in his leg was a mere itch, and he had thought that in fact all pain was as nothing, and that all one had to do was enter a certain state of mind by sheer effort of will, and then anything was possible for the body. It had seemed to him

that his mind was as sharp as knives and clear as crystal.
And he knew that all this was the effect of the drugs, and
he had better not believe it, because any moment he could
turn the other ankle over a stone, and his mind had better
shut-up, because it was a dishonest, traitorous mind. It
could not be trusted, just like the body, and if neither
body nor mind could be trusted what could be trusted?
What was there to trust? If it was all illusion anyway;
light, darkness, truth, untruth? What were colours but
vibrations at a certain wavelength of the electromagnetic
spectrum? And what were sounds but the action of
compressions in the air on certain tissues on the inside
of his head? And what was all of this but a construction
of the neurons in his brain, presenting the information
in a certain way to…what? Himself? What was that?
Consciousness? What was the 'I' that knew? The 'I' itself
could only be a construction of the brain, which meant
that it too was an illusion. It was an illusion that perceived
nothing but illusions, constructions built out of nothing,
castles in the air. And how had all this come about? From
the very beginning of the universe it had all been an
accident. There had been an explosion, and all that existed
had emerged from that point of light, and everything that
had ever been over billions of years had emerged out of
that single point of light, and the cones at the back of his
eyes and the hairs in his inner ear were merely accidents,
like sticks fallen in a pile, all thrown in the air and then

landing at random, and all he was was an accident
watching other accidents; an ongoing series of accidents
that was going to all end in what? And with this question
he had felt a great dark lump of despair descend upon
him, as if he had suddenly been covered in a tarpaulin
that weighed not only on his shoulders but even within
the organs of his body. He told himself it was one of the
effects of the drugs. They made you feel quick, awake,
optimistic, but they could also make you hallucinate. You
had to watch out for that effect, and it could be more
or less pronounced depending on the personality of the
soldier. Is that what he was now? A soldier? Again? Was
he on his way to kill? Was there going to be blood? Where
was his gun? As they approached the woods that covered
the end of the peninsula and surrounded Endpoint
House, the feeling of despair deepened and widened,
to include both the future and the past. He felt he was
heading towards some terrible fate, tramping through
this heather that kept brushing at his feet, and was leaving
behind light, happiness, beauty, locked in the castle,
unable to ever escape, because what surrounded Eamon
Ansgar was only darkness and despair. He felt his feet
grow heavier, and the sound of them against the heather
roots was a loud tearing, and the wind from the west was
growing stronger and whistling in the trees ahead, and the
moon was dying and fading now, but the day ahead would
be dark. And his incessant gums began to mumble a half-

remembered prayer because somewhere there had to be a meaning to all this. His mother had believed that. It could not possibly all be an accident. The lips moved and a low mumble emerged; 'Hail Mary, full of grace, the Lord is with thee…'

'Are you alright?' said Stevie, for the third time.

'Fine,' said Eamon, and walked a little further off from his brother so he could mumble in peace.

They entered the dense, green darkness, of the pine forest, filled with astringent scent and the hissing of wind in the tops, following the firebreak that led due west, downhill. They knew the route; they would follow this east-west break, which would lead to the north-south break, the one where they had come across the altar-like platforms and the stone cups; this lead to the track along the loch-side to the farm buildings and Endpoint House. When they were still at the top of the first firebreak they saw a grey-haired figure below them in the distance, walking away. Eamon and Stevie stepped into the tree shadows.

'It's Nyst,' said Stevie. They watched him through binoculars. Nyst was dressed in a long tunic over wellingtons and carried a colourful cloth bag. Eamon could see that his lips were pursed. He could not hear anything above the wind, but he was sure Denis Nyst was whistling as he walked and out of their sight.

They descended, keeping off the track in the centre, and it took them half an hour to reach the junction of the firebreaks. They paused and listened, but only heard from the tree-tops waving at a sky that was turning from grey to blue. Eamon could not decide if the cup and altar ahead was an ugly or beautiful thing. The altar was nothing but a pile of big stones with a large, flat stone on top, but it would not have been an easy thing to build. It looked like something out of an *Asterix* comic. The cup, perhaps, was what made it sinister. It was a crude copy of a chalice engraved with Celtic patterns, reminding him of childhood Sunday masses, the cup raised above the priest's head at the consecration, full with the blood of Christ. The last time they had been here the chalice had contained flower heads. He left his brother to look inside.

'Look at this,' he called back.

Stevie came over. There were two figures of men, made of grey, shiny plastic, at the bottom of the cup, among the daisy and dog-rose heads, and several abstract shapes, half-crescents and cuboids of the same plastic. Eamon took out a figure and held it up.

'Weird,' said Stevie.

'Man in a suit and tie.' Eamon put it back.

'Voodoo stuff, kind of.'

'Kind of. Look out!' Nyst had appeared above them in the firebreak, heading downhill at a nonchalant walk.

They tripped over roots and scratched faces and arms as they scrambled into cover.

Nyst was whistling and humming an aimless tune. Eamon and Stevie watched through a spiders-web of branches as he paused at the altar above them, reached into his bag and took out a small grey object and placed it in the cup. He reached into the bag again and took out another.

'Figures,' said Eamon, 'That's those figures.'

Nyst carried on down the break, humming and whistling. He stopped the altar they had just left, put something in the cup, and carried on down the hill to the next where he did the same. When he was almost at the last altar before the edge of the forest and the track to the house, Eamon and Stevie crept out of the trees and Nyst turned to look back.

Nyst set off at a half-run and Eamon called after him, but in seconds he was out of sight. Eamon and Stevie began running down the slope but when they were only half-way a quad engine started ahead.

'He'll be on the track back to the steading.'

'Just keep moving,' said Eamon.

As the dawn crept into the castle Harry fell asleep and the tall one was careful not to wake him as he laid him on the couch.

'You need to cover him,' said Rona, nodding at a blanket on the back of the couch.

'You are a good mummy,' said the tall one. 'I never had a good mummy. Can you be my Mummy?' His eyes moved to her exposed breast and he knelt next to her trussed legs. 'You know what is capitalism?' Rona shook her head. 'It means you only give milk to your own baby. He gets all the milk, and there is none left for all the babies in the world that have no milk. Is that fair?' Rona tried to swallow. 'You know what is communism? It means you give me some of your milk.' He grinned and moved his face closer to her breast. As she recoiled her eyes moved past him and caught her mother's.

Harriet was sitting up in the fireplace. She had brushed the ash-dusted hair from her face and was staring at her daughter with her mouth set in that unfamiliar, serious line; her mother without a sneer or scowl or insincere smile. Her mother's true face. Rona kept her eyes on it, so that it filled the whole of her vision, and the room, the man in black kneeling, the furniture and the fireplace that framed Harriet disappeared.

'Come on now! Just a little bit of milk, for the masses, for the people!'

The tall one became only a shadow and she did not see the top of his head beneath her jaw but felt the tongue and lips on her nipple. She slumped against the back of the couch and kicked out, but he brushed her legs aside

and placed his hands on her stomach and neck. She felt
the rasp of stubble on her breast and uttered a tired groan
that did not sound like her own voice and wondered
why she felt so weak. He pushed against her jaw and
was turning her head, but she kept her eyes on the face
of her mother. It seemed to rise then move towards her
until it was above, floating, disembodied, still with the
straightened mouth and steady eyes. She saw another
shadow above her mother's face, something blocking out
the light from the chandelier, and saw her mother's face
framed by her arms which she had raised above her head.
Then her eyes shut of their own accord as something wet
and warm splashed across her face. When she opened her
eyes she was looking down. She saw her own nipple wet
from the tall one's mouth and his broken-open skull on
the couch. Blood was pulsing from a wound the size of
a child's fist. On the floor lay something misshapen and
broken, round like the skull but glistening metal.

'Mum,' said Rona, looking up to find her face, but
Harriet was at the desk, opening a drawer, then Harriet
was at her feet, kneeling, shaking, and getting blood on
her dress as she cut the tape from around her daughter's
legs.

'The others,' said Rona, half to herself. She walked
automatically to the desk, opened a drawer and felt for
the bronze key with a green tassel. The key opened the
cupboard in the wall behind the desk and in a moment her

hands were on the stock and barrel of a shotgun and she was fumbling with cartridges. She turned and closed and cocked the gun in one movement. Harriet picked up the awakened Harry in her arms and the two ducked behind a couch as footsteps came from the spiral stairway.

When the boyish one saw the body his mouth fell open. He looked up as he heard a gurgle from Harry, and his eyes met Rona's. Rona swung up the gun and fired. The shot splintered a chunk out of the wall behind him. He ducked and scrabbled on all fours to the doorway.

'Jurgen!' he called. Rona fired the second barrel after him into the doorway and her hands shook as she lowered the gun to re-load.

'He came from the roof,' said Harriet.

'Yes, one was on the roof and one was sent to the basement. You stay here.'

'Where are you going?'

'I'm going to get them out of my fucking house!' She marched towards the door to the main stair, holding the gun tight into her shoulder. There was another cry of 'Jurgen!' as she went out onto the landing above the hall, and she fired again at a movement by the front door, but the door was open and as she descended the stairs she saw the two men framed in the archway, running across the front lawn into the dark. She slammed the door, drew the bolts and slumped to sit with her back to the door, drawing deep breaths to calm her shivering. Then

she remembered the tower door and went to check the
lock. Her phone was not in her pocket, and the phone
in the kitchen had been smashed off the wall. She ran
upstairs to the study. The phone on the desk had also been
smashed. Harriet pointed at Rona's feet; she had walked
through the pool of blood that surrounded the body and
was marking red footprints across the room. Rona forced
herself to look at the corpse.

The tall one was lying with arms and legs spread in an
expression of surprise. She recognised the broken thing
on the floor. It was the statue of Atlas, the one pilfered
then returned by Kosma and David to the table next to
the fireplace. Rona wondered at the force that her mother
had mustered. Harriet had shattered the statue into pieces
greater than the sum of its parts, and pieces of grey,
lustrous, blood-stained metal lay scattered around the
broken globe. Rona covered the corpse with the blanket
that had covered Harry. She tried to wipe the blood from
her shoes but it had soaked in above the soles. She took
them off.

'We should get out of here,' she said. 'Let's go upstairs.'

'We should call the police.'

'We can't. No phone. We have to wait for Kirsty. She'll
be here at eight.' The thought of Kirsty was enough to
calm Rona. All would be well when Kirsty arrived, and
she had a phone. They would call the police, and Eamon,
and he would come back.

Chapter 23

Eamon and Stevie were almost at the Endpoint steading when they heard the boat on Loch Nish. They took cover behind a grove of larch. The boat was about a hundred yards out, moving fast but they could see clearly at least ten young men and women. A thin girl with a flat face and dreadlocks was standing in the bow.

'Where are they off to?' said Stevie.

'Don't know. But there's no Denis Nyst on board.'

They slowed to a walk as they approached the steading and did not enter by the track but crept around on the forest side of the buildings, listening, hearing only the wind in the tree-tops and the slap of the waves on the shore.

Stevie peered into a shed through a web-covered window and saw Nyst through a window on the other side, in the yard. They ran to the end of the building, but Nyst had gone. They continued on the forest side of the steading but came to a chain-link fence stretching back into the woods and had to retrace their steps. They crossed the yard where they had seen Nyst, and found the path leading to the house. Eamon saw movement in back window, and at the back of the house they found the door open.

The house smelled of dust and damp. A corridor led into a hall where a dust-covered staircase climbed into grey light. Beyond the hall lay a drawing room with furniture covered with sheets, and the half-dismantled head of the torpedo. Plates of aluminium, components and trailing wires lay on the carpet.

'They found it,' said Stevie.

'We found it,' said Eamon. He took out his phone. When RB answered Eamon switched to a video-call and angled the phone at the remains of the warhead. 'You getting this?'

'Loud and clear old boy.' His voice was flat.

'That enough for you?'

'I'll call you back.' RB ended the call. A door slammed at the back of the house. Eamon and Stevie ran. Nyst was turning a corner into the steading.

'Denis!' called Eamon. Nyst turned his head towards them with his mouth slightly open in a half grin and the wind catching his grey curls. He did not stop.

In the yard they saw a shadow move in one of the sheds and they entered a dark corridor. A steel door was still moving on its hinges. Eamon pushed it open they entered a long room carpeted with straw. There was no other door, but a low hatch at the end leading outside. There was a strong smell of dog. They were half-way to the hatch when the steel door behind them slammed shut and a bolt was drawn. Seconds later the hatch slid shut.

'Denis!' Eamon yelled. Stevie examined the hatch and found it made of thick steel.

'Mr Ansgar? Can you hear me?' Nyst's voice came from all around them. 'I said can you hear me?'

'Yes.' They looked up. Nyst's face appeared behind a window high in the end wall.

'Don't worry, you are safe now. We don't want anything bad happening to you. Not yet.'

'Denis, what are you doing? We know about the torpedo. The government knows about the torpedo. They are on their way.'

'Are they? That is interesting. But not my problem. I'm not even thinking about that. I know nothing about the torpedo. That's all her doing.'

'Who is she?'

'She is Brigitta. "The Chosen One."'

'What is she doing? What does she want?'

'You look tired, you should rest. Do you know where
you are? Don't worry, they can't come in, not by the
hair of my chinny chin chin!' He sniggered. 'You should
have just let me release them. None of this would have
happened, if your stupid councils and agencies hadn't
interfered, and that peasant Murachar! He'll regret it!'

'What are you doing Denis?'

'I know how you think. You think we can save the
planet, and all the people on it. You think there can be
billions more. You don't want to hurt anyone. You want
all the gain but none of the pain! I know you Eamon
Ansgar! You are a nice man, a gentleman!'

'Why are there cups in the forest? What are they for?'

'Ah, you like my cups? I had them made specially! The
cups for administering the sacrament. Did you know
the little lady-boy stole them? Can you believe it? In
broad daylight! He was seen by my guards. He got his
comeuppance though, in the end. Nothing to do with me!
Don't accuse me of that! I would never stoop to anything
as pathetic as murder. It is not the solution to anything.
But Brigitta disagrees! She thinks murder is the solution
to everything!' He grinned and chuckled. 'Can you
believe it? She thinks we can murder our way out of our
predicament. "Kill the pig! *Schnell! Schnell*! Kill the pig!"
she says. "Death is purification. Ze purity of *ze aktion*. The
ontological significance of Shock and Horror," and so on

and so on. Too much philosophy! I suspect she is simply a bloodthirsty psychopath. Her only talent is a penchant for violence.'

'And you Denis, what is your talent?'

'Ha ha! Good question! I have none. No talent, but a clear vision, and practically infinite funds. I own a lot. Ha ha! Is that a talent? I have certainly spent more than ten thousand hours on it. I own a very large part of Eastern Ghana, for example. Much more than I own here. This little corner of the world is merely a prelude, an experiment.'

'What kind of an experiment?' There was a pause before Nyst answered, and his face grew serious.

'If I tell you I will have to kill you. So be it. What do you know about Chernobyl? You were still children when it happened. You probably don't know much, but I know a lot. I have been there several times. People are afraid of Chernobyl but it is my favourite place in the world. I heart Chernobyl! Environmentalists place all their hope in the rainforest. They worship it. The rainforest is their cathedral. Chernobyl is mine. The beauty of it is that it was created by man. It was created, and thus it can be re-created.'

'You worship an exploded nuclear power station? A colossal accident?'

'Not the reactor itself! The Zone! The area around Chernobyl. Hundreds of square miles. They evacuated

it. They made an exclusion zone. And the animals, the
bears, the wolves, the deer, they couldn't be excluded.
Chernobyl is the future! Humans dare not live there. They
can never live there. It is the only way to keep them out.
But at Chernobyl nature has blossomed. The buildings,
the fields, the roads, are overcome by nature. Plants and
animals thrive, and all this was given birth to by man!
Chernobyl is a special place, a magical place, because it is
the apotheosis of mankind. It is man giving birth to his
own demise, all that is wrong giving birth to all that is
right! It is the pinnacle of our civilisation! At Chernobyl
we have crucified ourselves for the greater good!' Nyst
was breathing heavily and flecks of spittle had wet the
window pane.

'You want to make a Chernobyl here?' said Eamon.

'Oh yes. Yes, yes, yes!'

'How?'

'You saw what was in my cups?'

'Figures, plastic figures.'

'Models of my enemies. I put in all the council
members, the entire board of Scottish Natural Heritage,
and a nice rendition of the First Minister, and of course
Johnny and his merry band are in there. Nothing but
plastic! Because I am surrounded by incompetence! It
was Pik's job to find the source and he assured me he
could do it! He had it all worked out. He even hired the
Muslims, all the way from South Africa, as a decoy! Can

you imagine? So that when it happens there are three mysterious Muslims in the area, and the first thing that occurs to everyone is that Isis has attacked! That is his cockamamy plan, but I don't care, because he assures me he can find a source! "How?" says I. "Don't worry," says he. "On the internet." "Fine," says I. But he's a bit thick is Pik. Always has been. Fails miserably! Thank God for Brigitta! She finds a source, and right here! On our doorstep! It is Providential. I think Mother Nature has arranged it. Anyway, as I said, I now have to kill you.' There was a click and the sound of the hatch in the outside wall moving. 'They can smell you. They have a great sense of smell, and I don't know how long ago they were fed. Everyone has left apart from me. Here they come! My children! My lovely children!'

Eamon and Stevie moved towards the wall below the window as a black nose and grey snout appeared at the hatch, followed by a thin foreleg, then a large wolf was in the room.

'I don't suppose you have some sort of weapon?' whispered Eamon.

'I've got a pen-knife. How about you?'

'A thermos flask?' The wolf raised a lip, showing long teeth.

'Children of the Forests!' Nyst raised his voice. 'From Northern Canada! The Hunters! The apex of the food chain! For thousands of years we have feared them, killed

and persecuted them, and now it is time for them to
return! It is time for them to reclaim their land!' Another
wolf slunk in behind the first and sidled along the wall.

'Make a run for the hatch,' said Stevie. He took one
step, tripped and fell flat into the straw. Eamon froze as
the largest wolf stepped forward and sniffed Stevie's head.
Then it lay down on the straw and panted.

'Attack! Attack!' screamed Nyst.

Eamon crouched and made a tutting noise. The second
wolf stepped forward to sniff his outstretched fingers.
'I think it's OK,' he said to the motionless Stevie. 'They
seem pretty tame.'

'Attack!' Nyst yelled, thumping his fist against the
spittle-flecked pane.

'Quick before he closes the hatch!' Eamon whispered
and they both crouched and crawled out into the
sunshine. Three more wolves started and drew back as
Eamon and Stevie stood up in the yard surrounded by
chain-link fence.

'Bad case of false advertising. These beasts look
pretty used to humans.' Stevie patted one on the head.
Somewhere behind them a heavy door slammed. Eamon
looked back at the building and then up. The sound was
coming from somewhere to the west but at the same time
from all around, as if working its way out of the ground.
It was a roar and a heavy thud and a scream, then a dark

ugly shape with two sets of scything blades; a Chinook between themselves and the sun.

'Well done RB!' said Eamon.

'They'll be coming down behind the house,' shouted Stevie. Eamon began to scramble up the fence but Stevie opened the gate at the end of the yard and Eamon climbed down to follow him.

On the patch of open ground between the steading and the house the Chinook was landing. Eamon had witnessed this a hundred times in Afghanistan, and it had always inspired awe. It was obvious, to any sane person, that this was a monstrous heresy against the laws of physics, a collection of magics guided by some sorcerer in an eyeless helmet. The thing was landing at an angle, the rear touching the ground as the nose tipped skywards, like a beast rearing on its tiny, deformed hindlegs, screaming at the sky. The rear door was open, about to void something revolting onto the earth, and the hurricane that came with the machine was casting swirls and tornados of dust against the blue and sunlight. Eamon and Stevie flattened themselves against the ground, shielding their eyes. Above the roar of the rotors they heard another sound; a grinding, whining, crunching, amid the shouts of men, but they were still staring into the grass and spitting out dust when they heard the voice. It was amplified and stilted; the voice of a well-trained robot.

'Which one of you is Eamon Ansgar?'

Eamon lifted his head and looked up at a hulking, grey, green figure; a mass of something plastic, bug-eyed, wearing wellington boots. He raised a finger like a schoolboy.

'Where is the device?' The voice was not coming from behind the gasmask that covered the man's face but from somewhere on his chest. Eamon pointed towards the house, and the green figure signalled to others that were being disgorged from the ramp along with the source of the grinding and roaring; a kind of gun-less tank, with tracks and a turret. A line of men in NBC suits carrying rifles jogged past them into the back door of Endpoint. Others were fanning out, forming a perimeter around the Chinook, now with its forelegs on the ground and the scream of the rotors diminishing. Eamon and Stevie followed the soldiers into the house.

They passed an armed, suited figure at the door. The house was quiet and cool. In the drawing room shadows hunched around the skeleton of the warhead, half-lit by torches and tablets. Something beeped. Eamon realised they were the only ones not wearing gasmasks. He reached into his pocket but could not find a handkerchief. The men around the warhead squawked to each other with electronic voices as a probe was inserted into the structure.

'Nothing?' said one.

'Nothing,' said another.

A mask turned towards Eamon. 'Who had access to this device?'

'Denis Nyst, Brigitta. Their men.'

'Where are they?'

'Nyst was here, before you arrived. Brigitta and the others took a boat, towards Duncul. What have they done?'

'What does Nyst look like?'

Eamon described him and Brigitta. The man touched a button on his neck and four bug-eyed men left the room.

'What have they done?' said Eamon.

'This is a nuclear device sir. They've removed the plutonium.'

'That's the radioactive bit?'

'Correct.'

Eamon could feel his mind slowing down. The amphetamines and the codeine were wearing off. He closed his eyes and felt as if he was beginning to fall. He sat on a couch. 'You can detect the plutonium?' he said. In his mind's eye he was looking down a well. The well was dark and cool, and endless.

'Yes.'

'It's not here? In this room?'

'Not in this room. But it's an alpha emitter. It can't be detected from long range. You have to be within a few metres.'

'Within a few metres,' repeated Eamon, struggling to open his eyes.

'Do you have any more information about the whereabouts of the plutonium sir?'

'Nyst must have it.' When he closed his eyes he could see the bottom of the well, a point of shimmering water a mile below. The pain in his ankle had returned, like a twisting knife. 'No, not Nyst, perhaps Brigitta. Brigitta has gone.'

'What is her destination? Sir?'

'I don't know. How is it dangerous? If it is not going to explode, and it is radioactive only for a few meters, why all the suits?'

'The danger is if a particle is inhaled or swallowed.' The voice was muffled as the man touched his neck. He spoke on a radio to his men, then out loud; 'A man wearing a smock you say?'

'Yes.'

'He's been seen on a boat.'

'Going in which direction?'

The hand reached for the neck and the voice was muffled, then returned to the speaker on the chest. 'East. On Loch Nish. Towards Duncul.'

'East. On Loch Nish,' Eamon repeated.

'Where is he going?' said the speaker.

'Going away. Getting away. Unless. I don't know.'
Eamon closed his eyes and felt the coolness of the well

around him. He was falling. At the bottom of the well was water, and something else. A stone cup. The sound of the rotors was suddenly there, filling the room. Eamon opened his eyes as a soldier entered with the smell of woodsmoke.

'Fire,' said Eamon, suddenly awake, getting up, moving towards the back door.

The whole steading roof was burning and flames were moving back from the building across the dry, overgrown lawn towards the Chinook and the house. The wind had grown stronger, straight from the west, and the day was the latest in a month of bright, dry days. The forest beyond the steading had already caught. He turned to the bug eyes looking over his shoulder. 'What does it look like?' he said.

'What does what look like?'

'The plutonium. What does it look like?'

'It's a metal. It looks like metal.'

'What colour?' The man touched his neck and consulted a soldier holding a tablet.

'Grey. A grey metal. Like lead, but shiny. The Chinook has to take off because of the fire. You need to come with us.'

'Does it melt?'

'What do you mean?'

'Does it melt? Will it melt in a fire? Like lead? Or is it hard? Like steel?' Again the man touched his neck and turned to the other.

'It melts at six hundred degrees. We need to go.'

'No. Not melt. Does it burn? Like…aluminium?'

'We have to go now!'

'No!' shouted Eamon, above the roar of the Chinook. 'Does it burn?' Again, the man touched his neck and consulted.

'Burns at four hundred degrees.'

'How hot is this fire?'

'What do you mean?'

'How many degrees? This fire! A forest fire!' The man turned to the man with the tablet and turned back to Eamon.

'A thousand degrees plus.'

'You need to warn Duncul, the conference on Murachar's croft and everyone downwind. They need to get out. It's here. It's in the cups. Nyst put the plutonium in the cups!'

Chapter 24

It was still early when Sergeant Peters realised that today was going to be one of those days when he thought about leaving the police. For others, older than him, it was often the only subject of conversation. Peters had not yet reached that level of disillusion. If the idealism of his youth could have been weighed against the encroaching cynicism, the balance would still tip, he was sure, in the direction of idealism. But he was also sure that the balance had begun to move the other way. It was being moved by things like the chopper ride to Halan.

It was something to do with it not being a police helicopter and not being piloted by an officer. Since Peters' childhood the world had always divided into civilian and non-civilian. Police and not police. He was

sure that if there had been a police pilot he would not
have faced a dilemma about the other aircraft, the one
that the pilot had said had left the imprint of its landing
gear on the grass. He would have known what to do
about it. But now he could not make up his mind whether
to tell anyone. He was not a detective. He was not meant
to do a detective's job. Detectives didn't like you to do
that. He wasn't really meant to think about these things
at all. There had been a report of a body there. Then
there had been no body there. In the meantime, there
had been another chopper there. This fact had been
spotted by a civilian pilot. The civilian pilot would have
to be interviewed by a detective. Then the detective
would have to be flown out to Halan. Then the detective
would have to decide to fly in a forensics team. And all
this would have to be justified, in writing, against his
own observation that what had happened at Halan was
a bunch of teenagers from Inverish had got drunk and
smashed windows. The whole system, Peters considered,
was just so clumsy. So inept. So unprofessional. That
was why he had not told anyone, he was sure. And yet it
bothered him, even now as he stood at the entrance to the
long drive that led into the woods and the gate of Johnny
Murachar's croft. It bothered him because he realised he
was part of that apparatus that did things so clumsily. It
bothered him because he knew he had missed something.

He knew he had made another mistake, just like the one that had led him to be the only one here.

One officer, and there were hundreds of civilians lining up to enter the Alt-Scot convention. And the parking was all messed up. The cars were lined up barely off the track all the way back to the head of the loch. That was going to cause chaos if they needed to get an ambulance or more police in. If there was trouble, some kind of protest, it could all end very badly. He considered how trouble was a real possibility as he watched the security guards at the make-shift barrier.

They were three Eastern European body builders, two with shaved heads and one with a sort of Hitler haircut. They were passing a hand-held metal-detector over everyone and frisking anyone that set it off, men and women. All of this was bad, bad practice. No-one had objected, yet. But if there was a problem, if a woman objected to the search, for example... Sergeant Peters could feel the beginnings of a kind of panic in his throat, and he had to swallow hard. He watched the crowd. They were young and old, black and white, rich and not-so-rich. All sorts, but all smartly dressed. The men were in tweed jackets and suits and ties. The women in smart skirts and jewellery. They were not the same crowd that he watched when he was on duty at the music festivals. There were no men in tights and novelty hats, no women in bras and wellies. No smell of marijuana to add a sweet note to the

stench of seaweed from the shore. No-one was drunk.
Quite a few of them had greeted him with, 'Morning
Constable!' They all looked like upstanding citizens, until
the guy in the boat arrived.

There was a fresh wind from the west, whipping frothy
waves onto the shore that masked the sound of the
outboard until the boat hit the rocks below the road. It
slid up the beach with an ugly collection of crunches and
cracks as the propeller destroyed itself. The line of men
and women turned their heads as one to see the man in
the boat lurch forward and fall flat, out of sight into the
bilge. He stood up dripping wet and shook himself like
a dog. He had untidy, curly grey hair, the head of a man
who had never grown up; a long smock, of some kind of
earth-friendly colour, and green wellies on bare legs. He
was a music festival man. He stumbled out of the boat
and over the weed-covered boulders onto the road and
stared with disdain at the queue. Peters only had enough
time to think the word 'Trouble,' once, before Denis Nyst
had walked up to the three thugs with a metal detector.

'There is a line. You must wait in line,' said Hitler
haircut. 'And where is your ticket?'

'Ticket?' said Nyst. 'I don't need a ticket. I am on the
list.' Hitler haircut grinned a little in disbelief but took out
his phone and thumbed the screen.

'What is name?'

Denis Nyst gave it. The security guard stared hard at the screen, then hard at Nyst. He showed the screen to his colleagues. They shrugged and nodded. Nyst started to walk past them.

'One moment,' said Hitler haircut. He indicated that Nyst should stretch out his arms. Nyst complied and the detecting wand was passed around the dripping tunic. There were no beeps or squeaks, and in a moment he had passed the barrier and was walking up the road towards the croft, whistling.

The eyes of the Alt-Scot delegates followed the strange man until he was small in the distance, then their eyes returned to the guards carrying on their business, or to the sunlight jumping from the waves on the loch behind, but mainly to the screens of phones, where they found themselves, the conference, Acturus and Murachar, beginning like the first crackling of flames at the base of a fire, to be the subject of the day. They were trending; eliciting the ever-ready sparks of anger, motivating news-anchors and pundits, bloggers, vloggers, tweeters, influencers and trolls, all caught up in the great maelstrom of vitriol. There were perhaps fifty delegates in that line at the barrier and not one looked up, skywards, westwards to the tower of smoke emerging over the Ardven hill, still below the sun, but building, flourishing and yearning to encompass it.

At the doorstep of the Old Schoolhouse Guesthouse Mo, Solly and Qualin did not need the finger of the taxi driver to show them the fire consuming the Ardven forest. They had already watched the beginnings of the blaze from the bedroom window. Solly had spotted the smoke and had paused the game. Someone had said, 'That's right at the house.' They had watched in silence as a Chinook had risen from the smoke and descended again. Mo had checked his watch and looked down the road for the taxi. Solly had called Eilidh again, making sure of where she would meet them at the airport. Qualin had made one last effort to tidy the room.

'It's a big one,' said the taxi driver as he put their bags in the boot. 'It's in the trees now.' There had been no comment from his three passengers. The driver sized up the two in the back seat via the rear-view mirror and the one in the passenger seat via the corner of his eye. It was going to be a long drive. They didn't say a word until they had reached the end of the mile-long straggle of houses along the loch that was the village of Inverish and were passing the stone jetty at the end where a bright orange RIB was moored.

'Is that Malky's boat?' said Mo.

'Yep. Police impounded it here,' said Solly.

'Pull over here *bru*,' said Mo. The driver pulled over and listened, which turned out to be useful, as the police were to ask him for every detail of the conversation several times in the coming days.

'What's up?' said Qualin.

'I'm going back.'

'Mo, the plane is at five. We don't have time for this.'

'I can take Malky's boat.'

'There's gonna be police, army even. That's an army helicopter.'

'You go on. Get on the plane.'

'What's your problem *bru*? What the hell is your problem?'

'I know something you don't. Leave it at that.'

'What?'

In reply Mo touched his phone screen and held it up so Qualin could see a yellow trefoil.

'This sign. You know what this means?'

'Nuclear. Radioactivy.'

'Precisely my brother. This sign was on the torpedo.'

'You're kidding me.'

'I saw it. Malky never told me that. He said "torpedo" not "nuclear torpedo".'

'Check this.' Solly showed his phone screen to the others. It showed the three of them wearing *kufis* and carrying rifles across their chests, looking serious. They were on a hilltop, with mountains and a loch behind. Three Muslims with high-powered hunting rifles.

'This comes from Pik,' said Mo. 'He took this picture when we were hunting. What is this on?'

'My Facebook! It's on my Facebook! It's on Twitter too.'

'What's it say?'

'In the name of Allah the most merciful…Shit Shit Shit! Operation carried out against the *kaffur* at Ardven Peninsula in vengenance for the attacks on the Caliphate…Isis. It is basically saying we are Isis!'

'We gotta go. Driver! We need to go.'

'They can't put anything on us. We didn't do nothing.'

'I'm going back. You go,' said Mo. He got out of the car and began walking back. Mo and Qualin followed, calling his name.

The driver wound down his window. 'Hey, this is a booked car eh?'

Qualin jogged back to pay him.

'Guys, take the cab,' said Mo. 'You're right. I'm going to be arrested. You are going to be arrested if you don't leave, now! Eilidh is waiting for you Solly.'

'Eilidh is a big girl. She can take a plane by herself.'

'They can arrest us, but we haven't done anything,' said Qualin.

'We gave her a torpedo. A nuclear torpedo.'

'She made us find it! We are not Isis! I'm not even a Muslim!'

'It doesn't matter. We gonna lose the money. When it is terrorism everything is different. All the money, all the bank accounts gonna be frozen.'

'I can transfer money to my cousin now.'

'OK, your cousin is going to be arrested and lose all his money. And if he sends it to his cousin that cousin is going to be arrested. Trust me, don't transfer any money to anybody.'

'What we gonna do?'

'I don't know. What we can.'

Chapter 25

'It is in the cups!' Eamon said, and repeated, and explained, to the masks and bug-eyes, who touched the buttons on their necks and took time to converse.

Outside, the Chinook raised its nose from the field as the flames crept windwards, and lowered it, and raised it, lifted off and landed closer to the house, while the flames advanced across the dry grass between the house and steading.

'The cups are spread out on altars along the fire-break,' said Eamon. 'About a quarter-mile into the forest. Nyst told me his plan was to make this place like Chernobyl. He wants to irradiate and poison the whole of Ardven so that it can be abandoned to nature. That is his goal! What happens if he puts the plutonium in the cups, and the fire reaches them?'

'According to the scientists here, the plutonium will burn. It will oxidise and go up in smoke.'

'And it will still be radioactive?'

'Yes.'

'And anywhere the smoke goes will be a radioactive zone! Am I right?'

'Yes.'

'For how long?'

'As far as we are concerned, forever.' The gloved hands unclipped a strap and tore off the mask to reveal the sweating, reddened face of a man half Eamon's age. 'Captain Aidan Bartell,' he said in a clipped Northern accent, offering a hand. 'Is there a road or track to the altars?'

'Yes.'

'Then we can take the vehicle.'

As left the house they raised their arms against the heat of the fire. The Chinook was almost airborne, an Armageddon of noise challenging the flames with its portable storm. But it had backed right up to the house as the fire had crept across the lawn and as Bartell was about to order his men up the ramp the rear rotor blades struck the roof of an out-house. The nose fell and in ten seconds the pilots had left the cabin.

'Get out of here!' shouted Bartell to the soldiers, 'Get beyond the house, down to the shore, and take cover!'

The grass was burning around the tracks of the gun-less tank and the door-handle hot to touch.

Inside the heat was stifling. Bartell pressed switches, and cool air filled the chamber. He sat in the only seat and gunned the engine as Eamon and Stevie held onto straps hanging from the ceiling. The only window was a small pain of greenish glass at driver's eye-level but around him were a row of screens showing a panorama of the burning steading and forest, the house behind them, and the Chinook, the blades of the forward rotor still flickering shadows. Bartell pulled on a joystick and the machine lurched and hit something hard. He pressed some buttons and the images changed to the ground before them.

'Tricky thing to drive. Still not quite got the hang of it.' Then they were moving at a surprising pace, bouncing over the lawn and crashing through a picket-fence. Eamon guided him to the track that ran along the shore. Bartlett slowed as they neared the gate at the end of the track.

'I'll open it,' said Stevie. Bartell revved the engine and knocked the gate off its hinges.

'Just follow the firebreak,' said Eamon. But the smoke had brought the visibility down to a couple of metres. 'You need to move faster! Faster!'

'The police in Duncul have been notified,' said Bartell. 'They'll have started evacuating the conference and the village.'

Eamon thought about 'the police in Duncul'. That meant Sergeant Peters, on his own. He took out his phone and called Rona's mobile.

'Hello honey!' The voice was sarcastic and masculine.

'Who's that?'

'Don't you recognise me honey? It's me! I want you honey! When are you coming home?'

'Where's Rona?' said Eamon. The call ended. He re-dialled and got voicemail. He called the castle landline but there was no answer. The tank swung and bounced up the firebreak.

'Someone has her phone. That means they're at Duncul,' said Eamon.

The tank stopped. 'Is this what you are looking for?' said Bartell.

Eamon peered at a screen. 'Yes. I'll get it.' Wreaths of smoke twisted around the altar and cup.

'You can't take the cup in here,' said Bartlett. 'There's a container on the side of the vehicle. Put the contents in there.' He gave Eamon and Stevie gas masks and opened the door.

They emerged into the sound of their own breathing, the crackle of burning branches and a subtle roar from all around. The pines disappeared into smoke above. Ash drifted and fell like snow. Eamon lifted the cup and found it heavy and cold to the touch. He looked in at the figures and grey shapes before tipping them into the container.

'One down. How many are to go?' asked Bartlett when they were back in the tank.

'I don't know. I've only seen three. I'm assuming there are more, further up,' said Eamon. Beyond the crackling of the fire, they heard a series of explosions.

'That'll be the Chinook,' said Stevie.

On the high ground of Johnny Murachar's croft with a view over tents and marquees among the vegetable-patches, fields and barns, now teeming with delegates, technicians, film-crews and catering staff amid the women in head scarves and men in dungarees, Acturus McBean was sitting beneath a gazebo, smiling for the camera

'What kind of a man is Acturus McBean? We see a lot of you on television but this morning, I want to go a little deeper than the politics and find out about the real you.'

'Fire away Andrew! But I warn you, I'm a very dull fellow!' McBean sunk lower into the bright leather armchair.

'You were born in nineteen-seventy-three, into a working-class family in a former mining village in Fife. Yet you say you are a lifelong fan of Margaret Thatcher. How did that go down with your family?'

'I have been blessed with a wonderful mother and father, and brothers and sisters who have always supported me. When I started my own business, they were there to support me, and when I went into politics, they supported me.'

'And yet I have here a quote from your older brother, from an interview last year, notoriously he said you were "a traitor to your class." And he said your father hadn't spoken to you for a decade. How does that square with your idea of support?'

'Well, as you know Andrew, families are complicated, and everyone in a family is entitled to their own ideas. Of course, we in the SIC have always embraced and welcomed diversity of opinion. We are not a homogenous, lickspittle cult like our opponents, the socialists and unionists. We stand for freedom of speech, economic freedom...' His voice trailed off. Andrew followed his gaze to a tall figure walking up the croft; a man with grey hair, wearing a tunic and wellington boots, looking at the ground, oblivious to the stares of delegates.

'Crikey!' said the interviewer, 'Denis Nyst! Cut this! Sorry Acturus, we'll come back...You, whatever your name is, get him!' he urged a young woman assistant who jogged after Nyst.

'Mr Nyst! Mr Nyst!' she called, but he did not turn until she was standing close enough to smell the sweat and woodsmoke from his tunic. He turned with a scowl.

'Mr Nyst, we would like to interview you, if possible? We're interviewing Acturus McBean right now…'

'Where?'

She pointed. Nyst followed her finger and grinned.

'I'll be with you in a couple of minutes.' He continued along the path. The assistant turned to Andrew and Acturus to give a thumbs up. But Acturus wasn't looking at her. He was looking up at the sky as he sniffed the air.

'Something burning,' he said.

Sergeant Peters was also smelling the air and looking west when his phone rang.

'Sergeant Colin Peters?' said a smooth voice.

'Yes.'

'This is Chief Superintendent Macdonald.'

Peters had once heard the Chief Superintendent make a speech but had never been personally addressed by him.

'Colin, are you currently at Johnny Murachar's, at the conference?'

'Yes, Sir.'

'How many delegates are there, so far?'

'About four hundred.'

'Four hundred?'

'Probably more. There's a queue.'

'Colin, I know you are on your own, but they have to be evacuated.'

'Evacuated?'

'Yes. Everyone has to leave the croft. Immediately. There's a fire.'

'Yes Sir, I've noticed. I can see smoke on the hill.'

'Colin, have you got a HAZMAT kit in the car?'

'Yes.'

'Put it on.'

'Yes Sir. Why?'

'Put it on. Don't breathe the smoke.'

'Why?'

'There's a possibility of a release of radioactive material.'

'Oh.'

'I'm sending a team, now, from Inverness. But you have to get the people out. Turn them around.'

'Where are they to go?'

'It doesn't matter. As far away from Ardven as possible. But Colin...'

'Yes?'

'Don't panic.'

'Yessir.'

'Good man. You can call this number. It's my direct line.' The call ended.

Peters went to the boot of the car. He tried not to hurry but was half holding his breath against the growing smell of smoke. Not actual smoke yet, he told himself. Only the smell of smoke. He popped the fasteners on the lid of the HAZMAT box that had never been opened. It was for chemical spills; in case a truck carrying chemicals crashed. He put on the full facemask, bodysuit and the long, luminous yellow gloves, and turned to the queue and the security guards. Those that weren't staring at the thick clouds of smoke billowing up in the west had watched him change from a comforting, friendly policeman into a species of alien.

The tank was at the second altar when the smoke ahead became brighter with a dull, shifting light. They were at the third when Eamon and Stevie stepped out of the tank and felt the heat of the fire.

'How much further?' said Bartell, when they were back inside.

'I don't know,' said Eamon. 'We've never been further up the hill.'

'The fire is already up there.'

'We have to go,' said Eamon. 'We have no choice!'

Bartell moved the tank forward. 'The air temperature out there is almost fifty,' he said.

Eamon watched the screens. There was smoke on all sides; a grey wall punctured with flashes of orange.

'I can't see a thing!' Bartell shouted.

'Just keep going up the path! You can follow the path!'

'Look!' said Bartell. He pointed at a screen. There was a clear image of trees wrapped in flames whipped to a frenzy by the wind. 'We've got to go back!' He swung the tank to the side, knocking Eamon and Stevie off their feet. Stevie picked himself up and placed his hand over Bartell's on the joystick, moving the tank back to the track.

'We're almost there,' he said. The altar and cup loomed on a screen.

'You can't go out there. It's pointless!' said Bartell.

Eamon's ankle was a ball of pain, and he told himself again that it was only a sprain. It was only the inflamed tissue pressing on nerve endings. There was nothing broken, no serious damage. His mind had stopped flickering but he felt hollowed out. Coming down from speed was all about not being afraid of the fear, he told himself. But he knew he was a shell of a man going out into the furnace, a scrap of flesh in rags of clothes, like an animated corpse.

'Leave it Eamon,' said Stevie.

'You stay here,' said Eamon, opening the door.

It was like opening an oven. The heat surged over and through him and the grass beneath his feet was smoking. He turned to the leeward side of the tank, sheltering for a few seconds. Yes, the drugs had worn off, but this still did not feel real. The breathing inside the mask sounded like the breathing of another man. The body of the tank was warm but the tracks were cool and wet from the churned-up forest floor. For a moment he felt safe and worried that he was still caught in the unreal world conjured by heroin and meta-amphetamine. That was always the problem, he remembered from Afghan; how do you know when things are real again?

He moved along the tank-side into the withering heat. There was smoke rising from the bowl of the cup on the altar. He could smell burning rubber and put his hand to his mask to find it too hot to touch. He approached the altar on his knees, keeping in the lee of the stones and reaching up for the cup. It was hot, but not too hot. It was almost cool, he told himself. He could feel the coolness penetrating his hands as he brought the cup down and looked into the bowl. The contents had melted into a pool of smoking liquid; smoke was also rising from his fingers, and as he dropped the cup skin tore from the flesh. The liquid spilled into the grass. He was too late. He fell back and curled into a ball around his burning hands. It was too late. He looked up at the track of the tank and saw it moving. His mind sought out the cool darkness of the well. The tank was not moving: he was moving. Someone was pulling him by the ankles. There was a loud bang as a burning branch fell onto the tank and showered him with sparks. He was too late. Stevie pulled him through the rear hatch, slammed it shut and pulled off both their masks. The tank rattled and bumped downhill.

'There's more!' shouted Eamon.

'It's too late,' said Stevie, calmly.

'The fire is across the break behind us!' said Bartell. 'We can't get back down!'

'There's a way; another break, there!' Stevie pointed at a screen. All the screens were bright orange.

'It's nothing but flames!' shouted Bartell.

'Calm down. Go into the centre there, where it's darker. Go through the flames. They can't have got that far up the hill yet. Put the boot down! Drive man!'

Chapter 26

The wind that drove the fire was a steady, dry gale, whipping froth from the top the sharp waves that moved in ranks from the Hebrides to vanish in a puff of spray on the mainland shore. If the wind had had its way the flames would have behaved as orderly as the waves and climbed the hill of Ardven in line abreast. But the fire fought back and blustered, sparked and roared in the face of the wind.

First it devoured the Endpoint steading, chewing even on the stone walls until they grew dry in its mouth and were left like bones on the ground. Then it seized the abandoned Chinook, seeking with its many tongues the taste of aviation fuel, sucking it in and spitting out flame-balls. In half an hour the aircraft had become a skeleton.

The fire rewarded itself with another delicacy; a gas cylinder, at the back wall of the kitchen, exploding it with an exuberant pop. The house, which was old and tired and depressed by its recent inhabitant, went up with gratitude, like a bundle of sticks. The fire only lost enthusiasm for its journey west when it came up against the sea. Then it bent all energy to the east, and growing drunk with power on this front, became whimsical, moved in fits and starts, and wanted to move along the forests of the shore, on both north and south sides of the peninsula, while leaving the interior to last. It tore fastest along the northern face of the hill and the clouds of smoke rose up over the sun to darken the faces of the delegates at Murachar's croft, and cars began to start at the edge of the road along the loch-side. In Duncul phones began to buzz, beep and sing, and messages pile up:

'Don't breathe the smoke!!!'

'Stay inside!!!'

'Get out of Duncul!!!'

'Chemicals in smoke!!!!'

'Terrorist attack outside Duncul! Something to do with the fire!'

The first to leave were the TV crews. The antennae retracted and dropping all association with the locals, without even pausing for a tweet, the occupants of the white vans sped east.

The smoke entered the village like an army of
phantoms. Clouds appeared in gardens and on the roads,
puffed in through kitchen windows and wafted over
rooftops, making shadows chase across the lawns.

Morvin Mackay closed his windows, switched on the
television, and made a cup of tea. Lydia Smythe came in
from the garden but carried on knitting. Olivier Martin,
on holiday from Paris, put his two children and wife in
the car and took the first corner on the road to Aberfashie
at eighty-five miles-per- hour. David and John Nicolson,
builders, donned full face masks and went house to
house banging on doors. Donald Johnson took the school
minivan without filling in the log-book and began picking
up pensioners. Edwina Murray consulted Dr Simmonds
who told her to pack a suitcase. In the woods behind The
Avenue a thin boy with curly hair covered his face with a
scarf and aimed his long lens at the panicking villagers.
In Duncul Castle Rona Ansgar and Harriet McColl were
watching the smoke when they saw the young men and
women spread out along the wall at the bottom of the
drive. A girl with black hair was eating an apple. A thin
man was leaning on a baseball bat. Rona recognised the
sad one and the boyish one. A young woman with blonde
dreadlocks began leading them across the lawn through
the wisps of white.

'Look in the cupboard behind the desk for shells,' said
Rona. She picked up the shotgun. 'They can't get in the

front or tower doors, not unless they have a battering ram, and there are no windows on the ground floor.'

'They know about the window to the cellar,' said Harriet. Rona handed her the gun.

She ran down the tower stair to the cellar door. The ladder was still in place beneath the open window, where smoke was filtering in. She heard a shout from outside as she brought the ladder clattering to the floor, then locked the door behind her. As she climbed the stair, she heard two shots.

The study was filled with smoke. Harry was on the couch expelling a regular cough from his tiny chest and Harriet was pointing the shotgun out of the window.

'Caught one trying to climb the drainpipe onto the porch roof.'

'You shot him?'

'I shot over his head.' She re-loaded the gun.

'I have to take Harry out of the smoke,' said Rona, coughing.

Harriet fired again. 'Go upstairs to the bedroom. Lock the door and window.'

'What do they want? What on earth do they want?'

'It doesn't matter what they want. They're not getting it!' She fired again. The shot was replied by a thumping from below.

'What's that?'

'The front door. Or maybe they're in the cellar.'

'Get up those stairs!' shouted Harriet. She took a pair of cartridges from a bulging pocket in her dress and re-loaded.

The tank roared up a dark, smoke-filled tunnel between the pines. Eamon lay on the floor, curled into a ball around his hands. Stevie kept his eyes on the forward view, hoping for the gate that would open onto the hill, but Bartell slowed as flames appeared, clearing the air around them and leaping across the firebreak

'There's no way out!' Bartell's face was pale.

'Go back down!' said Stevie.

'It's behind us too!' Stevie looked at the screens. The rear facing camera showed only flames and smoke.

'We're going to burn!'

'Go left, down the hill! Look there!' Stevie pointed to a gap in the trees. Bartell swung into a path that was too narrow for the tank and it slammed against a tree. 'Reverse!' shouted Stevie. The tank reversed into another trunk.

'Put your mask on, open the door!' Stevie pulled Eamon to his feet and forced a mask over his face. They opened the door to a torrent of smoke and heat. 'Downhill! Follow the path!' They ducked beneath low branches, followed the twisting, falling deer track and hoped that it was leading away from the flames.

'We need to run! Get to the shore!' Stevie picked up Eamon and swung him over his shoulder. 'Move!' Flames leapt from tree to tree above. Through the branches Stevie saw the silver of Loch Nish. He ran and lost the path, crashed through branches, fell, dropped Eamon, dragged him, picked him up, while Bartell scrabbled in his wake, losing his mask, coughing, falling, and running the last few yards along the spine of a rocky promontory. Behind them the forest roared and felt their backs with heat. The sea was twenty feet below, a high tide, licking the base of the rock.

'Jump!' shouted Stevie.

In the water the waves lapped over their heads, and they tore off water-filled masks. They swam, still with the heat of the flames on the back of their heads. A hundred yards out the smoke had thinned, and they turned to look at the burning forest.

'It's too late,' said Eamon.

'They're evacuating Duncul. The police will have everybody out,' said Bartell.

'The Police in Duncul is Sergeant Peters,' said Eamon.

By the time Denis Nyst arrived at the top of Murachar's croft the smoke had swarmed into the lower part and he could look down with a grin on the chaos.

A continuous blare of horns sounded from the shore as a hundred drivers started on the single-track road to

Duncul at the same time. Others had turned back along the road to the croft, mistaking it for another way out. Cars had been abandoned, doors left open, and people were hurrying up to higher ground to get out of the smoke. Nyst turned his back on them to walk further up.

When he came to the twig marker, the sock and the cartridge he took a clumsily made plastic gun from the pocket in his smock. It looked like a toy gun and was made of grey plastic cubes and cylinders produced by the 3D printer, but a piece hinged upwards from the handle to accept the real cartridge. Nyst's grin widened.

Below on the croft the paths were thick with coughing, spluttering delegates, holding handkerchiefs or parts of their clothing to their mouths. At the top someone had clipped a hole in the chain-link and people were ducking their heads to climbed through. Nyst cursed as he saw Acturus McBean step into the woods.

The far shore of Loch Nish was a half-mile away and Stevie doubted his brother was up to the swim. He was barely able to tread water, and the waves were washing over his head. Further out the waves were higher, and the tide fast. They would have to stay as close into the shore as the heat would allow until the fire burned out. He was wondering how long that would take when he heard an outboard.

Malky's bright orange RIB was casting up beats of
spray and heading straight towards them. Stevie raised
his arm, fearing they would be run down, but the note
of the engine lowered and the boat slowed. There was a
soldier wielding a boathook on the prow and ten soldiers
crouched on the deck, and two Chinook pilots, and in the
stern at the controls three men in civilian clothes that he
did not recognise. A black man with a sleepy expression,
another with lighter skin and a worried look, and another
with a moustache, at the helm, looking like he was in
charge.

'Put on your masks,' croaked Eamon as they pulled him
on board. 'Turn the boat! Get out of the smoke!'

'Who are these guys?' Bartell asked his men when he
had been dragged over the gunwale and laid on the deck.

'They came from Inverish,' said a soldier. 'The heat
from the burning house was too much so we were in the
sea at the end of the jetty. They picked us up there.'

'Do as he says,' said Bartell. 'Get out of the smoke.
Take us further out.'

'Sir we have a reading on the Geiger counter. Several
readings.'

'Turn the boat!'

'There is no radioactivity in the smoke. Nothing. Dr
Jenkins here says it is highly unlikely that there was any
plutonium in the cups in the forest.'

Eamon raised his head and Stevie pulled him to a sitting position.

'Not in the cups?' said Bartell.

'No sir.'

'That's, good news.'

'Aye, but if it's not in the cups where is it?' said Stevie.

'Brigitta,' croaked Eamon. 'Brigitta must have it.'

'Where?'

'She went to Duncul.' Stevie pointed east.

Mo turned the boat and told them all to lie down as the prow lifted and they sped up the coast. As a soldier bandaged his hands Eamon raised his eyes above the gunwale to see Sergeant Peter's car, blue lights flashing. The solitary policeman in a gas mask was waving his arms in a futile attempt to sort out the traffic. Cars had been abandoned in the ditch. Men and women were running towards the head of the loch.

As the boat neared the end of the loch it slowed and Stevie directed them to the mouth of the Ash, then the engine was opened to full throttle as they sped up the river.

At the Ash Bridge they heard gunfire. Mo ran the boat up a shallow bank and the soldiers ran ahead through the woods. Stevie helped his stumbling brother follow. When they caught up with the others at the wall between the woods and castle grounds Bartell and Stevie pulled themselves up to look across the lawn and Eamon peered through the doorway.

Harriet was standing at a battlement on the roof, a thin figure in a grey dress with long grey hair trailing in the wind, firing a shotgun down into the clouds of smoke, reloading, taking aim, firing. Beneath her in the smoke the *Autonomass* were assailing the castle. There was one on the porch and another one on the kitchen-wing roof and another climbing a drainpipe. There were several cowering in the wisteria along the back wall.

As Eamon watched a tall, lumbering figure came running from the back of the castle, carrying an axe handle. Mike Mack swung it into the torso of a thin young man. The youth crumpled and Mike raised the club above his head. The youth raised his arm, and the axe handle cracked against it. Mike raised the handle and brought it down again and again.

'Mike!' shouted Stevie. Mike stopped.

Bartell led his men through the door in the wall, arranged them in a line with rifles at their shoulders, and started across the lawn. It was all they had to do. The figures in black began to run in the opposite direction, some towards Tarr Bow, some towards the main gate. Eamon felt himself falling, closed his eyes, and saw the bottom of the well rise towards him.

When Eamon came conscious he was lying on his back on a swaying stretcher looking up at blue sky through smoke, and the fire in his leg and hands was being held at bay by morphine. The view changed to the arch above the front door. He was sure he could smell the oak of the door and feel the iron handle in his hand. Then the vaults swayed above him as they crossed the hall: old, red sandstone, worn smooth at the edges, the oldest part of Duncul that had been built, destroyed and rebuilt over hundreds of years. He felt the great pile of history above the vaults, and even more ancient, below the flagstones, in the cellar; lies, truth, sins, loves; history fading into the world before history. The stretcher swayed and tipped as they carried him up the main stair. She came down to the first landing with her son's face pressed to her shoulder. She seemed taller and stronger; a towering woman. Then he saw that her face was marked with trails of tears, and the fingers that held Harry were stiff and white-knuckled. Her mouth opened but he could not hear her voice above the shouts and clatter of boots on the stairs. They took him up another flight to the sitting room, then up another. He imagined that for some reason they were going to lay him on the roof, but they stopped at the study. He tried to hear what the voices were saying, but the words were broken up into dull notes without meaning.

He saw Stevie, Bartell, then Rona, then Harriet, smiling, and soldiers. Then there were loud shouts, all the soldiers put their masks on again, and he felt himself lifted, lurching down the stairs, and into the drawing room above the hall, the one they never used because it was cold even in summer. Rona's face swayed above him.

'Who is DM?' he said, 'Ask Mike!'

'Shhh now. Rest now. They've found it. It's over.'

'It's not over. I've seen it. I want to speak to Kirsty, and Mike.'

'Leave it now.' She stroked his face and he felt the morphine bringing in sleep and he passed into things that he recognised as dreams, wherein he floated on a bed through a vast Duncul, up and down stairways he had never known existed, into rooms that had lain centuries unopened.

The sensor beeped like a smoke alarm, and somewhere behind his mask and in the back of his mind Stevie thought that this was wrong. In films Geiger counters always clicked, like dolphins. Bartell, also in a mask, squatted, moving the sensor back and forth over the tartan blanket that had absorbed a dark red stain into its pattern. At the edge of the blanket towards the window a pair of boots emerged and towards the couch, a hand; a pale island emerging from the red. Bartell took one corner of the blanket and gestured for Stevie to do the same. It stuck to the fluid and resisted as they pulled. The man was face down. A statue of Atlas lay next to the head. The globe of the cosmos had broken open and crudely made cubes and obscure shapes of a dark grey metal lay like an archipelago in a port-coloured sea. Bartell's sensor rose to a scream as he placed it on one of the cubes. He switched off the noise and stood up.

'For future reference,' the voice came from his chest. 'This is what plutonium looks like.' He pressed a button on his neck. 'They've caught four of them, in the cellar, the work of your man the gardener.'

'Mike.'

'Mike saw them enter through the window, and jammed it shut.'

'Sir,' a soldier held up a phone. 'Orders to arrest Mohammed Landa, Solomon Matobela and Qualin H Bremner. They're wanted by the Counter Terrorism Unit.'

Towards the summit of Ardven the silence was punctuated by sobbing, coughing, and men and women calling out to each other through the smoke. From somewhere below and far off a voice was repeating that it was OK; something was OK. Nyst was running between shadowy figures, holding out his child's gun. He brought it up to the chin of a woman with tear-stained cheeks, then grabbed the lapels of a man in a suit but saw a moustache and pushed him to the side. But he became sure of his man on the top, where the smoke was thin enough to reveal a pale glow in the west. Acturus McBean

was talking into a phone and walking with purpose
towards the sun.

'We can talk about this later if you like Andrew, but I
am quite happy to finish the interview now. *Carpe diem*
and all that! I was born in a council house! I went to a
state school! I know what it is like to be on the wrong side
of the tracks! If you want a man of the people, that's me!
It is the liberals who are elitist! I represent the aspirations
of the common man; working hard, studying, achieving,
going to a Great Scottish University. Don't tell me what
the people want! I am the people! The people want
Freedom, Family Values, Opportunity! The people want
to be able to speak their mind!' He turned towards Nyst.
'Uhoh!' he said, 'I'll call you back Andrew!'

'Denis! Fancy seeing you here! I'm glad you could
come. It's a pity about this bit of trouble, but it will clear
up! All publicity is good publicity!' Nyst levelled the gun.
'Good God! What on earth? Like something out of *Star
Wars!* You're not going to shoot me with that! Look,
I've been meaning to sit down with you Nyst. Enough is
enough and bygones be bygones, let's bury the hatchet!
What do you say? You and I, we're the same! We both
have ideals. We both have ideas! I admit I might have been
a bit of a *provocateur* etcetera etcetera Devil's advocate and
whatnot, but no need for firearms!'

'We are not the same. The difference between us is I
care about something other than myself.' Nyst pulled

the trigger and the gun made a cracking sound. Acturus
flinched and looked at his chest, but before he could raise
a protective hand to the small hole that had appeared
in his shirt Nyst had grabbed his throat. Acturus fell
backwards. Nyst's face was purple and streaked with mud
and spittle. Acturus fought back, grabbing at the grey
locks with one hand and slapping an ear with the other.

'You shit!' said Nyst into his face. His breath smelled of
something dead. 'You destroy! You destroy the world!'

'Oh, give me a break!' began Acturus, and found it
strange that he could not finish the last syllable. He tried
again but found the stench coming from Nyst's mouth
overwhelming. Nyst's teeth were yellow. His lips were
flaccid and wet. What an awful way to die, thought
Acturus McBean.

When Acturus was still Nyst let go of the lapels. He put
the gun in his pocket, took hold of the body by the ankles
and pulled it downhill into the top of a spruce plantation.
Below him the fire was crackling merrily. He began
walking in the direction of Endpoint and when he reached
the edge of the fire making its way through the heather
he threw the gun into the flames and watched it melt.
He stepped back, pulled up his tunic and took a running
jump over the band of fire to the blackened ground on the
other side. When he heard a wolf howl in the distance he
grinned and skipped.

Chapter 27

One week later

Eamon lay on the couch in the study trying to hold a newspaper with bandaged hands.

'Fallout Panic in Duncul. Forest Fire False Alarm on Ardven Peninsula. While National News crews fled the scene at the first whiff of smoke, Stuart Macrae, 14, a local photographer, braved the "radioactivity" in Duncul to take these stunning shots of the fire and panicking residents.' The pictures were of the ballooning smoke above the hills and, looking down into the village, people running from their houses, the queue of cars on the road out, the police car with a flashing blue light and Sergeant Peters in a gasmask.

Kirsty came into the room with a tray of tea and biscuits.

'The intrepid local photographer is one of yours, isn't he Kirsty?' Eamon brandished the paper.

'Yes.'

'Mhairi's son.'

'Yes. My grandson.'

'He's talented. You must be proud.'

'He's always taking photos.' Her mouth was set in a thin line as she closed the door behind her.

Eamon's phone rang and he struggled to touch the screen with his one unbandaged thumb. Sergeant Peters was on his way to the castle, this time in his role as 'Victim Support.' As soon as Eamon had been deemed a victim of the crimes of the *Autonomass* he had discovered he was entitled to enquire as much as he liked about the case and the police were obliged to respond. 'If I had known this, I would have become a victim much sooner,' he had remarked to Rona.

When Sergeant Peters had settled into a wingback chair Eamon poured him a cup of tea.

'What news Sergeant?'

'The four *Autonomass* we caught are still not saying anything. They've got expensive lawyers. But this was published on the internet.' He took a sheaf of paper from a folder and put it on the coffee table. 'A kind of manifesto, written by Brigitta.'

'I've already read it,' said Eamon. Stevie came in and shook hands with Sergeant Peters. He set up a laptop on the desk. Rona arrived with Harry asleep on her shoulder.

'As we know,' said Stevie, 'Malky's body was cremated. The police pathologist hadn't been looking and didn't find a chip implanted in the body. I went to the undertaker though, Ian Fraser, in Inverness. They have a protocol for earrings, rings, studs, anything attached to a body. He had found the chip, removed it, recognised it as a camera memory card, and sent it along with all the other stuff that had been attached to Malky to the next of kin. He gave me the address of Malky's mother, and yesterday I took a drive to Kilmarnock.

His mother's name is Morag Macleod. She showed me what she had been sent. Most of it was still in the envelope, on her mantlepiece. Rings, studs, bolts, but no SD card. She said she had seen an SD card, but Janasha, Malky's wee sister, must have nicked it for her phone. We had to go and find Janasha in the park. She said I could have the card, 'cos there was no room left on it, and she couldn't delete anything, and the photos were all of machines and stuff, apart from the ones of Loch Houn and the hill. She asked if that was where Malky had lived and when I told her it was, she wanted copies of those.' Stevie touched a key on the laptop and turned it so they could all see the screen.

'He took a lot of photos. As you can see, he took pictures to show each step of how he dismantled the warhead and removed the plutonium, and then put it all back together.'

'Why?' asked Rona.

'I think, if he was going to sell it, he wanted to assure a buyer that it was the real thing. Or maybe he wanted to assure Kosma. It looks like he did this on a beach at night. I'm thinking down at his van, but it could have been anywhere along the coast, some out of sight place. Then he took pictures of exactly where he hid the torpedo.'

'So he took out the plutonium and gave it to Kosma,' said Eamon.

'Yes. Tariq told you Kosma's job was to befriend Malky, and that he had done a good job. He must have convinced Malky to hand it over to him.'

'And then Kosma hid the plutonium in the statue of Atlas. Why?' asked Rona.

'The *Autonomass* had already visited the manse once, to take back Nyst's precious cups. And Malky must have told Kosma they knew about the torpedo. That night, the night they came here for dinner, he was looking for a way of keeping the plutonium safe, but easy to find again, and he was in a hurry, because he knew the *Autonomass* would be visiting soon.'

'But how did the *Autonomass* know about the torpedo?' asked Rona.

'It was Mohammed Landa who told Malky to sell the torpedo to Brigitta,' said Eamon. 'Mohammed said it as a joke, but Malky took the idea seriously. Then he changed his mind, again. Malky didn't know about Denis Nyst's plan to release radioactive material. He didn't realise his offer must have seemed like fate, destiny, too good to be true. When he changed his mind and refused to give them the torpedo they didn't just forget about it. They followed him, stole the chart-plotter, and, we assume, in the end, kidnapped, tortured and killed him.'

'We don't know that,' said Sergeant Peters. 'The cause of death was drowning.'

'So on the night that David and Kosma came here,' said Rona, 'Before they came to dinner, Malky delivered the plutonium, Kosma hid it in the statue, and brought it here. If the *Autonomass* were following Malky, they would have known he had gone to the manse, and known David and Kosma came here. But they didn't know the plutonium had been handed over.'

'No,' said Eamon. 'That's why they spent the next three weeks looking for the torpedo.'

'But then why would they murder David and Kosma?' said Rona.

'We know they went to the manse,' said Sergeant Peters. 'We have forensics now.'

'But we don't know when they left those traces. It could have been the first time they went, to get back the cups,' said Rona.

'Malky went to the manse that day. Tuesday. Mrs Murray saw him,' said Eamon.

'OK.'

'Then Shem went,' said Eamon. 'The next night, the night he's supposed to have murdered them. We don't know when the *Autonomass* came. But if they were following Malky, and Malky went missing on the Tuesday, you would assume they went to the manse on the Tuesday. But it wasn't until the next night David and Kosma were killed. That is why the police think it is Shem. He was only one seen on the night of the murders. And the *Autonomass* couldn't have planted the bat at Murachar's croft unless they had been to the manse after the murders.' There was a silence in the room.

'Any news on Acturus McBean?' said Rona.

'Nothing. He was last seen on the top of the hill, heading towards the fire,' said Peters.

'And Nyst?'

'Nothing. Both he and his side-kick have gone. The RSPCA managed to catch three of the wolves, and if they don't catch the others they'll starve to death. They have no idea how to hunt; they traced the supplier to a suburb of Kansas City.'

'Have you read this?' said Stevie, taking the sheaf of paper from the coffee table.

'Yes,' said Eamon.

'It blames you for everything. You, and people like you are the pigs. You are responsible for climate change, poverty, the slave trade, sexual abuse of women, homophobia, the lot.'

'Yep.'

The long evening was beginning when Eamon walked out of the castle gate. When he had crossed the Tarr burn he turned into the council estate of Tarr Bow and knocked at the door of one of the grey, rain-stained cubes. Siobhan Macdonald came to door with a cigarette in her mouth.

Eamon asked his questions when he was sitting at the kitchen table with a mug of tea before him.

'Tell me about that night.'

'The first I heard of it was Angus came running in here.'

'What time?'

'Late. He was supposed to be in bed. After ten.' She took a long draw on her cigarette, stubbed it out and lit another. 'He came running in not saying anything at first. His face was all white. "Mum! Mum! Come on!" he didn't tell me what he'd seen but took me up the hill to the manse and showed me.'

'And what did you do?'

'I called the police.'

'Before that. The first thing you did. You took pictures.'
Siobhan looked down at the table.

'One picture. I took it for the police.'

'But you tweeted it, before they arrived.'

'Aye.'

'To who?'

'When you tweet you send it to all of your followers.
I've got a hundred and ten followers.'

'So they all saw the picture?'

'Not necessarily. Some of them, if they were on
Twitter. But when the police arrived Sergeant Peters told
me to take it down, and I did. It had only been re-tweeted
four times.'

'By who?'

'Four people in the village. But when I took it down,
they couldn't see it.'

'Kirsty Macrae?'

'Kirsty? No, she doesn't follow me. I doubt she's on
Twitter.'

'So she didn't see your picture?'

'There's no way of telling. If someone takes a screen
shot and stores the picture, that's them got it; I can't
delete it from their phone. I explained all this to Sergeant
Peters and he said something about contacting Twitter
but I told him that was a waste of time, because they can't

stop someone taking a screenshot or saving the picture so I don't know who saw it.'

'So, it could have gone anywhere, everywhere, all over the world, then got to Kirsty?'

'I suppose so.'

'And you took one picture only?'

'Only one. I didn't think it was appropriate to take more.'

'And did anyone else take a picture?'

'I don't know. Other people came up and looked in the window.'

A small boy came into the kitchen and began rummaging in a cupboard. 'Mum, where's ma wagon wheels?' he said.

'Say hello Angus. This is Mr Angsar, from the castle.' Angus stared at Eamon with his mouth open but did not speak.

'I need to ask him a few questions, if that is alright?' said Eamon. Siobhan nodded her assent.

'The night the boys were murdered, Angus. Why were you there? Why were you looking through the window?'

Angus stared blankly, then turned to his mother. 'I'm feeling uncomfortable!' he wailed, 'Where's ma wagon wheels?'

'I'm sorry,' said Siobhan, rising and taking a packet of biscuits from a drawer. 'The psychologist told him he didn't have to talk about it if he didn't want to.'

'Ah don't want to talk about it!' The boy took the biscuits and ran out of the room, slamming the door.

'Does he have his own phone?'

'Aye.'

Eamon muttered an 'excuse me' and stood up. In the living room the boy was sitting in front of an enormous screen.

'Angus, why did you go up to the manse?' The boy ignored him. Eamon picked him up by the shoulders and shouted over the noise of a machine gun. 'Did you take photos? Did you take photos with your phone?'

'Mum! Mum!'

'You can't do that!' said Siobhan from behind him. 'That's abuse!'

'You're hurting me!' wailed the boy.

Eamon put him down.

On the doorstep he turned to Siobhan as she closed the door. 'The photo you took. You've still got it haven't you. You deleted it from Twitter, but you still have it. Just in case the police need it.' Siobhan stopped closing the door. 'It's still on your phone, isn't it? I need to see it.'

She took out her phone and touched the screen. The body was lying face down, hair splayed out amid the broken ornaments, glass and furniture. 'Kill the Gays!' was written on the wall in paint, or was it blood? No stone cups were visible, but part of the room was obscured by the astragal of the manse window. The picture had been

taken in a hurry. Siobhan took the phone from his hand
and shut the door.

Eamon walked, and looked ahead, up at the manse, and
The Avenue behind on the hill. He took out his phone and
touched the screen.

'Kirsty?'

'Aye.'

'The photo you showed me the morning of the
murders.'

'It's deleted.'

'I know but who took it? Where did you get it?' There
was silence. 'Who took it Kirsty? Goddam it!'

Mhairi Macrae lived in the last house at the western end
of The Avenue, set back from the road, on a hillock,
at the highest point in the village. It had once been an
impressive house but had not been kept up. The owner
did not live in Duncul. He had divided the building into
flats, but had had trouble finding tenants, then he had
had trouble with the tenants he had found, and for most
of the time the house was empty apart from Mhairi and
her son. There were cracks in the stonework, and the
iron railings around the balconies on the first floor were
blistering. Eamon tried to recall what he had heard about
Mhairi. Mhairi had become pregnant as a teenager. He
remembered Kirsty's grave face the morning that this

news had reached the castle. The father of the child had been twice Mhairi's age, had a reputation for bestowing the gift of motherhood, and could be found easily enough in a pub in Inverness, but had never troubled Mhairi or his son with his attentions. Mhairi had initially borne up well, supported by a large extended family of Macraes in Duncul and surrounding glens, but had later faltered, tripped perhaps by some subsequent failure of love, and descended into a quiet but profound alcoholism that had thinned her to a bird-like appearance. Eamon had seen that she only emerged from her eyrie above the village to collect supplies from the village shop. From time to time, he had encountered her climbing back up the hill with a clinking plastic bag.

For the second time that evening he introduced himself to a thin woman smoking, leaning on a door jam. He was invited in. Yes, Stuart was home. Stuart was called down from his room. Eamon sat at table in a kitchen and waited. Stuart did not appear.

'You can go up,' said Mhairi, finishing her cigarette. 'Top of the stairs to your right.' Eamon thanked her.

There was no answer to his knock on the bedroom door. He pushed it open. A thin boy with wild dark curls wearing a school-shirt and trousers was sitting on a neat bed. A computer and printer stood on a desk before a bay window that overlooked the village. The walls were covered in photographs.

'Hi,' said Eamon. 'I saw your work in the paper. I was impressed.'

'Thanks.'

Eamon looked at the pictures on the walls. They were almost all of people, taken with a long lens. He could tell most had been taken from the window of the bedroom. Many had been taken at night, through lighted windows. His neighbours sitting, lying, eating, dressing. He crossed to the window. The whole village was laid out before him, the castle, the loch behind and directly below, through a gap in the trees where a sycamore had been newly de-limbed, the manse. He was looking right down into the rear window.

'You want to be a professional photographer?'

'Yes.'

'You can't take pictures like this, through people's windows. It's not right.'

Stuart lowered his eyes.

'You took a picture through the manse window, didn't you?' said Eamon. Stuart did not look up. 'And you sent it to your grandmother, Kirsty. Why did you do that?'

Stuart shrugged. 'Just to tell her.'

'Did you send it to anyone else? Your Mum?'

The boy shook his head. 'No.'

'Just your gran?' Eamon sat on the bed next to him. 'I've already seen it. She showed it to me. But she deleted it from her phone. Do you still have the original?'

Stuart switched on the computer. 'It was me who deleted the one on Gran's phone.' he said. He typed in a password and scrolled through files, then the picture lit up the screen. Eamon studied the image and remembered it. It had been taken from this high angle, with a long lens, with the astragals of the small-paned manse window clearly visible. It was not the same photograph that Siobhan Macdonald had shown him. That had been taken from a lower angle, taken from close in, so that the astragal was out of focus. The similarity was the subject on the floor, splayed out, hair around his head, blood in the hair. Broken furniture, glass and ornaments all around. Same scene, different image. With something missing; no writing on the walls. And something added, on the floor, next to David's outstretched hand, a stone cup.

'Is this the only one?' said Eamon.

Stuart did not speak but touched the mouse-pad. Variations of the image sprang up, taken from slightly different angles, some showing more of the blank walls, with no graffiti; tens, scores of pictures. 'And you showed none of this to the police?' Stuart shook his head. Eamon felt anger rising, but it was checked by the title of the folder that the pictures had emerged from. Twelve / Six/20--. The twelfth of June. David and Kosma had been killed on the thirteenth. On the evening of the twelfth, the Tuesday night, they had been having dinner at Duncul Castle.

'The date is wrong,' he said. Again, Stuart shook his head. 'That's not the right date. Doesn't your camera record the time and date?' Stuart touched the mouse and a box popped out of the foremost photograph. 13/06/20- 04:31. Half past four in the morning on the thirteenth. 'The murder happened on the evening of the thirteenth…' Eamon trailed off.

'But their bodies weren't found until eleven in the evening of the thirteenth.' Eamon sat on the bed. Surely the police can tell time of death? He almost said it out loud. And Shem had been at the manse on the evening of the thirteenth, but also the evening of the twelfth, as Mrs Murray had said, he came almost every night, so it doesn't matter. They were killed the night before and had been dead a whole day before they were found. Killed after they left the castle. But that was not important. What was important was that there was no writing on the wall. Whoever killed them didn't write 'Kill the Gays!' That was written afterwards. Before Siobhan Macdonald took a photograph. After Stuart Scott took a photograph. Malky, brings the plutonium. David and Kosma go to the castle. Shem visits. David and Kosma come back from the castle. David and Kosma are killed. Then the *Autonomass* come and take the cups, write on the walls, because they know about Shem's visit. Then Shem visits again, and sees the bodies, but it is not until Angus Macdonald sees them that the police are called. He gave Stuart his email address and instructions to send all the images.

In the twilight he walked fast along the avenue and banged on the door of Edwina Murray's house. He heard shuffling and a man's voice and called out his own name before the door was opened by Justin. Edwina cowered behind him in the hall.

'Who was there the night before the murders Edwina?' Eamon pushed his way in.

'The night before? I don't remember.'

'Think!'

'I don't know exactly.'

'Calm down Eamon,' Justin raised a hand.

'Think. Tell me all the people who visited that night. There was Malky Macleod. Yes? Then later on, the *Autonomass*, the hippies, yes? Then the next night, the night they were found, Shem Murachar.'

'Shem Murachar was there almost every night.'

'Yes, but no-one else?'

'Only…'

'Only who?'

'Your man. He was there all that week.'

'My man? What man?'

'He was cutting a tree.'

Eamon entered the Ash wood by the door in the south wall. The midges were thick in the still air. A thin stream of smoke was rising from the chimney of Mike Mack's cabin.

Mike was sitting on a stool in front of the fire, his wide back hunched. Eamon sat on the armchair and stared at the back of his gardener's head.

'Finlay might be coming home soon,' said Eamon. 'I spoke to his doctor.' He breathed in the familiar woodsmoke and the scent of the earth. 'Your man,' Edwina Murray had said. 'The engraving on the statue said "Presented by DM" Donald Mack. Is that your great grandfather?'

'Grandad's grandad,' said Mike. My man, thought Eamon, and my father's man, my grandfather's man.

'The statue was nothing Mike. It didn't matter.' He waited for a reply. Again, nothing. 'Tell me what happened.'

Mike's back shifted as he let out a sigh. 'They stole it. I went to get it. It wasn't there. There was a fight.'

'It wasn't there because they had already given it back.'

'I didn't know that. It was Duncul's. Not theirs'

'It didn't matter Mike. It was nothing.'

Mike leaned forward to adjust the stove. 'Donald Mack and the others saved every penny for a year. They went hungry. It's not nothing. You don't care about Duncul if you think it's nothing. Your grandfather didn't think it was nothing.'

Mike had gone for the statue when he knew David and Kosma were at the castle, and it had been the wrong thing to look for. Kosma had returned drunk; falling off his chair drunk.

'You hit them with something. With what?' An arm raised and pointed to the corner of the room. Along with a spade and a rake an axe handle leant against the wall. 'Quite straightforward.' Maclean had said, and he had been wrong, and right. A theft, an argument, someone drunk, and a fight. And then the *Autonomass* had found the bodies, and their cup, and had written on the wall, knowing about Shem's nightly visits. Then Shem had visited, he had seen them already all smashed up, and had said nothing, told no-one, and had come again, the next night, to visit his dead lover. How long would he have done that for if wee Angus hadn't looked through the window? And all the time, Stuart Macrae had been watching, taking pictures, telling no-one, until even he couldn't bear it and had to tell his gran. Eamon looked up as Sergeant Peters entered the room and unclipped a pair of handcuffs from his belt.

Eamon timed his journey to the head of Loch Houn to coincide with the low tide. He parked at the pier and walked across the sand as far as the bend in the river's track and the pool under the bank of birches. The decapitated torpedo was visible, cables protruding from its neck. A rainbow streak of oil was leaking into the stream. Bits of metal and wire protruded from the sand. He picked them up and turned back towards the car. The Ardven peninsula stretched out before and above him, a mass of blackened, barren ground. He had read Brigitta's manifesto through several times, and parts kept replaying.

'Pigs and lovers of pigs. Wannabe pigs. Piglets, sows and boars. Multiplying, devouring, poisoning, owning. You have brought the world to the brink of destruction, for what? To make yourself a little bit more comfortable, to make yourself fatter, and for your food to taste a little bit better, so that you can go a little bit faster to your pointless job. So that your piglet children can wear new clothes every day. So your house can be a little bit warmer, your shower a little bit more powerful, and your soap more gentle on your skin. So that your wife can wear the latest underwear and moisturiser, so that you can take a pill to make you feel you love her. You are destroying the planet for this.'

In the village he stopped at the bins in the carpark near the old school. The sky was dark and the radio was warning of a freak storm gathering in the north. For the first time in two months it looked like they were going to get some rain. The bins had been unable to cope with the influx of Alt-Scot delegates and were overflowing with bursting black bags. As he put the metal and wire into a recycling bin and wondered if it was the right one, rat ran across the tarmac. His phone buzzed and he remembered he was expecting a call from the builders at the Ash Wood Cottage. They wanted to know about the underfloor heating for the bathroom and he was going to have to make a trip into Inverness to choose the tiles. He turned the car in the direction of the petrol-station on the road to Aberfashie. He had to remember a mega-pack of nappies from the mega-store. As he took the road along the banks of Loch Cul a small boat was leaving a wake far off at the south bank, and the image of Brigitta came back to him, standing in the prow raised above the cloven water, a figurehead without a flicker of a smile.

Epilogue

Kwa Zulu South Africa

Eilidh Macdonell had never felt warmth like this. It was warmth that held you like the embrace of a mother. In the early morning it was a promise and perhaps a warning but as she walked along the track of red earth she let the promise fill her up and meet with the promise she held within her belly. There was the smell of the earth, of the fields on either side of the track, the rustling sugarcane, the scrubby trees, the small houses further off, and beyond them she was sure the smell the sea. She could smell the paper and ink of the letter she held in her hand.

'Dear Eilidh,
I know you will be surprised by this, but it is the only way to talk now. Our lawyer says everything is monitored that

we send by email and text and so-on, but he can post a
letter and there is nothing they can do about it.

I hope that the stay in my cousin's house in Durban
was OK. I know it was not luxury, but it was the best in
the circumstances. I do not know when all this stuff will
end. Mo was right, we are really in deep trouble now. We
have Captain Bartell and Eamon Ansgar and his lawyer
on our side, but still, they say it is going to take a long
time to sort out. Meanwhile we are in jail, and all the
accounts are frozen. They are asking us questions about
everything back to when I was a child at school. Mo has
to answer questions about all his business dealings going
back forever, and they have interviewed his Dad and all
his family in Nelspruit. But I am a Black African, and they
do not expect me to know so much about my family.
For them, I emerge out of darkness. So enclosed is my
mother's address. You will be safe there, because there is
no way that they can find her and track you. She is 'off
the grid'. I have written to her and she is very happy to
welcome you as her daughter. You will be safe, and you
can go to the hospital in Ulundi to have our child.

I hope that you can mend things with your family in the
future, but for now, sorry to say, you should not let them
know where you are.

I love you and am thinking of you all day and night.
Solly.'

Eilidh breathed in the singing grass, hills and sunlight. Over by the trees stood a small, white single-storey building with a tin roof, surrounded by the smell of a woodfire and a green garden. For now, that was home.